Settler's Prairie

A Family Triumphs Over Tragedy

By

Robert Connerly

ISBN: 1-4033-3103-0 (e-book)
ISBN: 1-4033-3104-9 (Paperback)
ISBN: 1-4033-5218-6 (Dustjacket)

This book is printed on acid free paper.

1stBooks - rev. 09/09/02

Table of Contents

Chapter One

There was a roar coming from somewhere above him, but he could not quite locate it. He thought he could hear words, but he wasn't sure of that. For a moment he was too terrified to do anything but lie where he was as though frozen to the dock. The last thing he remembered was that two men had pulled him into this narrow alleyway. He was not aware that all activity around him stopped, and men who had been minding their own business, turned to watch the scene they expected to unfold at any moment. He remembered a blinding flash and a major headache. The next thing Eddy Foster was aware of was strong arms lifting his crumpled body from the morgue like boards where he lay in a semi fetal position.

"Lad, can ye hear me?"

The voice had lowered a decibel or two, but there was still enough volume to rattle the timbers of the dock. Eddy groaned, and squinted in the direction of the noise.

"I asked are ye hurt bad?"

The voice seemed to ricochet from one of Eddy's ears to the other, and rattle the ear bones between.

"Uh…I…uh…don't…know," Eddy mumbled, "my head hurts" somethin'…awful.

He raised his right hand and carefully explored a large lump behind his left ear. He saw a light patch of blood on his hand.

There was a bench with shade where Eddy felt himself lowered, and he was able to look at his rescuer. He wasn't sure this giant-man with large sinewy arms and a black beard could be trusted, but he remembered his tenderness as he had lifted him from the dock. For a long moment neither of them spoke.

"Do ye think ye kin walk naow?" The bearded giant asked.

"I think so," Eddy replied.

"Well come along then and I'll git ye acquainted with the cook on me scow." As the bearded monster walked, he introduced himself. "I'm Shamus O'Bryan, and I been pushin' me barge up and down this canal all me life. Me auld father was the Cap'n before me. Me men call me Cap'n to me face…what they call me behind me back is no concern of mine."

There was the loudest guffaw Eddy Foster had ever heard. The Cap'n stopped beside a crane that was loading lumber on a nondescript barge by swinging it over the flatboat and lowering it to the hold. He abruptly turned to Eddy who was trying to catch his breath.

"Ye got to have a name, Lad. What is it?"

"I'm…breath…Eddy…breath…Foster."

Eddy was exhausted, and his doubts that he wanted to cast his lot with this giant were overwhelming as he meekly followed the Captain aboard the barge.

"Where're ye from?" O'Bryan roared. Eddy hesitated. "Speak up, lad, I asked ye where're ye from?"

"Ver…Vermont." Eddy hoped he spoke loud enough.

"Cap'n," Eddy hesitated. His voice was barely a whisper. "Cap'n," he tried to speak, but there was no sound.

O'Bryan ignored him. "Joe, I want ye to meet yer new helper," he boomed. "This here's a lad who thinks he can be yer pot licker. Come out and look him over."

At first glance Eddy thought this fat bellied man with the greasy apron that had once been white, wore a constant sneer, but as he approached, he could see a scar that cut across his left eyebrow down his left cheek to the corner of his mouth. The cook was wiping his hands on a corner of the already dirty apron.

"He don't look like much to me, Cap'n. He's too thin," the cook said as he walked around Eddy in the manner of a buyer appraising a beef for market. He poked Eddy in a few places, and felt his arms. "Seems like yuh better throw him back in the water. There ain't enough to him. A good wind would blow him off the barge." the Cook turned his attention to Eddy.

"Kid, you ever been on a flatboat?"

Eddy did not have time to answer.

"He's a rube from the back country and he's still wet behind the ears," the Cap'n roared. To Eddy he said, "That yer gear in that carpet bag? Ye can stow it where the Cook bunks."

The Captain left Eddy and Joe and walked over to four men who were guiding slings of lumber to the hold of the barge.

"I guess I'm stuck with you," the cook said resignedly. "You can call me Joe or Cook. I bunk in the cookhouse, but most of the time I sleep on deck. Stow yer stuff on a top bunk, and we'll git to work gettin' supper ready fer the crew."

Eddy threw his carpet bag on a top bunk, and reported to the cook for whatever duty a greenhorn kid had to do.

"Git a knife for peelin' outen the drawer of my work table, and then git that half sack of taters and I'll show yuh where to peel 'em. Let me know when yuh finish."

Eddy found the knife and potatoes and returned to the cook. Joe led Eddy to a bench in front of the galley.

"Set there," he told Eddy. "Let the peelin's fall where they may. Jus' push 'em over the side when yuh finish. Put the peeled taters in this kettle. Peel about twenty, and then I'll show yuh where to git water to wash 'em."

Eddy sat down and went to work while the cook returned to the galley. When the potatoes were peeled, the cook secured a bucket with a rope tied to the handle. He told Eddy to fill it from the river side of the boat opposite the dirtier water near the dock.

"Try to git the cleanest water yuh can," he muttered. "Lord, knows that ain't easy, the port side has too much stuff in it."

He paused in his attempt at humor, but did not see the desired response in Eddy.

"Wash the taters in the water from the river, bring 'em in and pour 'em in this kettle. Git another pail of water, and set it on the stove. When it comes to a bile, pour the hot water in the kettle with the taters. We'll be feedin' the crew as soon as they finish loadin' lumber. Now git wood from the stack outside the galley and keep the fire goin.' That'll be an all day job."

Eddy noticed a large reddish brown spot just outside the wheelhouse, but knew that he best ask no questions at that time. He found the wood stacked along one wall of the cookhouse, loaded an armful and returned to the galley. He thought his chores were finished, but was directed to go out side and chop more wood. Eddy secured the axe, and began splitting wood. When that task was finished, he reported to Joe.

"Time to set up for chow," Cook announced.

He ordered Eddy to get plates, knives and forks for seven from the galley cupboard and place them on the bench outside. Eddy saw that the crane was no longer loading and the crew was washing up for supper. Good naturedly they began a mild hazing aimed at Eddy.

"Hey, Cap'n where'd you get this pollywog from?" asked one of the men Eddy later learned was Jack Blade.

"I'll bet he don't know starboard from larboard," said one called Ford. Eddy never learned his given name.

"He ain't bigger than a Pennsylvania toad, an' he looks like a scared rabbit."

So it went until the Cap'n bellowed that they keep their opinions to themselves.

"Did you make sure he won't steal from us like the last pot licker did?" Jack Blade asked.

A brief silence that was broken only by the sound of water splashing against the barge and pier settled over the group.

"Another word from any of me crew about that and I'll throw the man who says it overboard," O'Bryan glared at the crew, and an ominous quiet settled over the men.

"Come and git it," Cook yelled and the silence was broken.

Joe placed a large kettle of stew on the bench outside the galley, and ladled out portions for each man. Warm oven baked bread was added to each man's plate by Eddy. The men sat on the gunnels of the barge using the lumber they had just finished loading as a table. Eddy and Joe ate after the men were finished. Eddy noticed the Captain talking to the crew in an almost normal tone so that he could only get the gist of what he said, but he knew that the talk was serious.

"Men, I want ye to lay off Eddy...a lad from the back country...he ain't never bin on the river." His voice rose as he continued, "any man of ye that gits it into his head to do what ye done to Charlie will answer to me." He changed the subject, and his voice assumed its usual bellow.

"Ye done yerselves proud loadin' lumber in good time. We'll take the evenin' off and go to town and celebrate," he paused briefly for effect, "drinks are on me"

The mood of the men changed from somber silence to their normal joking and banter as they made themselves ready for an evening of drinking paid for by the Captain.

When Eddy and the Cook finished the evening chores, they sat together for a time of relaxation. Cook told Eddy he thought he "would do" as a helper. "What happened to the helper you had before me?" Eddy asked. "Kid, it's best you let that be," Cook replied. "In the first place he was a dock roustabout the Cap'n hired just like you, but that was afore our last trip down the river. Right now I want to go into town and drink with the Cap'n and the boys. Ye'r welcome to come along, if yuh don't mind the drinkin'."

The cook winked and Eddy felt a camaraderie that he had never known. Having nothing else to do, Eddy decided to go along with the cook. The sun had set and the moon had not risen. In the dark of early evening the two disrobed and jumped into the river. Joe had a bar of brown soap that he had made and they bathed in the privacy of the night. Bathing finished they donned their best clothes and journeyed forth. Cook knew the waterfront bar where the men had gone, and there were loud greetings when Joe and Eddy entered.

"Come on ye auld alligator," the Cap'n roared at Joe, "Eddy ye come here and set by me so's I can keep me eye on ye."

A waiter was passing by. "Bring whiskey fer me cook an' a beer fer the young lad here."

Eddy wanted to protest but felt overwhelmed by the voice and manner of this monster man. For the first time in his life Eddy drank beer. He was surprised that the first taste was partly sweet and mildly bitter. True to his word the Captain kept his glass full. After two beers Eddy felt his head spinning and his vision blurred. With the third filling his tongue thickened and his speech was slurred. After the fourth glassful, Eddy heard nothing more that was said as the crew talked lustily of life on the river. Next thing he knew he was being shaken awake, and as far as he could tell it was about midnight.

"What time...?" Eddy realized his voice was weak, and he felt nauseous. The answer surprised him.

"It's four o'clock. We got to have breakfast over by six. That's when we're castin' off. Git outta yer sack and git the fire goin.' We got lots to do. I don't want to keep after yuh about gittin' up"

Memory told him that was Joe's voice, and that he was on the barge where he had been drafted into service as cook's helper. He started to rise and fell back on the bunk nauseous, bewildered, and head-achey. A tall, blond, bearded man Eddy had not noticed before shook him awake for the second time.

"You yust help Cook." The voice was gentle.

"Who are you?" Eddy asked bewildered.

"I bain Olaf, I verk on this yere barge."

Eddy rolled out of the bunk and realized that he had slept in his clothes. He could not recall when he returned to the barge the night before nor could he remember how he got in his bunk. When he asked Joe, he laughed and told him he didn't climb in, they poured him in.

"Git the fire started right away." Cook yelled from the work table. Eddy began whittling shavings, then he got larger pieces of wood and placed them in the stove. Soon a good fire was sending smoke and wood sparks up the chimney.

"First the fire then more water," the Cook ordered. "Yuh got to keep a pot bilin'. We never know when we can use hot water."

Eddy filled the pail and poured it in the kettle on the stove as he was told. Meanwhile, Joe had cooked sowbelly in thin strips. Eddy noticed the sowbelly threw spurts of hot grease out of the pan, and landed unnoticed on Joe's apron.

"No wonder his apron stays greasy," Eddy thought.

Joe mixed flour in the grease and added water and made a thin brown gravy. He added a handful of salt and a spoonful of pepper.

"Now git a cup of coffee from that red can and pour it in the water." When Eddy had done that, Joe gave him new orders. "Git out the plates an' stuff an' set them up."

Eddy thought the cook sounded as grumpy as he felt, but he obeyed. Joe had baked biscuits, and Eddy was surprised to see that they were light and done to a turn. While Eddy and Joe worked, the Captain and crew were busy casting off and maneuvering the barge to head down river. Joe and Eddy fed the crew breakfast as the barge entered the main current of the river. The Cap'n steered while the men ate.

"Now we'll put a tub of water on the stove and throw in a bar of soap I make," Joe stated after the meal. "Then we'll scrub the galley and clean everthin' up until it's ship-shape. We may eat sowbelly, but we don't live like pigs."

Eddy laughed and Joe grinned, satisfied with the boy's response to his river barge humor.

After breakfast cleanup, Joe and Eddy had time for conversation. The barge was headed downstream and the morning mists had cleared. The Captain was at the wheel, the river was calm, and there were new sights for Eddy to see at every bend of the river, but at the moment he was more interested in the fate of his predecessor.

"What happened to the boy who had the job I got?"

"I told yuh before not to bring that up. He was caught stealin' by Oley, the Swede, and Tex," Joe replied. "Before any of us could help Charlie, they dragged him out to the front of the wheelhouse where you see that brown spot and stabbed him. He bled to death right there." Joe could not pass up the opportunity to warn Eddy and added, "Let that be a hard lesson to yuh. Don't steal on this barge."

"I been learnin' hard lessons all my life," Eddy stated.

"Who hain't," Joe replied sardonically.

"What happened to Oley and Tex?"

"We was goin' through open country when it happened, an' there weren't no place to report to. As far as we knew Charlie didn't have no kin. We beached the barge and went ashore and gave him a decent burial. The Captain judged that Oley and Tex had a right to protect the crew from stealin,' but he didn't agree with what they done. This will be their last trip on this barge. They asked that they be allowed to stay till we reach Kayro, Illinois where they'll help us unload the barge. That'll be the last we see of them."

The Cook paused in his story and Eddy remained silent. Since there was little to do until they must prepare the noon meal, Eddy moved to the starboard gunnel and watched the shore pass by. For the moment, memories of Chloe Myrtie, and the words of her father flashed through his mind.

"You are too young, and you have nothing to offer a young lady. This money will take you back to your family in Vermont where you belong."

He had given Eddy enough money to buy tickets for the trip and had sent him to the railroad station. There was no time for a long reverie on the barge.

"As soon as one meal's over we start gittin' ready for the next. Right now we got to git potaties and stew ready fer noontime."

So Eddy's chores went from day to day. It didn't take Eddy long to realize that there was a routine to the job he had taken on. Get up at four, start the fire, get water, set up utensils for meals, wash pots and pans, and do that process over and over for every meal. The more routine it became, the more bored he became. Evening chores were usually finished an hour after the meal, and then there was time to listen to the tales the crew told of life on the river.

Eddy was fascinated by the operation of the barge. Cap'n O'Bryan was the wheelman who steered the barge to the best channels. Poles and the rudder were used to push off the docks, while in mid-river a crewman with a measured and weighted line threw it ahead of the barge, and as the barge moved forward, the line dropped to the river bottom. The crewman hollered measurements of river depth to the Captain with a kind of sing-song chant and the Captain steered to the best channels according to the information he had just received.

"Mark one port." The man with the marker yelled as he moved quickly to larboard, and the barge was steered left until a measurement was called from the port side of the barge.

"Mark twain to port, steady as she goes," and the barge stayed on its course. When the river changed, the crewman rushed from side to side shouting measurements, and the Captain maneuvered the boat in the direction indicated as the barge moved smoothly into the best water according to the call of 'mark twain' from the steerman.

"It takes years on the river to do what they do," Joe remarked when he saw Eddy watching. "Do yuh think yuh could ever learn how to do that and be a riverman?"

"My family's in Nebraska and I want to be with them," Eddy replied. He saw surprise in the Cook's expression.

"Did yuh tell the Captain that?"

"No, he didn't ask me anythin'."

"Yuh best tell him first chance yuh git."

At that moment the Captain hollered orders for Eddy.

"Kid, come stand beside me, and I'll show ye how to steer me barge. Pay attention to the man with the plumb bob. He measures the water depth in the river, and I steer the barge to best water."

Eddy made his way to stand by the Captain who showed him how the wheel affected the direction of the barge.

"Cook tells me ye know how to work," the Captain said. "There ain't no time for lazy bones on this barge."

Eddy felt tongue tied in the Captain's presence, but he knew it was now or never so he mustered up his courage enough to speak.

"Uh. Cap'n…" there was a long pause.

"Speak up, lad, ye got somthin' to say, spit it out."

"Cap'n, what's the best way fer me to git to Nebraska?" Eddy blurted, his tongue feeling thick.

"Why?" There was anger in the Captain's tone.

"I have cousins there…" Eddy was not prepared for the Captain's outburst.

"Ye pot washers are all alike. I gives ye a job and what do ye do? Ye leave first chance ye git. If I didn't need ye, I'd put to shore and dump ye right now."

The Captain maintained the roar that was his custom, which made Eddy feel about as small as a cricket's knee. The Captain waited for Eddy to speak until his patience ran out.

"Well kid, speak up. How long ye gonna be with me?"

"I don't know, sir."

"I'll be a damned shantytown Irish. Ye'll eat me grub and do as little work as need be, and then ye'll jump ashore first chance ye git. What kind of lad are ye?"

The gruff Captain and the greenhorn kid stared at one another to see who had control.

"Sir," Eddy yielded, "where's the best place fer me to go so's to git to Nebraska?"

The Captain stared at Eddy coldly before he spoke.

"Well Kid, I'll count on ye to stay with me crew till we git to Kayro. We'll unload our lumber there and take on a load of Bohunks that wants to homestead near Saint Joe, Missouri. We'll make our way upstream on the auld Mizzou as far north as Saint Joe where we'll unload the Hunkies. Ye ought to stay with me till we git there. From there it's up to ye how ye git to the place in Nebraska ye wants tuh go to. As for me, ye can do as ye please after that."

"Cap'n I will stay with the crew until we git to Saint Joe." Eddy had no idea where that was, but he continued, "and I want to thank…"

"I'll have none of that, ye do yer work, and ye'll git yer pay. If ye leave at Saint Joe, its no concern of mine."

Before he gave it a thought Eddy blurted, "What is my pay and when do I get it?"

"Ye eats me grub. Ye sleep in me cabin on a dry bed, and ye wants pay. I'll pay ye ten dollars a month an' no questions asked. Naow git back to yer work."

Eddy left the Captain feeling like a cross between a whipped dog and a blessed cat. Dogs get the lashings of their masters while cats live nine charmed lives. Back in the galley he told the cook his side of the conversation. When he finished he asked Joe how long it would take to get to Saint Joe, and asked where it was.

"It's north of Saint Louie, Missouri. Countin' layovers fer loadin' an' unloadin' it'll take about two months."

In silence Eddy weighed that piece of news against his desire to get to Nebraska. He decided that he could stay with the barge, and earn money for a railroad ticket to Nebraska, and "mebbe have some to spare," he told himself. As he worked that afternoon, the words of Franklin Foster pounded through his head:

"Your future is doubtful at best. You have nothing to offer a young lady."

The tightness of rejection, and the feelings of loneliness he had known since the age of five, when his mother had left him in his grandfather's home returned. For a time he lost interest in his surroundings. Scenes on shore that he had enjoyed watching were now lacking color. For a week he did his work on the barge as though he were in a daze until the Captain took charge.

"Lad, if ye're gonna mope around here, ye best go ashore."

The Cap'n sang an Irish song and did an Irish jig which made Eddy laugh. Right then he decided that he wanted to see his mother, but that could wait, and he would write a letter to Chloe Myrtie.

Chapter Two

Lazy days settled on the barge and the river, and time slowed to the tempo of the current as it slowly swirled around the barge. The cook had told Eddy that the barge could make forty miles on a good day, but when the river was against them, they might spend a day or two on a sandbar or caught on an underwater snag, which could be a fallen tree or a large underwater root that they couldn't see from the surface. On a day when the barge had moved close to shore in order to stop at a pier, it suddenly lurched to a stop. A couple of crewmen dove into the water to see what had caused the problem, and reported to the Captain that there was underwater debris wrapped around the rudder, "Mike, git the buck saw, an' ye an' me will git it free in no time," the Captain ordered.

There wasn't much that anyone on the barge could see except that from time to time both men surfaced for air, and gave a report. In a couple of hours the barge was free, and the two men were hauled aboard. When the barge docked at the pier, Eddy and Joe went ashore and bought supplies. That finished, the barge moved into the mainstream once more.

There were many and varied craft plying the waters of the river. One that was shaped like a dragon caused the crew to laugh and yell insults at its crew.

"Are ye fire breathin' river rats?" O'Bryan yelled.

"We're dragon slayers," came the answer.

"Have yuh got scales and fins?" Joe hollered.

"Yuh landlubbers know nothin' of dragon men." came the answer.

The two craft moved side by side and the banter continued until both crews tired, and the dragon boat pulled ahead.

Dual stacked steamboats that belched angry plumes of black smoke shoved smaller craft aside as though they owned the river. Eddy noted that they always seemed to be in a hurry and that they disregarded other craft. He watched as the dragon boat capsized in the wake of one of these steam powered boats. Eddy heard the steamboat crew laughing and jeering at the hapless landlubbers. The crew of the barge pulled these unfortunates from the water, retrieved their craft and unloaded them at the next pier. These dragon travelers were immigrants going west where they hoped to get free land.

Eddy's fascination with the changing scenery along the river banks grew as the days passed. At times there were bluffs that narrowed the river and made the current swifter. Around a bend there might be valleys with small villages and farms. In broader valleys there were piers where farmers and vendors sold their wares to the passing rush of humanity. Crew members told Eddy there were river "pirates, river rats, and alligator men" who laid in wait for the less wary travelers. These men hailed the unwary claiming a need for help, and many times robbed and killed them for whatever they possessed.

"Has this barge ever been attacked?" Eddy asked the cook one day when they had finished their work.

"Cap'n O'Bryan has made this trip so many times he knows most of the pirates by name, and they know him, and anyways, he's the fightingest barge man on the river. Mostly the rats leave him alone."

"How do they know this is his boat?"

"He bellows and roars at his crew, and he sings them Irish songs loud enough to be heard for miles. He scares them back to their holes."

There was no reason to expect that O'Bryan's barge would not be attacked. Pirates chose that very night when there was no moon and the barge was moored close to shore. After midnight a ball of fire arched from shore and landed on the deck near the wheelhouse. There were banshee yells as six half naked pirates began climbing aboard. The fireball had roused the crew and the Captain, who was the first to meet the intruders. His bellowing rage and great size caught the pirates off guard. The crew joined the melee with swinging fists, and for half an hour there was a violent struggle for control of the barge. Eddy grabbed the bucket with the rope and began dousing water and extinguished the fireball as the last pirate was thrown yelling into the rolling depth of the river.

"Next time think before ye attack O'Bryan's barge," the Captain bellowed into the night. In the darkness he called the roll of his crew.

"Oley, Tex, Frank, Joe, Mike, are ye all alright?"

"Yeh," each man responded.

"Cap'n, ye forgot Eddy," one of the crewmen said. "He dumped water on the fireball and put it out."

"He did a fine job of it just as the rest of ye did. We'll talk more about it in the mornin."

Without another word the Captain went to his bunk, but the excited crew sat around the deck and talked over their part in the melee. After breakfast the next morning, the Captain looked each man over, and joked with them about their scratches and bruises.

"Tex, that's a nasty lookin' eye ye got. I don't know if a pirate hit ye or me that done it."

"Mike, ye look like ye were clawed by a mad civet cat."

"Cook, ye got quite a bruise on yer cheek."

"Oley, those bumps on yer knuckles look like ye hit a tree stump, did ye take as much as ye gave?" Oley nodded.

Captain turned to Eddy. "Eddy I don't see a bruise or a scratch on ye. Are ye sure ye didn't stay in yer bunk while we was out here fightin'?"

Eddy grinned, and felt a camaraderie that he had never experienced before as one by one the crew told him "he was alright."

After the midnight encounter with the pirates, O'Bryan decided to remain moored at the spot where the fight occurred in hopes that the rascals would try "agin to high jack me barge." It never happened. Inactivity for two days, and obvious restlessness of the crew, made the Cap'n decide that it was best to move.

Days blended together for Eddy as he began to see a sameness in the scenes along the shore. However, the variety of crafts on the river and the people they carried kept his interest. He was glad when he and Joe were able to market with the vendors on shore. Joe and the Captain were always impatient to be on the water while they bought cooking supplies, so there was never enough time for Eddy to visit with these settlers Lazy summer days with plenty of sunshine and little rain continued as the barge made its way downriver. Eddy and Joe went to the market vendors along the shore for supplies when the barge docked, and there were frequent stops in wooded areas where Eddy and the Cook chopped and sawed wood for the cook stove, while the crew cut logs for the small steam boiler when needed to provide power for the small paddle wheel.

"Goin' up the Mizzou can be an uphill struggle," Joe told Eddy one morning. "We'll need all the wood we can cut for times we hit calm water, but we'll need to stop nearly ever' day to chop more wood. When we go against the current from Kayro to Omaha, we may have to hire mules to pull us over sandbars we can't see until we're stuck."

"Cuts the time we can make in half," the Captain boomed from the wheelhouse.

"When we're in Kayro, ye may want to go ashore, if ye ain't workin'." he told Eddy later. "We'll be docked there, an'we'll unload the lumber, an' stay a day or two."

They stayed a week, and Eddy was glad for time on shore. He roamed the streets, and came across "Mary O'Linn's Boarding House—Bed, Bath, Breakfast—Twenty-five Cents." The Boarding house was the largest residence in Cairo and Eddy decided to ask O'Bryan if he could stay there at least one night. The Cap'n told him he could "so long as he was on board to do his chores in the mornin." For the first time in weeks Eddy was able to take a bath in a metal tub and spend the night in a bed with a mattress and clean sheets.

Cairo was a busy town on a point of land where the Ohio and Mississippi rivers merged. Early mornings were misty with fog that usually cleared away by nine or ten. Eddy walked the streets exploring the town in the warm and brighter afternoons. On such a day he was passing a saloon when he heard someone inside calling his name. He turned around and there stood Tex leaning against the door post with a silly half-sober grin.

"Tex, I thought you an' Oley left to go to Texas two or three days ago," Eddy said.

"Caint leave here when they's so much good drinkin' to do," Tex replied with a laugh. "Me an ol' Oley have been on a tear for two days. We done drunk up most of our money."

"Where's Oley?"

"He's inside, come in. I'll buy you a drink."

Eddy had not been friends with these two river rats, but he did not want to be unfriendly so he entered the saloon. Inside he found Oley at a table with his head on his arms. Tex walked over to Oley and gave him a slight punch. Oley looked around the room, and did not seem able to focus his vision on Eddy.

"Look who's here," Tex said. "We got to have a drink with the best pot licker on the river." He yelled to the bartender to bring another round. An' bring one fer the lad."

Three glasses of a brown liquid that passed for whiskey were brought to the table. Eddy had made it a rule in Pittsburgh that he would take no more than two drinks, but by the third drink he could barely "hit the ground with his hat." He soon realized that he was the only one paying, and slowly rose to his feet.

"I got to go back to the barge," He said.

"Yuh greenhorn, yuh jus' gonna walk out on your friends," Tex's tone was as ugly as his expression. "Before I let yuh do thet, I'm gonna teach yuh a lesson."

"Yew leave my frien' alone," Oley stated. "Yew fight Oley, yew don' fight my frien'."

Before Eddy moved a muscle, the two men began sparring, and soon began seriously punching each other. To Eddy it seemed that the whole bar had chosen sides, and the fight spread from table to table. Barely able to stand, Eddy chose the quickest way out and made his way back to the barge. The first person he met was the Captain.

"Lad, ye're not in any shape to do yer job tonight," he boomed at Eddy. "Ye best go sleep it off, and we'll talk about it in the mornin'." Next morning Eddy was roused out at the usual time for helping the cook get breakfast. After they had served breakfast and cleaned up, Joe was curious about Eddy's activities that made him come back to the barge under the influence the day before.

"What made yuh go on a binge yesterday?" He asked.

"I met Oley and Tex in a saloon in town and Tex bought me a drink," Eddy stated. "I guess that's what started it."

"I'll bet yuh ended up buyin' more drinks than they did." Joe said disgustedly "Them two is good workers, when they're sober, but when they drink, they's bad business. Yuh best stay away from their kind."

The Captain joined them. "Aye Lad, ye've been a good help for Joe. If ye want to git to Omaha, ye best stay away from river rats in saloons. We'll be pullin' up stakes and headin' up river as soon as we git all them bohunks on board. We'll need ye all the way to Omaha." The Captain made this speech in a normal tone. "Naow do yer job and keep yer nose clean."

Eddy had not paid much attention to the happenings on the barge during the time the barge was moored in Cairo. He had noticed that the lumber was unloaded, and he had seen that the crew had built a shelter over the hold. When he asked the cook about it, Joe said that was for the "Bohunks." That morning a crowd of people wearing costumes Eddy had never seen, began to gather on the dock. By noon the barge had become crowded with people who spoke a language Eddy had never heard, and they brought sausages and breads that were new to him. Eddy learned that these passengers were from a camp he had heard about outside Cairo, and they had stayed in their camp until that morning. He heard of gypsies and wondered if bohunks were gypsies.

"Where are these people from?" Eddy asked Joe.

"They're Bohunks from the Old Country." Joe replied.

"Where will they sleep?" Eddy asked.

"They'll sleep on the floor of the hold."

"Looks to me like it'll be crowded."

"Yuh got to realize these people came to this country on a ship in steerage, where they wuz as crowded as cattle with no fresh air. Some of their relatives died on the boat. On this barge they'll have fresh air and a dry place to bed down. We have to cook for our crew, and for the thirty eight Bohunks." Cook said.

Joe set Eddy to work peeling potatoes and doing his chores. While he worked Eddy thought about these new passengers.

"What's a Bohunk?" he asked.

"As near as I know, a Bohunk is somebody from Bohemia," Joe said. "They're settlers goin' west to homestead."

"I thought you had to be a citizen to homestead," Eddy stated.

"These people were sworn in on Ellis Island when they got off the boat that brought them to this country."

Eddy noticed that the Bohunks seemed content to eat bread and sausage for their evening meal. After they ate, they produced musical instruments Eddy had never seen, and sang songs he did not know in their own language. The instruments were playing a tune with wild rythm, and three young women and three young men rose and danced their native dances.

"This is gonna be some trip up the Missouri," Eddy said. While they had been docked in Cairo, the Cook had bought sacks of yellow and white corn meal, potoatos, flour and onions. He had cooked some of the white meal in loaf shaped pans. The first morning on the Missouri Joe and Eddy prepared bacon and then cooked the mush in the grease, which they served to the Bohemians. After the crew and passengers had eaten, one of the Bohemian leaders asked to speak to the Captain.

"What's on yer mind, Petrovsky?" the Captain asked.

"Me and brother-in-law Rostov, verk barges in Old Country," Petrovsky stated. "Ve know rivers. Ve vork for you."

"We need two good men," O'Bryan stated. "Kin ye start naow?"

Petrovsky agreed and then continued, "These people my family. Ve haf Momma und Poppa Petrovsky, Momma cooks Hungarian."

"I am the cook on this scow," Joe stated emphatically.

"Momma makes best Hungarian goulash. You vill like."

"Me barge already has a cook," the Captain stated.

"Momma vill help cook. She vill show him Hungarian. She cook cornmeal better, and make Hungarian goulash. You vill like."

"When does she want to start?" O'Bryan asked.

"Today. Your cook can verk vith her today. Vhen she cook, makes you feel better."

"Me cook and me will have to talk this over," the Captain stated before Joe could object. "We will let ye know."

The two went into the wheelhouse and Eddy could see that they were having a heated argument. There were heads shaking and hands waving, and loud voice sounds. When they emerged, Joe went to his bunk and began packing his belongings. Eddy joined him there.

"No way I'm gonna let a Bohunk take over any galley of mine. Eddy, it's up to you, if yuh wanta stay on this scow, but I'm gittin' off right now. You can stay or go, it's up to you."

In less than two hours he was put ashore at a small village.

"Ed," the Captain now assigned Eddy a more adult name. "Ye must show Momma around the galley." He then spoke to Petrovsky,

"Ed will show Momma around the galley, and he will be her helper. I'll pay her cook's wages if she will cook for me crew."

Petrovsky said he would have to ask Momma, and went into the hold where another session of excited voices could be heard. He returned to the Captain.

"Momma vill cook," he said.

Working with Momma soon became one of the happy experiences of Ed's young life. She called him "Honi" which was as close as she came to honey, and she expended her entire English vocabulary with him, which was "Honi, do dis vay." Ed learned more about cooking from her than he had ever known. She stewed a hen and made dumplings with flour and broth for moisture, and then cooked the dumplings with the chicken. She removed the fat from another chicken and made noodles with eggs, flour and water. Her Hungarian stew was just as good as her son said it would be. She told Ed the Hungarian names for all she cooked, but he couldn't pronounce them, so he tried to teach her the English for them. The crew of the barge were getting meals the like of which they had never had.

"Momma could let a chicken walk through hot water and make noodles and dumplings from the broth," Ed told the Captain later.

"No wonder them Bohunks look so well fed." The Captain grinned as he changed the subject. "I've hired a mule team and driver to help go against the current. Where there is a towpath beside the river, he will hitch the mules to the barge and help us go upstream. We can use the paddle wheel when we need it. When the river banks are steep, he will ride one of the mules to a place where there is a towpath, and we'll use the paddle wheel. He will eat his meals with the crew, but he will sleep where he can look after his mules on shore."

The next morning the barge cast off, and the journey up the Mississippi toward the Missouri began at sunrise.

Chapter Three

Going up the Missouri in those warm days of late summer was the best of duty for most of the crew. Mike and Frank tended the steam engine, and there was little difficulty so long as they had plenty of wood for the boiler to keep the steam up. The most work the crew did was to go ashore and cut wood when the wood supply was low. The evening of the second day on the Missouri the paddle wheel struck a floating log that broke three of the slats in the wheel. The Captain had laid in a supply of slats, but repairs could not be completed that late in the day.

The barge was moored for the night, and the Hungarians took up their usual evening serenade until it was time to turn in for the night. Suddenly, there was a hissing sound, and the barge began to shudder. Petrovsky immediately raced to the boiler and began turning knobs, until gradually the hissing and shuddering stopped.

"Youze no shut down boiler," he told Mike and Frank accusingly.

"We don't need no damn Bohunk to tell me what's wrong," Mike yelled above the noise of escaping steam from the boiler.

"I'll have none of that," the Cap'n intervened. "On me barge every man does what needs doin'. Stand aside Mike or I'll have to take ye into me own hands."

"Good thing the boiler had a safety valve," Frank yelled. "I was on my way to open it wider, but you beat me to it."

"Ya," Pretrovsky said. "Too much steam, boiler go boom, maybe barge sink and we all die."

"Frank and Mike, next time ye best remember to release the steam," O'Bryan roared. "We got plenty of troubles with the paddle wheel. "Petrovsky ye saved me crew and yerselves. I'll talk to ye in the mornin'. Best ever'body turn in naow."

Night guards were posted and quietness settled over the river and the barge. Eddy slept well that night, thankful the bohunks were aboard and happy to work with Mama Petrovsky.

Mama Petrovsky and Ed began the next day's breakfast at the usual time. By ten the slats of the paddle wheel had been replaced, and the barge began its slow progress up the Missouri. That late in summer river water was low and there were many sand and mud bars. On the fourth day out of Cairo the barge was grounded on a long and wide bar of mud and sand. The boiler was fired up, and the team on shore along with the paddle wheel only managed to move the barge forward three yards after four hours. Passengers were put ashore to lessen the load and to allow the barge to draw less water, but the sand and mud bar was too wide.

"This river gits too wide and makes sand bars where there weren't none before. I bin up it five times and it's allus the same. We'll have to hire more mules to pull over this'un. I'm an Irish son of the auld sod," the Captain bellowed his frustration, "this river changes its mind more than any woman I ever knew."

Looking ahead the crew could see there was a sharp curve with narrower water, but where the barge was grounded the river had widened and the flow of the current had left this bar.

"Cap'n, river is too shallow for barge. Maybe rains up river come and vater vill git deeper. You vait two t'ree days and see," Petrovski said. "Sometimes rains make vater rise."

"This time of year we could be here a month or more," O'Bryan replied wearily. "The only thing I know to do is hire more mules. If ye can't see through this muddy Mizzou, ye can't steer away from mud and sand bars. Makes me want to give up this kind of life and go back to Ireland where I could dig potaties like me grandfather did."

"Halloo, barge," a voice hailed from shore.

"What do ye want" roared the Captain.

"Oh it's you, O'Bryan," the voice replied. "Looks like I got yuh where I wants yuh. Youse are stuck pretty bad. I got mules if youse got ropes. I will hitch my mules with your'n, fer the right price."

"What's yer price?" O' Bryan demanded.

There was no answer from shore, but the crew could see the shadows of several men in the brush.

"Come aboard and we'll talk." O'Bryan ordered.

There was a thick undergrowth of brush along shore, and a rough looking frontiersman emerged from it.

"I thought it was ye, Chief. Ye hain't got me nowhere, but I will let ye aboard to talk."

The man called Chief paddled a canoe to the side of the barge where he moored it, and came aboard.

"What's yer price?" O'Bryan demanded without greeting.

"I wants five dollars fer each mule, I got four mules. Thet would be twenty dollars."

"I'll pay ye ten, and five fer the driver, but not until we are in clear water, and me barge is free."

The Chief nodded and the two men shook hands. A three mule tandem was arranged with a lead mule in front. Two more drivers appeared from shore and the mules were goaded and whipped until their bellies nearly touched the ground as they tugged against the weight of the barge. The barge was slowly moved to clear water. All the mules were unhitched, and the drivers made their way to the barge. The Captain tried to reach a settlement with the muleskinners and an argument began.

"I told ye I'd pay ten dollars fer pullin' me off that sand bar," the Captain roared, "an' five dollars fer one driver."

"Whatever yuh pay him yuh owes me," said the driver of the mule team the Cap'n hired in Cairo. O'Bryan stared at him coldly.

"I'll pay ye the same, but on me own terms," O'Bryan loudly stated. "When we agreed to my terms, that's all I pay."

Chief let out a loud whistle, and seven men emerged from shore.

"Yer loud yellin' don't phase me none, and anyways we got your crew outnumbered, and we aims to collect every penny comin' to us," Chief stated, thinking he was on safe ground.

"I'll pay ye what's fair and no more," O'Bryan stated loudly as he threw twenty dollars on the deck. "That's more than fair."

One of the shoremen quickly picked up the money. O'Bryan's crew and the Hungarians had gathered around the shoremen who had drawn guns they had in their belts. The Hungarians had separated the shoremen so that no more than two were together. Without any obvious signal the Hungarians attacked the shoremen suddenly and disarmed them. Just as quickly they methodically threw them, along with the driver the Captain had hired in Cairo, overboard into the deepest water of the river as the barge paddled away full steam.

"Youse"..gasp.."come..this"..gasp.."way…agin…"gasp"youse'll be sorry," Chief yelled as he rose and sank, and the barge crew and the Hungarians yelled insults at them.

The current of the river swept the shoremen further and further behind. The last the barge crew saw of them they were standing in waist deep water, still waving and hollering, on the very mud-sand bar from which they had pulled the barge.

"Thet Chief, he's a bad'un," the Captain told his crew and passengers that evening. "He's a renegade from the army. Looks like he's got a gang together." Anger began to cloud his face. "Them rascals tried to high-jack me barge," he roared. "If it hadn't been fer ye Hunkies and me crew, they mighta got away with it. Petrovsky, I owe yer people fer doin' me a favor."

For a moment the Captain and Petrovsky were silent while each man took the other's measure, and then took the other's offered hand and grinned their friendship.

"In Ol' Country ve know that kind," Petrovsky stated. "No goot. They rob and murder, no damn goot."

The barge docked for the night in a cove where there was a village. Early the next morning the journey up river continued. Mama and Ed prepared a breakfast of potato cakes and sausage with biscuits and hot coffee. After chores were finished, Ed saw that the shore was now dominated by willow brush. The barge had entered an area of low hills that formed cliffs where the river eroded its way through. Here the current was swifter, and the paddle wheel was their only means of going forward.

There were broad valleys with streams which added silt laden water to the swirling, flowing, majestic and muddy Missouri. At times there were villages at these confluences. Some streams contained more silt than the Missouri, and Ed decided that he could tell where storms had washed silt away and brought it to the already muddy river. Petrovsky had also been watching the shoreline and saw the broad valleys.

"Goot land for farming," he told Ed. "Just like Old Country."

Around a bend in the river there was a cluster of tepees along the shore on the west bank of the river. The village seemed peaceful enough and the barge continued on its way, but out of sight of the village, a band of seven or eight young braves began sending fire tipped arrows toward the barge. Several landed on the tarp covering the hold and others landed on the deck Those on the tarp roof were starting fires that threatened to set the barge afire.

"Git to those arrows the best ye can and toss them in the river," the Captain ordered as sparks and arrows fell on the deck.

"Ed, round up all the buckets ye can find."

Ed found eight buckets and two had ropes tied to the handles. He and Petrovsky began filling them while the Captain organized the bucket brigade to douse the fires that the arrows set in the tarp. Almost as quickly as the attack had begun, the fires were extinguished, and the barge continued on its slow pace up stream.

"Agin ye saved me barge," O'Bryan told Petrovsky. "I'd be glad to have ye as me neighbors." He changed the subject. "Tell Mama me men like her cookin', and so do I."

Petrovsky agreed that he would tell Mama. Among the Hungarians there were a couple of young men near Ed's age, and one day Petrovsky introduced Ed to them.

"This Petr, and this Igor, both my nephews, maybe you teach goot American Inglesh?"

"I ain't no teacher," Ed stated.

"Nephews must learn in this country," Petrovsky persisted. "You teach, I pay you money."

"I will do the best I can," Ed promised.

"That be goot, I tell them." He spoke to the two boys in their language. They looked Ed over as their uncle spoke and began to grin, which Ed knew was a challenge.

"How many years?" Petrovsky asked Ed.

"I'm sixteen," Ed replied.

"Petr seventeen, Igor fifteen. I leave you now," and Petrovsky withdrew to the hold to join the other Hungarians.

"Friend," said Petr.

"Friend," Igor repeated, but Ed saw challenge in his eyes.

"Do you know English words?" Ed asked.

Both boys hesitated "Inglish," each said in turn, "Hello, friend, cold, hot, no more."

In the six weeks they were together there was time to teach, but Ed had trouble getting them to focus on learning. The first days he followed a method of showing them objects and stating the name. He asked them to repeat the word. He would then form a sentence using the word and ask them to repeat it. But teaching was not Ed's biggest problem. Igor would sneak behind Ed, throw his arms around his chest pinning his arms to his sides. This bear hug would last until he was able to struggle free. He learned to let his body go limp which usually caught Igor by surprise. He then jabbed him in the stomach with his elbow, and Igor would release him.

"You call me Hunkie, I show you Hunkie," Igor said when he had learned that much English "I no like Hunkie, I am Hungarian."

"You have bigger arms than me," Eddy replied showing Igor his thin arms hoping that would stop the bear hugs. Igor imitated his action and showed Ed his larger muscles grinning that challenging grin all the while.

"You're stronger than me." Eddy conceded, but Igor forced Ed to spar and wrestle. He easily overpowered Ed and enjoyed the activity which he repeated often.

The barge passed by Saint Louis and went on to Saint Joseph, where Petrovsky and the Hungarians had decided to stay. There were many features of a frontier town in Saint Joe. Flatboats and barges, keelboats and vessels of every description were tied up at its piers. In some ways it reminded Eddy of Pittsburgh, but there was less order and more variety in its traders. There were fur traders with large bales of furs, buffalo hunters selling robes, railroad men moving to rail camps at the end of the line, and religious groups moving west with carts and many walkers with bundles on their backs. At Saint Joe the Hungarians left the barge.

"You one fine goot Captain," Petrovsky told O'Bryan.

"Ye're good people," the Captain responded. "Anytime I come this way, tell Mama to cook me some good Hungarian goulash."

Farewells were said and the Hungarians left the boat. The barge stayed in Saint Joe two more days while the Captain hired two new crew men. O'Bryan arranged to take another group of settlers up the Missouri to Omaha, Nebraska. When he returned to the barge, he called Ed to the wheelhouse to tell him his latest decision.

"We'll be loadin' another bunch of settlers in the mornin'," he said, "and I want ye to stay with me. If ye'll stay, ye'll be me mate, an' I'll pay ye twenty dollars a month and yer grub and bed."

"I'll stay as long as I can," Eddy replied, and he was thrilled for the promotion, even though it meant delaying his trip to see his mother.

Dave McGrew and Henry Iams were hired as the new crew members. They proved to be willing workers and helped organize the load of settlers who were going west. The tarp where arrows had burned holes in it needed repairs, and a section of new canvas was sewed in to cover those places. Henry Iams had been a sailor on a windjammer sailing the ports of the world. He soon came to be known as "Hank," proved to be excellent with a needle, and the job looked neat and well done when he finished.

"Ye done a nice job on me tarp," O'Bryan told him.

I was the sail mender on many a ship before I became a landlubber," Hank replied.

When they arrived at Omaha three weeks later, the weather had turned cold and the threat of snow was in the cold damp air. The settlers were unloading and the barge was secured at a pier.

"Ed, what do ye think?" the Captain asked him one day. "There's a boardin' house here where we can stay the winter, and in the spring we can take a load of furs down to Saint Louis. "We'll have the fur traders along with us, and they'll pay us well fer the trip."

"That would be all right with me," Ed replied. "The trip down river might not be so good in cold weather."

Ed was glad for a time to take stock of his life and to decide the direction of his future. He did not feel that he wanted to see his mother at that time, even though he was miles closer to her in Omaha than he had been for several years. There was a young woman school teacher living in the same boarding house and Ed prevailed upon her to help him write a letter to the girl he left behind, Miss Chloe Myrtie Foster. He told her where he was and asked her to write. That accomplished he spent his days exploring the town of Omaha and musing about his past. His thoughts drifted to Vermont and the large log house that had been built in 1832.

He thought of the young Hall boys who had harassed him and of his Grandfather. He barely remembered his mother as one of the ladies of that household, and the pangs of feeling rejected by his mother when she left him as a ward of his Grandfather. He realized a tightness in his throat whenever he thought of those times, and he knew he could not forget those bitter memories.

Chapter Four

First events in Eddy's memory were at four or five living in that large eight room log house in Vermont. Hall was the name of everyone else in that home except his mother and himself. Eddy did not remember his father and when he heard people talking about him, they seemed angry, he did not know why. One day he asked his mother why his name was Foster and everyone else's name was Hall.

"Before you were born I married Hiram Foster, and he became your father," she replied.

"Was your name Hall then?" Eddy asked.

"Yes Edward it was," she answered, "I married your father, and after that you were born. I named you Edward Prescott Foster. In honor of a great uncle who fought in the Revolutionary War."

"Where is my father now?" Eddy asked.

Julia Hall Foster showed rare patience with him.

"He died before you were three years old. It seems like a long time ago, but it was only two years. Hiram, your father, went to war with the "Green Mountain Boys" from Vermont, and he died while he was in the army"

"Are Ethan and James my brothers?" Eddy asked.

"No Ethan and James are your uncles. They are my brothers," she stated. She had daubed at her eyes with a lace handkerchief, and Eddy remembered that she bowed her head. "Please don't ask me about your father, it makes me so sad that he was taken away.

"Why was he taken away?" Eddy asked.

Julia Hall Foster stared blankly at her son. There was a sharpness in her voice and facial expression that warned him never to ask anything more about his father.

"To this day, I don't know why," she replied with a sob.

From that day forward Eddy became more and more aware of the beginning of a cold unresolved frustration between himself and his mother. From his earliest memories there were other children near his age living there. He remembered that he felt powerless and alone when they teased him. As long as he remained in that household they teased him and he still remembered their words.

"Eddy has no papaw, haw, haw haw. Eddy has no papaw," said the older children.

"Orphie, Orphie, Eddy is an Orphie, he don't know who his papa is," the younger ones teased.

When he went to his mother to get understanding, she was rude.

"Edward we are guests in your Grandfather's home, We must endure what we cannot change," she said.

When Grandfather Hall heard their teasing, he sternly said, "we will not have that in this house, I do not want to hear anymore of that kind of teasing," but the jibes just moved away from his presence.

Eddy's attempts to strike back were met with equal frustration. Older boys pinned him down and sat on his chest. Adults usually blocked Eddy from striking back, and his outbursts of frustration and anger were met with isolation without meals.

"Edward you will go to bed without supper," he was told.

He found that his only release was to sullenly obey, and meditate on what he would do "someday." He would run away and go so far that he would never see them again.

"Hiram Foster was a soldier, and not a very good one," he heard his aunt Lucy say. "He was a barroom brawler."

"He was killed by another soldier in a fight," his aunt Mabel replied with a knowing air.

"I don't know how Julia took up with the likes of him," Aunt Lucy stated with a superior lift of her nose.

"He disgraced himself and your family," they told his mother.

He often heard his aunts speak of the Fosters as though they were a step or two below the Hall family. Eddy learned that he and his mother lived with the Halls because she was the daughter of grandfather Gresham Hall, and had no other place to live. Julia Hall was the middle child of Nettie and Gresham Hall. Her mother, Nettie Cole Hall, had married Gresham when they were still in their teens. Nettie was fifteen and Gresham was seventeen. By their early thirties they had parented ten children, and Nettie died in childbirth with her eleventh child. Julia was the middle child in the Hall family.

"A man can't look after his farm and take care of a family as large as Gresham's without a woman in his house," neighbors said.

Remarriage was customary after the death of a husband or wife, and was approved by the church after a year of mourning had passed. Gresham took Cora Jennings to be his wife at the end of that year. She was the daughter of Squire Jennings and was considered a spinster since she was twenty when she married Gresham. He was nearing thirty when they married. Ten children were born to that marriage. Eddy and his mother had come to live in the Hall household when the youngest Hall child had just entered the world. Eddy was two years old and the new addtion to the family meant there were twenty three members in the Hall home living in the log house that had been built in 1735. That house had burned down and a new one replaced it one hundred years later in 1832.

A saying among neighbors was "a big family is a blessing of the Lord. It takes a big brood to help with the farm work."

In Eddy's memory there were two large spinning wheels and a smaller one beside the giant stone fire place. All three were kept busy spinning homespun cloth to make clothing. Older family members and girls were kept busy cleaning, carding, and spinning wool. Every child was taught to do necessary chores. Boys were required to learn to milk cows at an early age. Chores around the barn were assigned to the older boys who were also taught to harness horses and hitch a team to the rock sledge and then go into the fields and remove rocks. Eddy learned the hard lessons of the Yankee work ethic.

"If you don't work, you don't eat." was the motto of the Hall family. "In this house everyone must earn his keep."

Memory brought Eddy to realize that he was often the scapegoat for chores not done. When the barn stalls were not clean enough, when the milk pails were not stored properly, and even when Eddy was just there at the time, he was blamed.

"We told Eddy to put new straw in the stalls, but he didn't do it," Ethan and James said.

"We showed him where to put the milk pails, but he went off somewhere, and we had left the barn," James said.

Grandfather was not inclined to let chores undone go unpunished. He also would not let a boy or boys to whom he had assigned a task shift the responsibility to anyone else. Eddy often witnessed the whippings of the older boys who later passed the punishment on to him and the younger boys. An animosity developed between Eddy and the older boys which led Eddy to deliberately shirk chores when the older boys shifted them to him. Eddy knew they would be punished, and he was willing to receive their blows just to see them whipped by Grandfather. When he sought sympathy from his mother he received none.

"Serves you right, Edward. "You must remember the Golden rule, 'As ye would that others should do unto you, do unto them likewise.'"

To Eddy those words became an excuse for harshness, and in silence he transferred his resentment with the teasing of his uncles to his mother. Neither did his attitude toward those boys improve when his grandfather sent him out with the older boys to do heavier work than the chores he had been doing around the house.

"Edward, tomorrow you will go with the older boys and the rock sledge. Mebbe that will take some of the meanness out of you," Granfather Gresham told him. Eddy was seven years old, and those words and the consequences of them remained in his memory all his life. There was no choice for Eddy and he recognized the sternness in Grandfather's voice, but did not respond.

"Did you hear me, Edward?" Grandfather demanded.

"Y-yes," Eddy stammered.

"You will also help with the milkin'."

The next morning Eddy was roused from sleep at four o'clock and sent to the barn with a pail along with the older boys who felt freer than ever to tease him.

"Hey Froster, where do you think you're goin'?" Ethan asked. "You ain't never milked a cow before. You ain't even big enough to reach old High Pocket's tits. Anyways she'd kick you clean out of the barn if you even touched her.

All the boys laughed, but Eddy remained sullen and silent. He was given the task of trading empty buckets for those that were full as the older boys milked the cows. He was told to carry the full buckets to the cooler which was at the end of the barn. The full pails were heavy and Eddy sloshed some of the milk out of them. By six A.M., the milking was finished and Eddy's pants were soaked with milk, "Young man, you will wear those pants the rest of the day,"

Grandfather stated when the boys reported for breakfast, "and you must wear every pair you slosh milk on for that day."

Eddy endured the discomfort of the milk stiffened pants every day he sloshed milk on them.

Using a long bar and shovel to dislodge rocks in the fields and lifting and placing them on the sledge was a ritual of spring for farmers in Vermont. The loaded sledges were driven to the place where walls needed mending. As aYankee farmer Grandfather was proud of his stone fences and saw to it that they were well kept to outline his pastures and property. To Eddy's mind the problem with rocks was that they came in all sizes. Occasionally the older boys found the largest they could and pried them out of the ground only to call Eddy and tell him to load them on the sledge. Two days of that and Eddy experienced a severe pain in his lower right groin. His Grandfather made a pronouncement after he examined Eddy.

"Edward will need to rest for a day or two," he told Eddy's mother. "He has a slight swelling in his groin."

In the house the next two days Eddy helped move furniture, carried wood for the stoves, saw to it that the spinners had wool, and did other chores. When he returned to the rock crew, the teasing began again.

"Old lady Froster had to do girl's work," one said.

"Did you wear a skirt and an apron?" another asked.

Eddy stared at them sullenly, but said nothing.

At the age of ten it was decided that Eddy was just another mouth to feed, and he was apprenticed to a shoemaker in Saint Johnsbury, Vermont. Ethan was given the task of driving the wagon with Eddy and all his belongings to Saint Johnsbury, and while he drove to town, he took great pleasure in telling Eddy more than he ever wanted to know about John and Mary Alberts, proprietors.

"Ole man Alberts is about as mean as they come," Ethan told Eddy. "He worked his last apprentice to death. His name was Johnny Smith, and I saw him in church when the Albertses had him with them. Old man Alberts used to holler that he was a bastard and had no rights. He treated Johnny worse than a slave, and he'll treat you the same way. Johnny got tuberculosis, and he died in the room where you'll prob'ly sleep. Alberts didn't teach him anythin'about makin' shoes."

"Mebbe, it won't be any worse than it was on the farm," Eddy said with a tinge of sarcasm.

"You forget who you are, "Ethan said with anger in his voice. "We Halls have a chance to inherit somethin', but you have no chance at all. Seein' as how you are an orphan."

As they rode along, Eddy experienced the tightness that always rose in his throat when he thought of what might lie ahead. He had hoped that getting out of the Hall house would be a better life, but his hopes sank as he listened to Ethan.

"The Alberts never let Johnny out of the house if they could keep him in, but he was able to sneak out a time or two. I talked to him one time when I was in town He told me old man Alberts kept a buggy whip in his shop. If Johnny forgot to do his chores, the old man whipped him with it. That's what you got ahead of you."

Eddy sensed gloating in Ethan's voice, but had no time to react as they drove up in front of a small shop on Main Street where a small crude sign read JOHN ALBERTS, SHOEMAKER. Eddy lowered himself from the wagon seat and Ethan gathered his carpet bag of clothing from the wagon bed and handed it to him. Their parting was brief and direct.

"Goodbye, and good luck," Ethan said.

"Goodbye," Eddy answered.

If Eddy thought the shop was dingy outside, it was almost dark inside except for a lamp over a bench where an older man with grey brown hair was pounding with a hammer. As he drew closer Eddy saw that the man was pounding nails in the heel of a boot. The old man neither turned his head toward Eddy, nor did he stop pounding nails. Finally the old man turned toward Eddy, but neither of them spoke. Not knowing what to say Eddy remained silent.

"I'm too busy to vait fer you to tell me vhat you vant," the old man said. "Speak up or get oudt so I can go back to verk."

"I'm...," Eddy hesitated and then started again. "I'm Eddy Froster, I mean Foster."

The old man stopped work and it seemed to Eddy that he was looking right through him to his backbone, which he felt was none too secure at that moment in this strange place.

"So you're Eddy Foster," the old man said as he left the shoe last and the boot. "You're small fer a ten year old."

He came around the counter and felt Eddy's arm for muscle.

"You hain't got a lot of muscle," Alberts said shaking his head.

"Your grandfather said you vorked right along vith his older boys." He then began to list Eddy's duties with his German accent.

"You must rise by four thirty each morning, sveep the shop, straighten the verkbench, build a fire vhen needed, keep vood for the fire, und make sure the fire does not go oudt. Leather, hammer, nails und other supplies must be made ready for my days verk."

As he outlined these duties, he took Eddy quickly around the shop showing him where equipment and supplies were kept.

"Pay attention that I keep everything in its place. I expect my verk bench to be neat at all times, und don't bother me vith questions."

No further instructions were given and the old man went to the rear of the shop and pulled a cord. A bell somewhere above the shop rang and a wrinkled and bent old woman soon appeared. John Alberts told his wife who Eddy was and returned to his work. Mrs Alberts did not acknowledge the introduction.

"He looks too puny to be of much help. Vy do you have to take on such veaklings?" She did not wait for a reply, but spoke to Eddy.

"Idle hands are the Devil's playground," she said. "Vhen you are not doing chores in the shop, I expect you to help me vith the houseverk. Come along, I show you vhere you vill sleep."

Eddy thought she lifted her nose and sniffed as she led him to the stairway that led to their living quarters.

"I verk long hours with my husband und you vill see that there is oil in the lamps. Fuel for the fires is stored in the shed out back vhere you vill find the outhouse, the chicken pens und the cowshed. Keep the shed doors closed vhen you feed the cow or get vood for the house. See that the outhouse is supplied, and that it is cleaned. Do you know how to milk?"

Eddy nodded.

"Ven you milk you vill feed hay and grain for the cow and grain for the chickens."

Eddy thought she was finished with her instructions when she asked, "do you understand?" He acknowledged that he did.

"You vill keep vood for the kitchen in the bin beside the stove. You must feed the chickens morning und evening. Feed costs money so don't vaste any. The cow must have hay morning und night vhen you milk." She paused for a long time.

This time Eddy thought she was finished, but she repeated instructions about the outhouse and added, "the hen house and cow stall must be kept in clean straw, and eggs must be gathered daily."

"There is no time for idleness here," she stated. "Should you find your chores are finished you must come to me for other duties. Do you understand me? You vill be vipped if you forget."

Eddy felt overwhelmed as he nodded his answer. He remembered the things Ethan told him about Johnny Smith, "they worked him to death, and they'll likely do the same to you.," and again Mrs Albert continued.

"If things go vell here, you vill have time on Sunday to go to Church vith John und me. Ve are Christian family und ve expect you to sit vith us quietly. Scripture says 'Vatsoever thy hand findeth to do, do it vith thy might.' If you fail in your duties, punishment vill be sure." For the moment she stood and looked Eddy over from head to toe, shaking her head all the while.

"I'll say one thing for you, you don't say much. Your room is up that stairvay. I vill not go up since I am oldt. See that you keep your room neat. My husband vill inspect daily. Papa vill vhip you if you don't keep it neat. For sassing papa or me there iss vhipping."

She shook her head as she turned away, Eddy went to his room in the attic where there was a single cot, a mattress, a blanket, pillow and single sheet folded neatly at one end. Eddy glanced around the room which was lighted by a single small window in a dormer above the bed. There was barely enough room for him to stand, and there was just enough room to walk between the bed and the wall.

From age ten to fourteen there had been at least a whipping a week, and meals had been withheld at least three times a week. At fourteen Eddy wondered how he had survived the four years of limited suppers and whippings. He learned that he could not confront the Albertses face to face. That led to more whippings and loss of meals, but by setting the Old Man and the Old Woman to arguing with one another about chore priorities, he gained time and some pleasure because they never tired of arguing with one another. He inwardly laughed to see them at it. At fourteen he knew that no one else could or would solve his problems, and that, if action were to take place, he must act for himself. In the dark of one summer night he packed his belongings in his carpet bag and crept down the stairs and out a window of the shop.

Laws at that time favored the shop owner regarding an apprentice. Old Man Alberts had told Eddy that no apprentice of his would ever get far "avay." Posters with a description of Eddy soon appeared throughout the region along with newspaper ads offering a reward for the return of one "Eddy Foster, Apprentice to John Alberts, Saint Johnsbury, Vermont." Eddy travelled at night and slept in haystacks or barns during the day. He sucessfully made his way to Bennington, Vermont where he knew Uncle John Roberts lived. Uncle John had married Alice, a younger sister of Eddy's mother, and for the first time in his life he felt wanted.

When Eddy arrived in Bennington, he felt bold enough to inquire of the towns people for directions to the Roberts' farm where he was welcomed into the family. John Roberts was a kind man who saw in Eddy a potential farm hand and helper. Alice Roberts believed in education and was teaching her two daughters, who were five and seven, reading and numbers, and she welcomed Eddy as another pupil. She helped Eddy write letters to his mother, now living in Chicago with a distant cousin. Return letters from Chicago informed him that she had gone to Central City, Nebraska where she was living with another sister who was married to Jason Norton. His mother wished Eddy well, but she did not invite him to come to Nebraska. She did give him the address of cousin Franklin Foster who lived in Chicago. Eddy stayed with the Roberts family two years…years that brought him a sense of manhood and convinced him that he was ready for new sights and adventures. He talked to Uncle Johnny about setting off on his own, and Johnny gave him ten dollars and wished him well.

In 1879 westward travel was by Conestoga wagon, horseback, on foot or by railroad. Eddy started his journey on foot with ten dollars in his pocket, which was all Uncle Johnny could spare, but more than he had ever had. He joined a wagon train, and helped drive livestock belonging to the movers as far west as Ohio. At Toledo he decided to buy a train ticket to Chicago, and arrived there two and a half months after leaving Bennington. He had written to the Chicago Fosters before he left Bennington and received word that they would welcome a visit. He sent a telegram from Toledo telling them when he would arrive in Chicago.

Chapter Five

The Chicago Fosters traced their ancestry to David Foster who had settled in Vermont with his brother John in 1732. Four generations later the name of Franklin Foster was well known in business and social circles of Chicago. During the war between the states, Franklin had become wealthy trading in grain futures, and had been elected President of the Chicago Board of Trade. He directed his home with the pride and precision he had used to reach his business goals. He demonstrated his pride in his family by carefully overseeing the lives of his two daughters, Chloe Myrtie and Cora Elaine, and his young son, Franklin William. He was well pleased with the management of his home provided by his wife Myrtie. He believed that he could achieve more with "sugar rather than vinegar," and made it a point to praise those who took his goals as their own.

"I am especially aware of the way you have managed the lives of our children." he often told his wife. "You have given our girls great ideals. Chloe will become a fine pianist, Cora will become a manager just like her mother, and Franklin will walk in my footseps."

"The girls get along well and I am proud of them," Myrtie replied. "Right now I'm trying to get them ready for the Spring Piano Recital, and we're going to be late unless they hurry."

Franklin laughed at her anxieties, said his goodbyes and departed for his office. There was the sound of giggling girls coming from upstairs. Myrtie hurried to the foot of the stairway and called.

"Girls we should be leaving for the recital," she called.

Upstairs Chloe stood before the mirror as Jessamin fluffed her curls, and straightened her sash.

"You will be the prettiest chile in the recital," she said, "and you'll play the bestest of the whole program. Jus' you wait and see."

"Do you really think so?"

"I surely do honey. I've heered you practicin' an you really do knock the music out of that piano."

"I hope you're right."

"I knows you will" Jessamin said. "You knock the spots offa them piano keys."

Chloe curtsied to this woman who had cared for her since her earliest memory, and whom she cared about deeply.

"Thanks Jessamin, I hear mother calling me so I must hurry downstairs now," Chloe bounded quickly down the stairs where her mother inspected her costume and nodded approval. Her mother directed her voice up the stairway as she had before.

"Cora, please hurry. Aren't you ready yet?"

There was another rustle of crinoline and lace as Cora rushed down the stairs and joined them. The girls were dressed in the same fashion and they looked enough alike to be twins, except that Chloe was an inch or two taller and two years older. Both girls had light brown hair, a light complexion and the bright blue eyes that were characteristic of their family.

"Will father be at the recital?" Cora asked.

"We must hurry to the carriage. Franklin said he would try to be there, but he has important business today," her mother answered.

"He's always too busy to know what we're doing." There was petulance in Cora's voice.

Myrtie did not respond to her daughter as she shooed the young ladies to the carriage in the manner of a hen with chicks, while she directed the driver to their destination. Seated in the carriage, the girls began to chatter about the recital.

"I hope that awful Corinne Palmer doesn't play 'The Boatmen of Venice,' Cora stated.

"That would ruin the whole program for me," Chloe sighed.

"Well, you play much better than she does," Cora replied.

"Maybe I should have chosen a more difficult piece." "Honey, you will do fine." Mother was combing the rat's nests from Cora's hair. "You should brush and comb more often."

Cora winced and yelled with each pull of the comb.

Arriving at the auditorium, they quickly entered, and were greeted by many friends and neighbors. Cora and Myrtie found seats while Chloe made her way to the ready room with the other pianists. Mrs. Palmer was giving last minute instructions about the order of the program. When she saw Chloe, she came to her and put an arm around her shoulders.

"Chloe, I know you have practiced 'The Boatmen of Venice.' I prefer not to change the program at the last minute, but would you mind playing the 'Blue Danube.' You play that so well."

Mrs. Palmer did not wait for Chloe's answer, nor did she notice the shocked expression on her face.

"Students, there has been a change in the program," she stated. "Chloe is going to play 'The Blue Danube.' Corinne will play 'The Boatmen of Venice. Hurry now children we must seat ourselves while I announce the program to the audience."

Chloe thought she saw a smirk in Corinne's expression.

"Mother says I play "The Boatmen of Venice" much better than you," Corinne whispered, "and anyways I will win first prize."

To herself Chloe thought "I hate you Corinne, and I don't care about 'The New Book of Etudes, either." To Corinne she said, "I will do my best, and I hope you do too."

There were ten students in the recital and Chloe was the sixth to play. Her feelings were a mixture of anger and sadness when she finished. She knew she had made two mistakes that the judges couldn't help but notice. Winners were announced and Corinne won first prize just as she said she would. Two other students were awarded second and third prizes. Chloe received Honorable Mention.

To herself she said "horrible mention."

"That old Mrs. Palmer, I hate her," she said bitterly in the carriage going home. "I hate that silly Corinne most of all."

"Old lady Palmer shouldn't have changed the program," Cora stated as she tried to put her arm around Chloe's shoulder. Chloe shook herself free to hear what her mother was saying.

"Honey, you learned an important lesson today…"

Chloe interrupted her mother.

"I hate her and I hate Corinne. The judges were all friends of Mrs Palmer's. I couldn't have won no matter what I did." They weren't even fair." Chloe sobbed and daubed tears that were coursing down her cheeks already reddened by anger.

"I hate old lady Palmer too." Corinne said in sympathy.

"Disappointments come to all of us," Myrtie said as she drew Chloe close. "I know that you played your best in a difficult situation, but you can learn from that experience. You learned that you must do your best even when things are beyond your control."

Chloe often repeated those words to herslf in later years, but she changed their context to "Do your best regardless of circumstances."

Three days later she was practicing at the piano when Cora came and excitedly sat beside her.

"Did you hear that we have a cousin from Vermont coming to visit us?" she asked.

"What's she like?" Chloe asked disinterestedly.

"It's a boy and his name is Edward Prescott Foster. I heard mama and papa talking about him after dinner just before I came here"

"How is he related to us?"

"Papa said he's some kind of distant cousin."

"Did they say anything else about him?"

"They didn't know much about him except he's about fifteen or sixteen years old."

"When is he coming?" Chloe asked.

"He's due on the train tomorrow morning." At that moment Mrs. Foster joined her daughters. "I heard you talking about our visitor," she said. "We will be taking the carriage to the station in the morning and will meet him then. He will stay with us for a few days. His mother lives in Nebraska. You both met her several years ago. Her name is Julia Foster. She's my sister. You girls may go with us if you like."

"That should be fun," Cora stated. "Just think of meeting a cousin you didn't even know you had."

"It doesn't sound interesting to me," Chloe sounded dissident. "I would rather stay and practice for next year's Piano Recital."

"Please come with us," Cora persisted. "I would feel out of place going without you."

At first sight Chloe was not impressed with the young man standing by the information kiosk. He was slightly taller than she with a slender rather stoop shouldered stance. In the carriage he was shy and distant making comments only when he was asked a question. Chloe noticed two things about him. He had bright ice blue eyes that expressed more than he said, and his hands were rough and scarred.

When they arrived home, Franklin met them, and was introduced. He directed Eddy to a room above the carriage house, and informed Eddy about mealtimes along with an outline of the families usual evening schedule. Cora could hardly wait to have a conversation with Chloe about "cousin" Eddy Foster in their bedroom.

"How old do you think he is?" Cora asked.

"He can't be much older than I am," Chloe stated with obvious disinterest. "He's only just as tall as I am and he's very thin."

"What do you think of him?"

"There's not much to think. He didn't say enough for anyone to be impressed with his conversation."

"You didn't like him." There was accusation in Cora's voice.

"I neither liked him nor disliked him." Chloe was not aware of the note of superiority in her tone, but Cora was.

"Mother says you can't be neutral about anyone. She says that a person forms impressions about everyone they meet."

"Well, my first impression of Mister Edward Prescott Foster is that he seems like a frightened country rabbit."

That evening at dinner Eddy was unsure of which piece of silverware to use and how to use a napkin. He was awkard in his responses to the serving maid, and seemed embarrassed at his ineptness. Chloe began to feel sorry for him as her father directed one question after another to him about his background.

"What do you know of your line of Fosters?" Franklin asked.

"N…not very much, sir," Eddy replied.

"Since we have the same last name and your mother wrote that we are seventh cousins, I wondered where your line of Fosters settled. Was it New England or Marryland?"

"In Vermont, sir. That's about all I know about the Fosters."

"Do you know the name of the town where you were born?"

"My mother told me I was born in Newbury, Vermont."

"Your father and I were from different branches of the Foster family," Franklin stated. "As I see it he and I were seventh cousins which makes our children eighth cousins."

Franklin asked no more questions, and Eddy kept his eyes on his plate. He was silent for the rest of the meal as Chloe and Cora excitedly told their father about happenings at the recital.

"Edward, if you aren't too tired from your traveling, we would love to have you join us in the parlor. Chloe will play some of the old songs, and we will circle around the piano and sing."

The family did as Myrtie had directed and Eddy joined them. He knew neither the tunes nor the words to the songs Chloe played, but he was fascinated by her grace and poise while she played. Mrs Foster tried to make him comfortable by asking people to move so Eddy could see the words, but his discomfort became obvious as the rest of the family joined in singing. Finally Franklin asked if he would like to go to his room, and Eddy nodded that he would.

When the girls were alone in their room, Cora was the first to speak.

"What a country bumpkin he is. He is exactly what you said, a frightened country rabbit."

"He certainly seemed out of place," Chloe responded.

"He's a clumsy ox if I ever saw one." Cora giggled at the thought. "He was certainly not like the boys we know in Chicago."

In the morning the girls repeated their impressions of Eddy to their mother who mildly reprimanded them.

"Girls just remember that you don't know the character of a book until you read it. Try to get Edward to tell you more about himself, and you surely need to be friendlier," she added. "After all he is family. His mother and I are sisters."

We have just barely met him," Cora said as though that gave them the right to form an opinion about him.

Chloe decided to follow her mother's advice, and during the five days of Eddy's stay with the Chicago Fosters, she tried to talk to him as much as possible.

"Did you decide you liked him?" Cora asked her later.

"I don't know," Chloe stated, and there was a noncharacteristic bewilderment in her tone.

"Oh, oh, I think you love him."

Chloe hesitated. "No, I don't think that."

"You felt sorry for him then.?"

"I wouldn't say sorry…" Chloes voice sounded meditative.

"What then?" Cora persisted.

"He's a person…that's it. He's a person who doesn't know himself. And he was bewildered in our home."

"You mean he doesn't know anything about his family?"

"No, he doesn't know who he is inside…He hasn't found himself. He's like a cocoon that becomes a butterfly. He's still inside his cocoon struggling to get out as a person."

Myrtie joined her daughters in time to hear Cora summarizing their conversation about Eddy.

"I think you love him. He doesn't have much to offer anyone. Did you see the carpet bag he carried and his shabby clothes? I certainly would want the boy I fall in love with to be better off."

Chloe did not answer. Mother said nothing, but her determined expression indicated that was not the end of the discussion as she and Cora rose and left the room. Alone, Chloe reviewed the conversation Eddy had told her about between himself and her father, and she remembered unexpressed sadness in his manner.

"Mister Foster told me not to get interested in either of his daughters," Eddy had said. "He said I had nothin' to offer anyone at your family's level. He didn't ask me where I wanted to go, but he gave me money enough to return to Vermont. Then he told me he wanted to see me when I had a more suitable station in life."

There was embarrassment in Eddy's manner, and Chloe realized that he had been made fully aware of his lack of resources.

"He is a person," she absently mused, "and he's just as worthy as anyone I have ever met."

Later her mother lectured her about how to relate to young men.

"Girls your age often develop feelings for boys they think are handsome or cute, but at thirteen you need to develop interests of your own. There are many boys that you will come to admire and even feel sorry for, but you cannot base your life on those feelings. I'm glad you made Edward welcome in our home, but he has much to learn and earn before you should consider him seriously."

"Mother, he didn't ask me to marry him or even to wait until we were older," Chloe stated, "and anyway I'm not ready to talk about marriage to anyone."

"You have plenty of time to find 'Mr Right,'" Myrtie said, "and your father wants you to become an accomplished horsewoman, and along with your love of nature, you should plan to study that field later on. You have a whole life ahead of you, don't waste it on a boy like Edward. You may write to him if you like.

"I will write to him if you or father will give me his address."

"I see no harm in that," her mother stated. "I will talk to your father, perhaps he has an address for Edward…or his mother."

At that moment Chloe felt an emptiness, and she knew that Eddy was one person she wanted to see again.

Chapter Six

At seventeen Chloe graduated from High School as Valedictorian of her class. She chose the topic "America, Land of Opportunity," and cited her father and two other businessmen in Chicago as examples of success. She had dedicated herself to achieving her goals, and she felt that she had earned her first reward which was a full scholarship to Chicago Normal School where she planned to continue her education for a teaching career. It was customary that a dinner and debutante ball be held at the Chicago Country Club for the new graduates, and Chloe was elected Princess.

"I should have been elected Princess." Corinne stated as they were getting ready for the processional.

"You could have been, if your mother had been in charge."

Chloe could not keep the sarcasm from her voice and grinned as Corinne lifted her nose and swished her gown as she haughtily strode away. Parents and young people mingled on the ballroom floor, and there were excited greetings and congratulations for the young ladies and gentlemen who had graduated. The <u>Chicago</u> <u>Tribune</u> sent a photographer, and a picture of the elite of the city's young people appeared in the next day's edition of the paper.

"You were so pretty. You were magnificent. I'm very proud you are my sister," Cora stated in the carriage later.

"Guess what I told Corinne Palmer." Chloe gloated while a wry smile spread across her face.

"I hope you put her in her place."

"She whispered that she should have been the Princess, and I told her she could have been, if her mother had been in charge."

"A princess must learn to control her feelings," her mother stated. "You must remember that 'kindness is to do and say the kindest thing in the kindest way. Next time you see Corinne, I think you should apologize."

"After all the mean things she has said to me ever since we were little?" Chloe's anger flashed as she spoke. "I can never forgive her."

"For you to be sarcastic lowers you to the other person's level. Being kind puts the burden of bad behavior on the unkind person."

"Mother, There are times when a nasty person must be put in their place. You just don't know how mean Corinne has been to me."

"Meeting another person's nastiness with meanness of your own never makes a bad situation better."

Chloe knew her mother was right, but she couldn't help inwardly gloating to think that she had finally gotten even with Corinne. During that summer Chloe enjoyed more freedom than she had ever experienced before. There were nature hikes, horseback riding, tennis at the club, and dancing. Chloe limited her time to the things she liked to do most while she completed the procedures for enrollment in Chicago Normal. She arrived at the school early the morning of registration for all students.

"Why do you wish to enter Chicago Normal?"

Chloe had completed her forms, and was now called to the Registrar's office where she had been asked to wait while her papers were reviewed, but she had not expected to be asked that question.

"My desire is to become a teacher." Chloe stated.

"Many young ladies from your social circle enter our institution, but they do not complete the course for one reason or another. Most find too large a separation between the life they were living and the hard road to becoming a teacher."

"Ma'am, I am a person who finishes what I start," Chloe replied.

Attending college brought many changes in Chloe's social life. She spent an occasional evening with Cora at a concert or at the theater, but she limited her time to her studies and to her family. She had many opportunities to date very eligible young men, but her goal of becoming a teacher, and her memory of Eddy kept her from seriously dating anyone. She completed the requirements for a teaching certificate in two years, and could legally have taught, but she decided to obtain a four year degree at Chicago University.

"It was the proudest day of my life when I received the Bachelor of Arts degree with a teaching credential," Chloe told her family.

"You have pleased your father a great deal," Myrtie stated. "He especially appreciated your emphasis in music and language."

"The School Board has assigned me to South Side High School to teach Latin and English," Chloe replied. "I will report the last week of August, and will meet with the faculty. I will be given my class schedule then. Mother, I'm really frightened."

"I have confidence that you will do well," Her mother said.

South Chicago was an area in transition since the War Between the States had released many former slaves from plantations in the South who had traveled North. Many had settled in tenements near meat packing plants, or near manufacturing plants where there were many types of unskilled employment. Laws requiring education brought many black students into the classrooms of South Chicago. Into this milieu entered Chloe Myrtie Foster in September with her heart and mind full of eagerness to prove she was a teacher. She very soon found herself being introduced to her fellow teachers by Dr. Rubicoff, Superintendent.

"Ladies and Gentlemen, Miss Chloe Foster will join our faculty this fall as a teacher of English and Latin. She comes to us highly recommended by her professors and supervisors at Chicago University. Please stand Miss Foster so that the faculty will recognize you as one of our fine South Side faculty." He paused for Chloe to stand. There was polite applause as Chloe briefly stood and quickly sat down.

Dr. Rubicoff continued with announcements for the beginning of the school year. He then added a note to teachers.

"Our schools are receiving an increasing number of students from families who were former slaves. Most of these families have very limited incomes, and so they must live the best they can in older tenements, or makeshift shanties. Children from these families may be of High School age, but they have had little or no formal schooling. We do not have a great number of such children, but they do call for teaching that will give them the best foundation possible. Language classes will need to focus on the abilities of these students. Mathematics and science teachers will need to individualize their teaching to the needs of these pupils. As much as possible we will group these students according to their abilities, and we will try to make their classes as uniform as possible."

Room assignments and class schedules were given by the Dean of the Faculty. Department Chairpersons were recognized and the faculty for each department was dismissed to go to their assigned areas.   As she walked down the halls of this building that had survived many generations of students, Chloe was impresssed with the odor of floor oil, soap, chalk dust, and wood polish. The high ceilinged hallway, and the wainscoted walls made her aware that she was entering a career that was rich in the tradition of this hallowed hall of learning.   Her primary assignment was to the English Department. She was joined by Miss Froman, Language Department Chairperson.

"First morning embarking on a teaching career can be tense and frightening," Miss Froman said. "We older teachers have all been through it. No one can take away the feeling of fright and loneliness as you face your classes that first day. Our Department works together, if you have needs, you may come to any one of us and we will do our best to help you."

"I'm really eager to meet my classes," Chloe said as Miss Froman smiled in memory, and mentally compared it to her own first day, when she faced her first classes.

"Our policies have established that the teacher is in charge of the classroom. That means that you set the tone for study with discipline and control. It is much easier to be a disciplinarian in the beginning. You can ease up later, if your situation warrants it." Miss Froman said She and Chloe entered the Department meeting together where she was reintroduced to the Faculty of the Language Department.

For the first week of teachers meetings, morning hours were given to Department details and to area meetings for Latin, French, German, and English teachers. Afternoon hours were used by teachers for getting their classrooms ready. Chloe lined bulletin boards where she placed her theme for the year. "Language is Basic." Her teaching assignment included four classes of Latin and two of English. She attended a District reception for new teachers in the afternoon of her second day. Miss Froman piloted Chloe from group to group until she was called away to a meeting. A group of new teachers were chatting amiably when she heard someone behind her saying something that interrupted her thoughts.

"You beginning teachers still have the shine of idealism in your eyes." Chloe turned to face a white haired gentleman with brown eyes and a distinguished bearing.

"I am eager to start teaching," she said.

"My name is Paul Jones. I am Chair of the Science Department which is a department for men only. I teach Chemistry and Physics."

"I'm Chloe Foster. I will be teaching Latin and English."

"Lord, how green I was when I started teaching eighteen years ago. It didn't take me long to learn that you need a hickory stick as your best aid in the classroom, and another thing, I am an evolutionist and do not hold with all this creation poppy cock."

His comments made Chloe aware that he was itching for an attack on anyone who believed in creation or on anyone who held opinions opposite from his own.

"I am a believer in the Creator God," she stated, "but I do not debate that question openly in public places."

"Oh ho," Mr. Jones remarked. "Anytime you wish to discuss your beliefs in private I will be glad to meet you. By the way, I have an extra hickory stick I will lend you, when you need it."

"Teachers who make their classroom presentations interesting and appealing to their students should not need a hickory stick," Chloe stated.

"I like your spunk," Mister Jones stated. "I will agree, there are any number of methods of teaching and maintaining discipline. And I also know that you can't teach without it. When discipline is lax learning suffers."

"John Denton at the University believes teaching should be pupil centered," Miss Froman had joined the group and heard Mister Jones final remarks. "Mister Jones believes that subject matter is more important than student attitudes. He maintains good control in his classroom. His students do learn his subjects and many take top honors when they enter the University. He prepares them very well."

Teachers were dismissed to go to their rooms, and Chloe spent the rest of the day reviewing lessons, and by the day's end felt that she was ready for her classes which began the next morning. Students in her Latin classes seemed as eager to learn as she was to teach. Two children of color were in her third hour advanced Latin class. Their families had been in Chicago for two generations and they had been with most of her students through the lower grades. Chloe soon learned that their achievement equalled or surpassed most of her other students. Her Freshman English classes were made up of one third such students, one third immigrant students from southern Europe. and one third second or third generation students. Chloe soon found that the students who had been in the Chicago system from first grade were competitive, and those students were eager to learn. These students kept her busy planning studies that challenged them.

Freshman English classes proved to be the most difficult to teach and to plan. Many of the students who had been in Chicago schools were motivated to learn and their achievement levels were high, but for newcomers achievement was about the same, and most seemed to be street smart, but not academically inclined. She asked Miss Froman why, and was told that many of these students did not have a solid background because their families had been transient and many families were emigrants who had no schooling until they arrived in Chicago. One evening Chloe talked to her mother about the problem of teaching so varied a group of students.

"I'm having trouble finding how to start my Freshman English classes." She stated. "I have such a mixed group. Some of them barely speak English, and others have a mixture of English and street language. The rest of the school population teases the newcomers, and I've heard that there are fights after school. Several of these students would rather spend their time on the streets than in school."

"You stated that your motto was 'Language is Basic,'" her mother replied. "Perhaps, you need to teach the basics of Language."

"Yes, but I don't know where to start."

"What have you learned about Language?"

"Language is communication. Language can separate people or it can bring them together."

"There are mechanics of language such as spelling, parts of speech and tenses. You must find out how much they know of these and use that as your beginning point."

"I guess I best talk to Miss Froman as soon as possible."

Chloe was surprised that Miss Froman knew her dilemma.

"Do you see a solution to your problem?" Miss Froman asked.

"I talked to my mother about it and she says I should find the basic levels of the students knowledge and begin there."

"That's excellent," Miss Froman stated. "But you'll have to boil that idea down to a lesson plan. When you've done that return to me and we'll go from there. You must do that as soon as possible. You should begin by asking your pupils to write about things they do after and before school."

The next day Chloe asked her classes to write about their time away from school. She was surprised at their lack of knowledge of the mechanics of language. She found that these students could not form sentences, nor could they spell. The first response from the students was to ask questions.

"Miz Foster how does you spell after?" "How do you spell school?" Some of their written responses were simple word phrases.

"Play stret," "hom is grama," "papa gone," were samples.

Chloe noted their use of verbs such as, play, gone and is, and she felt she could begin by expanding that idea. The next Monday Chloe consulted Miss Froman.

"I've been thinking of reassigning several of your students," she said. She noted a frown on her young teacher's face. "How many language deficient students are in both sections of Freshman English?"

Chloe thought for a moment.

"About eighteen."

"Eighteen…, if we were to assign all those students to a new section along with the one or two others from your other sections, you could gear your teaching to their needs. We can select two advanced students to become your helpers who will work with those having difficulty. When you have done that, come to me and we will set up new sections, but your work load will be the same."

The next Monday Chloe met her new sections. At first progress was minimal, but by mid year these students were writing more correctly in simple complete sentences and their requests for help with spelling had greatly diminished. Miss Froman noted this progress.

"A teacher who can teach several ability levels of students and do it well is a great asset to the profession. Miss Foster you have taken a large step to becoming an excellent teacher."

At the end of her third year Chloe was selected Teacher of the Year. She was twenty-three and single. Each year she had worked as a teacher seemed better than the year before. She was pleased and surprised at the announcement her father made at the end of that year.

"My dear wife and children," he solemnly stated, "the time has come that I believe we need a change. We have all been cooped up in this house and we need a change of scenery."

"What do you have in mind, Franklin?" Myrtie asked.

"Tell us…tell us," Franklin, junior shouted.

"Well…" Franklin paused to savor this moment. "I must tour the grainbelt of the midwest, and I thought we might make it a summer of travel. We will tour Minnesota, Wisconsin, North and South Dakota, Kansas and Nebraska. Is everyone up for that kind of adventure?"

"Oh, yes papa, when can we start." Franklin answered eagerly.

"As soon as we can pack the things we need," he replied.

While his family experienced the wonders of the grainbelt, Franklin visited with the storage operators and grain growers. For the first time in his career he visited the heartlands and saw first hand the methods of harvesting, handling, and shipping their products that were the life blood of the Chicago Board of Trade. He was more than pleased that he had arranged the trip.

When Myrtie asked him to explain he replied, "I have seen first hand the growing of hard winter wheat and soft wheat and how these make a difference to processors and bakers. I have heard farmers talk of drought and its effect on harvests. I have seen fields blighted by smut and have talked to farmers who experienced losses because of that. These are experiences few grain dealers in Chicago have., and it has been a real education to me."

To Chloe the highlight of the trip was a visit to the Jason Norton farm and her visit with Eddy Foster's mother. After the niceties of getting acquainted, she had a most enlightening conversation.

"Has your son written to you?" she asked.

"No, and I don't expect that he will," Julia replied.

"You don't expect to hear from him?" Chloe wondered.

"Edward feels that I abandoned him as a child." Julia stated.

"I was glad he was able to visit our family in Chicago," Chloe said. "When did you see him last?"

"I've seen him once since he left the Hall farm in Vermont. He was about fourteen then."

Chloe thought she detected wistfulness in Julia's voice.

"Ed had very little to say about his past or his family, but I feel he would very much like to be with his family," Chloe stated.

"When you saw him, did he tell you where he was going or what he intended to do?" Julia asked.

"I only know that father gave him money to return to Vermont. I have had no letters from him, but I have sent him several."

"He hasn't informed me that he ever went back there, and I feel he should have written long ago to tell me what he is doing," "I have not heard from him since he left us. I was hoping you might have an address so that I could write to him." Chloe noted an expression she could not interpret, and Julia seemed uncomfortable.

"As far as Edward is concerned, I do not know whether he is alive or dead." Julia rose. "It seems he doesn't care whether I live or die."

"Could I write to him here?" Chloe asked. "Would you give him my letters if you do get an address for him?"

"You may write if you like. I will hold the letters here if he comes here, but I don't think you can count on his writing." Julia turned and abruptly left the room.

"I can better understand Ed's reluctance to tell us about his past after meeting his mother." Chloe told Cora later. "I have written several letters to him, but I didn't know where to send them. I will send them here, and hope that his mother will find a way to forward them to Ed."

The next day the Franklin Foster family departed for their home in Chicago. Before leaving Chloe wrote a brief letter asking Ed to write to her. She gave the letter to Julia with a prayer that she would find it in her heart to send it to Ed. She could not know that Ed would arrive at the Jason Norton farm later that same month.

Chapter Seven

There was a frantic hurrying everywhere Eddy went in Omaha. The railroad switching yard was one of the busiest places Eddy had ever seen. Just a few years before his arrival the transcontinental railroad had been completed to California, but the excitement of railroad building was in the air. Railroad workers were everywhere, and there was a constant sound of train whistles in the air which never ceased, even at night. Sport hunters from across the ocean stayed in the fanciest hotel, and Ed never tired of seeing their outlandish costumes. Most wore tan khaki jodhpurs, well polished riding boots, tan hunting coats, and jungle hats. Most of these gentlemen were accompanied by wealthy businessmen or executives from the railroads. Eddy enjoyed standing on the street corners and listening to the way they talked. He was not so concerned about what they said, it was the way they said things.

"I say old boy," one would say, "will there be a train to the plains in the offing this ahfternoon?"

"Hi've maide inquiry of our guide, Wild Bill (or is it Bill Buffalo?) about our shedule. We will depart before six in the A.M."

Eddy tried to imitate, but his Vermont twang got in the way, and his tongue did not always obey his will. Occasionally there would be an accent familiar to him, and he expected to find someone from the Vermont area, but whoever had spoken was dressed in the same manner as all the other "fops and nabobs" as Captain O'Bryan had labled them. Both the Captain and Eddy felt the same about men who put on "airs" just to impresss other men. They found a clothing store that sold the kind of clothing they were used to, which was dungarees or Levi Strauss jeans and blue chambray shirts. They had bought no clothing while they were on the river.

The boarding house where the Captain and Eddy were staying was on a back street. Through the winter there were eight men who boarded there including the Captain and Eddy. The Captain had warned Eddy that he should not ask questions of any of these men, but that could not keep the men themselves from chiding one another about their pasts. There was Jack Holcomb, who had lost his left eye.

Jack Blade called him "one eyed Jack." Apparently John Blade, who was called Jack, was the man who teased and played pranks on anyone he decided was a likely target.

"Jack," Blade challenged, "Do yuh see just half the world?"

"I see all of it, and I see the half that you don't," Jack replied with obvious annoyance. "I see the whole world, but you look at it without seeing half of it. In my case one eye is better than your two."

Eddy was glad he was with the Captain because no one bothered him, but when Eddy was on his own he came in for his share of pranks. He might rise in the morning to find his sox tied in knots, or when he turned in for the night, he could find anything in his bed, such as a toad or a broomstick under his mattress. The Captain warned Eddy to acept this kind of horseplay with a grin, "but if it gits out of hand, I'll see that it stops."

The Captain had decided to go to work as a roustabout loading and unloading barges on the river front. Eddy started work selling the <u>Omaha World Herald</u> and took up a stand outside the police station where he sold papers for a month until he heard of work as a runner for the Police Department. On that job he found himself learning about crime in Omaha. He was surprised to see paperwork on Jack Blade, and Jack Holcomb on an officer's desk. Neither of these men had talked about their past, and Eddy wondered how they came to have files in that department. He decided to ask the Officer on whose desk he had seen the file, and found himself in for a justified reprimand.

"Everything on my desk is private," John Runyon stated. "You may read any name you like on any notepad I have, but keep it to yourself. I guess I'll have to call you 'Curious Eddy,'" and the nickname stuck for as long as Eddy worked there.

The day came when Blade and Holcomb were brought to the station house. They were sullen and silent, but Eddy saw them staring at him with anger and betrayal in their expresssions.

Eddy spoke to them, but neither man replied with words he could hear. Both men were sent to jail and were placed in different cells. When Eddy had time one day, he went back to the cells and tried to talk to them.

"What did you rascals do to get in jail?" Eddy asked.

"I supose you told the cops where to find me." Blade replied.

"You little snitch," Holcomb stated. "You better be long gone when I git outta here."

"I had nothin' to do with your gittin' in here," Eddy tried to convince them, but they stubbornly held to their belief that he had told the officers where to find them. One day Eddy looked through the "wanted" posters where he saw that these men had been involved in shooting a man named Jules in a place called Julesburg, Colorado. A few days later a hearing of sorts was held in the jail with the Chief of Police and his three officers. Eddy was asked to attend on behalf of the two miscreants. He was surprised to hear that Blade had been in Julesburg, Colorado when the fort had been burned to the ground and Jules had been shot. Omaha police had no evidence that Blade had committed the crime, but the association of Blade's name with the act had been carried up and down the stage lines and later the Union Pacific Railroad. Jack Holcomb on the other hand had been in Deadwood, South Dakota when Wild Bill Hickok had been shot in the back. Again there was no hard evidence that Holcomb had done the deed, but the association was enough to convince the Omaha police that he was also an undesirable character. In no uncertain terms the Police Chief told both men to "git outta town by sunset."

"If I or any of my Officers see you around Omaha after six tonight, we'll run you in, lock your cell door, and hold you on suspicion that yuh might commit a crime or keep yuh until we get evidence both of you were involved in shootings."

The two desperados acknowledged that they understood, and when Eddy returned to the boarding house that night, they had checked out and their room was empty.

One day Eddy confided to John Runyon that he a was a fugitive from Vermont himself.

"How did that come about, Curious?"

Eddy related his escape from his apprenticeship to John Alberts, the shoe maker.

"I was fourteen," Eddy finished his narrative. Runyon laughed.

"Out here a fourteen year old is a man." John replied. "Fourteen year olds ride, rope and shoot as good as any man. How old are yuh now?" John asked.

"I'm seventeen," Eddy said.

"When he was eighteen, Hank Dalton shot his first man." John continued. "It aint killin' that makes a boy a man, it's the stuff he's made of inside. You may not have liked it but you got some pretty good training before you was fourteen."

"What do you mean?" Eddy asked.

"Them old Yankee Granpaws had a pretty strict life for a boy or girl," John said. "You can be glad you had one."

"I never thought of it that way," Eddy said. "I was glad to get away from the farm so I could go out and start a life on my own."

"What brought you to Omaha?" John asked.

"In Pittsburgh I got a job on a barge. Cap'n O'Bryan was the skipper. We come up the Missouri River about three months ago and decided to stay the winter here. The Cap'n works on the docks. We'll be goin' back down river in the spring."

"O'Bryan must be a good man," John said.

"He's the best barge Captain on the river." Eddy said with pride. "Mebbe you've seen him around town. When I first saw him, I was afraid because I thought he was a giant."

"Does he have a black beard and a voice singin' Irish songs you can hear for a mile?"

Eddy nodded that he did.

"I've got my eye on him," Runyon said. "Half the men on the dock are scared of him, and the other half would follow him to hell and back, if he asked them to."

Eddy grinned. "That sounds like him awright."

At the boarding house that night Eddy was surprised to see Oley and Tex in the room that had been vacated by Holcomb and Blade.

"This ain't Texas," Tex said. "We decided to go to Colorado and try minin' fer gold. It's a cinch yuh cain't git rich on the river."

"Ya, goot to see youse," Oley said and held out his hand which Eddy shook. He liked Oley, but had no respect for Tex.

"Where's thet no damn good O"Bryan?" Tex asked.

"He'll be along anytime now."

"Vat you doin' now?" Oley asked.

"I work at the police station. I'm a runner there." Eddy answered with a grin.

"Vat a runner does?" Oley asked.

"I go to the telegraph office and get telegrams, then I make the Chief and the boys coffee. I take pictures to the <u>Herald</u>, and I put wanted posters in the post office and around town. Besides that I don't have much to do." Eddy grinned, and Oley nodded.

"Where's the closest saloon?" Tex asked. "We been fightin' thet river since we left Saint Joe, and I got a throat as dry as west Texas."

"I guess the closest one is about three blocks toward town," Eddy stated. "Me and the Captain haven't been to a bar here."

"Come along," Tex said, "We'll buy yuh a drink."

"No thanks," Eddy replied.

"I'm savin' my money."

"Yer a damn cheapskate jus' like I allus thought you were," Tex turned to Oley. "Come along Oley we'll find that bar and leave this greenhorn here."

The weather that evening was calm and the regular boarding house members found it a good night for sleeping. Sometime after midnight there was a commotion in the hallway. Eddy could hear the scuffling of feet and there were grunts and groans as though men were fighting. He and the Captain shared the same room, but not the same bed. Eddy rose and started to dress, so he could go out to the hallway to see what the ruckus was all about.

"Go ahead and dress," O'Bryan stated, "But it's best ye stay here, lad," the Captain stated. "I'll go see what's goin' on outside." A short time later he returned. "Slip out the back and go for the police. There's bin a fight an' Tex has been stabbed. Oley is layin' in the hall out like a light. Naow be on yer way, hurry."

Within minutes Eddy returned with a policeman. Tex had been taken to the kitchen and was lying on the work table. Mrs. Klauss was tending to his wound which proved to be minor. Oley had gained consciousness and the Officer began questioning him. Before long the story of what had happened was pieced together.

Tex and Oley had come up the street staggering and singing. They had not noticed that they were being followed. They stopped under a gaslit street light when the two men following approached them and asked for a drink from the bottle they were sharing.

"I never drink with dogs and strangers," Tex stated.

There was a struggle, and Tex gave them the bottle, as he and Oley entered the boarding house. The two men followed them in and demanded their money. Oley and Tex tried to defend themselves, and a fight resulted in the hallway. Oley was knocked out and Tex was stabbed in the side.

"Can ye give a description of either of the two?"

"Couldn't see much," Tex answered. "But one of those yahoos had a patch over his left eye. The other one called him Jack."

"Jack Blade and Jack Holcomb," Eddy stated.

"Naw, them two left town two days ago," Thompson, the policeman said, and then paused…"or did they?"

"Prob'ly not," O'Bryan stated.

"We'll git out a wanted poster in the Mornin' an' we'll see if they are still around."

The officer left and Eddy and the Captain helped Tex and Oley get to bed. The next day Eddy was sent to the printing office with a description of Holcomb and Blade. By late afternoon Eddy placed posters in the stage and railroad stations, and on a dozen poles around town, but Blade and Holcomb were never found. Thompson learned that two men, one with an eye patch, bought horses at the livery, and rode away early the morning after the fracas. The livery man did not know which way they went.

"Them two're long gone by now, and it's good riddance," Eddy heard Thompson tell the Chief.

For two months Omaha was held captive in the grip of a cold and blustery winter. There was little traffic in or out of the city, and the few people who ventured out on the streets were bundled up so much they looked like erect apes or bears. Tex recovered from his wounds, so he and Oley did any job they could find. When Eddy was not at the police station on weekends he had nothing to do. He stayed in the boarding house or wandered around town. He decided one Sunday morning that he would go to church. He dressed in his best clothes, and walked past the sitting room where several men were talking and smoking.

"Hey, Prissy where you goin," Tex said loud enough so all could hear. "There ain't nobody dead so yuh cain't be goin' to a funeral. Mebbe yer goin to see a lady."

The three men seated in chairs laughed. Eddy said nothing, but continued on his way to the small church down the block. On the way he mused that this was the first time he had ever gone to church without someone nagging him to go. He found the experience exhilarating, and he felt an independence that brought a sense of pleasure. He listened carefully to the sermon and when he returned to his residence, O"Bryan asked him what it was about.

"He talked about the Gospel, and how God had raised up Circuit Riders to preach to settlers throughout the west," Eddy said.

"Did he tell ye what the Gospel was?" O'Bryan asked. "He said it was the Good News that Jesus taught people how to live better lives, and he asked people to put their faith in Jesus."

"Lad, there are too many things that lead you to perdition," O'Bryan stated. "When ye find somethin' that makes life better, ye best follow it. I was born Catholic an I believe in the Church."

While they were in Omaha, Eddy thought of getting in touch with his mother who lived less than three hours away by train, but when he remembered his mother, the pain of bitter loneliness crowded out his feelings that there might be some joy and pleasure in the reunion. He stayed with Captain O'Bryan on the river three more years. Years in which he traveled to Pittsburgh twice, Saint Louis, Saint Joseph, and Omaha three times. The barge traveled from Saint Louis down the Mississippi to New Orleans three times. Those years taught Eddy many hard lessons about his own nature and about getting along in the world, and he knew those lessons would last him a lifetime. During that time Captain O'Bryan taught him how to shoulder responsibilities he would apply the rest of his life. He made his last trip to Omaha knowing that he would leave the barge.

The Captain and Ed stood on the Omaha dock with little to say to one another. Both men shuffled their feet and stole quick glances at one another. Finally Ed broke the silence.

"Cap'n you've been like a father to me," Eddy stated, "but I think it's time for me to git acquainted with my family in Nebraska."

"Ye've bin a good hand." the Captain stated. "If ye ever want to return to the river, look me up. Ye've allus got a home on me barge."

The Captain handed Eddy a roll of bills. "Here's yer wages."

Eddy did a quick count, and knew that it was over a thousand dollars.

"That's more than we agreed on."

"Ye've earned every penny of it," O'Bryan replied.

"I'll be catchin' the train out of Omaha, and I'll be on my way to meet my mother in Central City, Nebraska," Eddy said.

"Watch yer step. There's plenty of shysters would like to git their hands on yer wages an' leave ye fer dead."

"I learned that in Pittsburgh a long time ago," Ed stated.

Silently the two shook hands, and as Eddy turned away he thought he saw a tear course down O'Bryan's cheek. He knew there were tears in his eyes.

For the first time in his life Eddy had more money than he had ever had. He found that O'Bryan had given him his wages and a hundred dollars besides. He went to the railroad station where he sent a telegram to Jason Norton, one cousin he had never met.

> Omaha, Nebr. 21 Apr. 1884 J. Norton Central City, Nebr.
>
> "Jason STOP Will arrive Central City four pm STOP Hope to meet you then STOP"
>
> Cousin Ed Foster

He bought a ticket for Central City, and hoped that he would find a welcome there. As the train rolled west, Eddy wondered about his feeling toward his mother whom he had briefly seen once since he was five years old. He hoped that their meeting would heal all the feelings of bitterness and loneliness he had harbored for so long. His expectation was that she had not changed. He hoped that he had.

Chapter Eight

With each mile the train traveled approaching Central City, Ed's anxiety grew. He had seen his mother only once since he was five had hardly remembered what she looked like. There had been no letters from her while he was on the flatboat, and he had written none to her. She had sent the Norton address to the Chicago Fosters, and Franklin had given it to him several years before. He knew that at age twenty two he had met the world on its terms, and he felt that he could cope with anything, except his mother. He was not ready for the reception she gave him when they met at the train station in Central City.

"Edward, why have you not kept in touch with your mother?" she asked even as she said hello. "I have been worried sick over you. The last I heard from Franklin was that you had gone back to Vermont. I wrote the family there, but no one had heard from you. No one knew whether you were dead or alive. Why didn't you write at least a note, if you can write."

"Mother, life on the river is not like livin' in a town…"

"What do you mean 'life on the river?' Surely there was some way you could have written if you had wanted to. Now what will you do? You haven't any money, I suppose. Land sakes here you are without a penny to your name, and needing a place to stay. You can't live with Jason for nothing. You must earn your keep."

In a flash of anger those words sent Eddy's memory back to the older boys at Grandfather's farm. Anger quickly faded, and he inwardly smiled when he realized his mother's subtlety about money. He turned away from his mother, and spoke to Jason.

"I'm glad to know you. It will be good fer me to work fer you, if you need a hand."

"Your mother truly did worry about you," Jason replied after acknowledging Ed's greeting. Changing the subject he continued, "we live three miles out along the Platte. Our farm is well situated on good land. I'll be glad for your help."

There was sincerity and friendship in Jason's greeting, but Ed was uneasy about his mother. He did not wish to share his life with her, but felt he had no choice. He knew that she would express her disapproval of him no matter what he did, and he especially did not want her to know that he had even a small amount of money. Her next statement surprised him.

"Edward, I have several letters addressed to you from Chloe Myrtie Foster. She was here with her family just this month, but I could not tell her where you were. You should, at least, have written me." There was accusation in her voice as she continued. "If you ever did earn any money, you could have sent me something for my needs."

"I could not have sent you money when I didn't have any."

"You could give me something now while we are in town. There are some things I need that I could get today."

Ed noted the shift to sweetness in her voice as he gave her five dollars. She happily left them, and went shopping. While she shopped, Ed went to the bank and deposited fourteen hundred dollars. His intention was to keep his business dealings as secret as possible because he knew that she would use every means within her power to get any money he might possess. He had already learned that she was not above wheedling and cajoling, and giving priority to her needs to get him to give her money. He resolved that he would give her no more than five dollars when she said she had need.

When they were in the buggy on the way to the Norton farm, Julia asked Ed what he had done with his life since he "ran away from his apprenticeship.

"He had a good opportunity there," she said to Jason."

"There ain't much to tell," Ed stated. "At first I was at Uncle Johnny's, and after I left there, I made my way to Chicago where I met you and Chloe Myrtie and her family. Uncle Franklin gave me money to return to Vermont, but I didn't go back there. I met Cap'n O'Bryan in Pittsburgh and he gave me a job on his flatboat. I worked for him until I decided to come here, and that's about all."

"I for one am glad to have you here." Ed noted that there was sincere welcome in Jason's tone. "We can use a good hand, if you're willing to work on a farm."

"I'll be glad to have somethin' to do that I like," Ed replied as they drove into the farmyard.

Jason stopped the team, and Julia took her packages as she stepped to the ground, but she did not go into the house. Jason indicated a tar papered one room shack with an arched roof which he told Ed was the bunkhouse where he could put his belongings.

"I'll take care of the team, and park the buggy," Jason said. "You'll find a pitcher and basin on the small table. You can get water from the pump in front of the house. We'll have supper as soon as I finish takin' care of my team and milk the cow."

Julia walked to the bunkhouse and entered with Ed.

"Edward, you are on your own here," Julia stated. "It's up to you to keep the bunkhouse neat and clean. Don't expect me to do your washing, but I will iron some of your things. Just remember that I'm your mother and your first duty is to me. You are a man now, but I'm still your mother, and I feel you owe me something for that."

"My first duty is to Jason," Ed stated, but she ignored his reply.

"I expect you to do everything you can to make my life comfortable while you are here."

"Mother, do you have those letters from Chloe Myrtie?"

"You'll get them when I'm ready." Julia stated.

"Mother, I want those letters. Chloe Myrtie is the only person who ever treated me decent." Ed could not keep anger from his voice.

"Well I never…I am your mother," she said, "and I expect you to show me respect."

Julia left the bunkhouse without another word about letters. Ed was seething, and knew that he would have a confrontation with his mother, but decided that he would set the time and place. Even in his cold fury he knew there was nothing he could do or say that would change his mother. Looking around the bunkhouse he mused that it was not a lot different from the flatboat. There was a cot, a small table with a basin and pitcher, a corner shelf with nails for hanging things on a board under it, and a couple of rustic chairs that had their legs held together with wire. There was a window on each wall and one in the door. A small pot bellied stove sat on a metal square that had once been painted with a design, but many years of heating had worn the paint away so that the bare metal was centered where the stove stood with a filigree of brown paint around it. The stove pipe rose straight to the ceiling where another square of metal was cut to allow the pipe to go through. Ed emptied the contents of his carpetbag onto the bed and hung his things on the nails in the corner, then he went outside and joined Jason in the barn.

Jason's fine team of draft horses was munching hay in their stall, and Jason's saddle horse was in a box stall of its own. Two cows were in stanchions along the other side of the barn. A straight ladder to reach the hayloft, which extended over half the inside of the barn was nailed to the wall along the horse stalls. The loft extended over the stalls and stanchions. Jason was pushing hay down to the cows on their side of the barn when Ed entered. He saw Ed as he forked hay through openings over the stalls, and began to outline a plan for the farm work that they would begin the next day.

"We'll look the farm over tomorrow. We're still puttin' up hay so we'll haul hay first thing tomorrow after chores. Old Ned and Charlie work together real good. They'll get a workout tomorrow," Jason said. "I'm finished here, so we can go to the house for supper."

Jason had milked the cow and carried the pail as they walked to the house side by side. A plain woman with pale blue eyes and hair streaked with gray was introduced as Jason's wife Edith. She was of average build and just a bit shorter than Ed. Two girls of ten and five were also introduced, but eight year old Amy didn't wait for an introduction.

"You must have stirred Chloe up some to get as many letters as you did," she said mischievously.

"I haven't seen any letters," Ed replied.

"Aunt Julia has them. She tells us what they say, but she won't let us see them." There was a twinkle in Amy's eyes as she spoke, and Ellen and Esther both giggled at her boldness.

"Well for heaven's sake," Julia stated. "Edith you must teach these girls not to be so outspoken. Edward we will have supper and then I will get your letters for you."

A typical farmer's meal of meat, potatoes and a vegetable was served, and when she was finished Julia rose and went to her room. She returned with a packet of letters that were bound with twine.

"Here are your letters," she stated as she handed them to Ed. "I will help you read them if you need me to."

"I know you have read them, but I will read them for myself."

"You can read then?" Her tone was drippingly sarcastic. "I know you never went to school as a child."

"Alice Roberts taught me to read and write when I lived with them," Ed replied. "She cared enough for me to do that."

He said goodnight to everyone and went to the bunkhouse where he lighted the lamp and sat down to read. His mother had arranged them in the order of the first received to the last.

Chicago, Illinois
September 23, 1878

Dear Edward,

I was very happy that you were able to visit us in Chicago this past summer. I was sorry that you could not stay longer, but father told me you wished to return to Vermont.

Cora and I plan to attend the Fall Cotillion for Young Ladies to be held in September. Father insists that we have new outfits so that we will be presentable to the eligible young swains who will be present.

(Ed was thrilled to read her next lines.)

I remember our times together which I felt were honest and sincere. The "young swains" father speaks about are shallow and foppish. There is more to living than cotillions and fancy parties.

I have resolved to write to you even though I may not receive a reply for months.

With kind regards, I am your friend,
Chloe Myrtie Foster

There were seven letters with the length of time between letters spread over the years since Ed had been in Chicago. The last letter was dated just a week before he had arrived at the Jason Norton farm.

67

All expressed warm friendship for him. As he read them, Ed remembered the promise they had shared and wondered if she ever thought about that. In his mind he reviewed that promise as he had for the last four years.

"Can eighth cousins marry?" He had asked, and he was aware that she had not rejected the idea of marriage between them. He paused at the thought as he sat reading her letters, and he remembered her reply.

"I don't know, but I will ask mother."

"That must have been the reason her father sent me out of Chicago the next day," Ed thought, and the feelings of self doubt that had haunted him since the age of five, entered his mind. He had not written to Chloe lest her family reemphasize the rejection he had felt when he left Chicago. It was then he realized that he did not have writing materials.

"First chance I get I'll ask Jason to loan me pen and paper," he promised himself.

Two days later he had the necessary writing tools, and he laboriously composed his first letter to Chloe Myrtie Foster.

Central City, Nebraska
September12,1884

Dear Chloe Myrtie,

    I had two supprises when I come to Central City day before yestidy. One was that you dint fergit me and you wrote to me.

    The other supprise was that my mother kept your letters for me.

    I did not go to Vermont when I left Chicago, but I went to work on a flatboat on the river. Plees write to me agin. I think I will stay here and work for Jason a long time. I think you have the address.

With deepest regards I am yer frend,
Edward Prescott Foster.

During the fall of 1884 Ed wrote two letters to Chloe, and each time he wrote he received a reply that lifted his spirits. There was a warm friendship with a promise of deeper feeling for one another in each letter. Both young lovers were afraid to exceed the bounds of propriety and make a declaration of eternal love. That winter Ed wrote that he had decided to return to Chicago to visit the girl he could not forget. When his mother learned of his intention, she expressed her feelings.

"How can you, a man who has never owned an acre of ground, pretend to be worthy of a girl who has had a life you can never give her? And besides, you are needed here. You can't go traipsing off to Chicago any time you feel like it. Jason needs you."

Ed's first impulse was to reply with a nasty tongue lashing for his mother, but his better judgment prevailed, and he simply ignored her.

"Jason and I talked it over and decided that work slows in winter and that he could take care of the farm for a couple of weeks." Ed stated. "I'm goin' to Chicago the first week in December."

Julia pouted about reasons he should put her first in his life, and take her with him, but that did not deter him from his desire to go to Chicago and visit Chloe.

"Mother, I want this trip for just Chloe and me," he said.

Chapter Nine

Even in December Chicago was much more the center of trade and industry than Ed remembered. There were more people scurrying through the railroad station. He guessed that some were going to outbound trains, but others were hurrying through from one train to another or to an El that would take them to jobs. Noises of hawkers and hucksters shouting their wares, and the clang of freight dollies and shouting redcaps echoed off the high ceiling and granite walls of the grey canyon lobby. There were no welcoming Fosters to greet him as there had been for his earlier visit. Ed stood alone beside the information kiosk. He had sent a telegram asking Chloe to meet him there, and he was surprised that the smartly dressed young lady standing on the other side of the kiosk was Chloe. He shyly walked around the Kiosk and stood facing her.

"Hullo," he said with some doubt that the person really was Chloe, but she offered her hand as she spoke.

"Hello Ed, It's very good to see you."

"I have thought about talkin' to you for years," Ed stated. "I did write a couple of letters to you, but I guess they were lost in the mail."

"I'm very glad you're here," Chloe replied. "You didn't receive letters from me because I did not have an address for you. I found scraps of letters I thought came from you in father's waste basket, and I did find your mother's address on father's desk. That's when I decided to write to you in care of your mother."

"I was workin' on the river, it was hard to give anybody an address," Ed replied. "We moved from town to town, but most of the time we didn't git off the flatboat."

Neither spoke for a moment while they peered deeply into one another's eyes. Ed was the first to speak.

"There's somethin' I need to ask you to do for me."

Hesitancy in Ed's tone reflected in Chloe's answer.

"You may ask," she stated.

"Farm hands and river men don't dress the way city folks do. I would like you to help me buy clothes that I can wear in Chicago."

Chloe became aware of the roughness of Ed's clothing.

"Clothes don't make the man," she said, "but a good suit with a shirt and tie makes any man more presentable. We can have a good time choosing your wardrobe whenever you are ready."

"Do we have time today?" Ed asked eagerly.

"Indeed I do. I have a carriage. We can go now, if you like."

She had noticed Ed's carpet bag, and knew that he could not have more than one or two changes of the same kind of clothing he was wearing. Together they made their way to the carriage, each trying to estimate the other's attitude from their brief conversation.

"Take us to Marshall's Clothing Store," Chloe directed the carriage driver.

They were silent as they sat stiffly beside one another. Neither seemed to be looking at the other, but she was aware of Ed's presence and he was aware that he was closer to her than he had been for a long time. Feelings of yearning to hold her and feel her warmth welled up within him. He awkardly made a gesture to hold her hand, but she apparently did not see it. Their strange silence was resolved when the carriage driver announced that they were at Marshall's. Ed was grateful that she knew her way around to the men's department. She quickly made his wants known to the tailor who measured and marked and showed them materials that were woven in the style of that time.

"How many suits would you like?" He asked Ed.

"I want somethin' for reg'lar wear." Ed responded, "and somethin' to take this young lady places in the evening.' I need two."

"Do you want more than two suits or just two?" the tailor asked with a wink at Chloe.

"Two," Ed answered.

Chloe did not object. Tailoring finished, they decided to walk to the Loop which was a short distance from Marshall's.

"I remember that your father was more than glad to get me out of Chicago." Ed stated. "So, I think it best that I stay in a hotel."

Chloe's face flushed as she replied.

"My father's home is my home. I must do what he wishes me to do. He has said nothing to me about you being here, but I think it best that you do as you have said."

"Are there hotels near where you live?"

"Not really close, but there are hotels along the lake front."

"Is that more than a mile from where you live?"

"There is one about a mile from our home."

"It would be best for me to go there and check in by myself," Ed stated. "When will I see you again?"

"I planned for you to come to dinner this evening."

"I won't have a suit until the tailor finishes puttin' it together day after tomorrow," Ed mused aloud.

"My parents understand about travel, and I want you to be with us this evening. After all, you are family."

Chloe gave Ed directions to the hotel, and he walked with her to the carriage where they shook hands and formally parted.

"I want you to be with us." These words repeated in Ed's mind, and he decided that he was glad he had made this trip. "You are part of the family." That warm glow returned, and he seemed to be in a dream, not believing that he was really near the girl he had dreamt about. Visions of Chloe's grace and manner danced in his head, and echoes of her voice rang love bells long silent through his mind. He was hardly conscious of the room or the young man who escorted him to it. He became aware that he had been asked a question.

"Say that agin," he murmured.

"Is this room satisfactory, sir?"

"Yes it's just fine," he replied and barely noticed the room at all.

Ed realized a tip was expected and handed the young man a dollar. He quickly stored his things in the wardrobe and decided to make himself ready for the evening. Freshened up he went to the lobby and asked the clerk how to find Chloe's address. Chloe had told him that dinner would be served at six, but Ed was anxious. Even though the time was only four, he left the hotel and began walking toward the Foster home. As he walked along the quiet streets his tenseness mounted. The further he walked the more unsure he became about the greeting he might receive from Franklin Foster, head of the Chicago Foster household.

When Chloe returned home, she told Cora and her mother about meeting Ed, and the events of their going to the tailor.

"We both felt so shy," she related. "I know Ed wanted to be near me, but he just stared straight ahead like a statue."

"What did you do?" Cora asked, and she giggled her amusement.

"I must have been as tense as he was. I followed his example. I stared straight ahead. We didn't even hold hands."

Both girls giggled at the vision of these inept love birds sitting as stiff as mummies. Their mother made no comment about that, but frowned as she changed the subject.

"Girls come to the kitchen, and we can discuss your meeting."

In the kitchen Myrtie asked Chloe what impressed her about Ed.

"They were too shy to hold hands," Cora laughed.

"Cora…" Chloe's face was flushed, but not with anger.

"They sat in the carriage like a couple of mummies." Cora smiled at Chloe's embarrassment.

"How was Edward?" Myrtie asked. "Did he mention Julia?"

"He was fine. He didn't say anything about his mother." Chloe stated. "He asked me to help him buy suitable clothing so that he could escort me to evening events."

"That was nice of him," Myrtie responded, and Chloe could not decide whether her tone was friendly or sarcastic. "He was a bit countryfied as I remember him. Did you help him?"

"Yes, we went to Marshall's and he bought two tailored suits with accessories…one suit for day wear and one for evening."

"That should make him look less like a scared rabbit than he was last time you saw him," Cora stated.

"Do you want to be his hostess while he is here?" Myrtie asked.

"Yes, mother, he came to Chicago to see me."

Time passed quickly as they worked, and they barely had time to change for dinner when there was a ringing of the doorbell. The maid ushered Ed into Franklin Foster's presence in the study.

"Hello, Edward it's nice to see you again," Franklin greeted him.

"Good evening, sir. I trust you are in good health," Ed replied with stilted formality.

"Yes, I am. I asked the maid to bring you to my study because I want to have a word with you privately." Franklin indicated a chair and invited Ed to be seated.

"As I remember, you talked to my daughter about marriage of eighth cousins, is that correct?" Franklin's brusque manner and the sternness of his expression caused Ed's throat to tighten till he could hardly speak.

"Yuh…yes…sir."

"At that time you were just a young hired hand who had worked on an uncle's farm, and I told you there was very little you could offer a young woman. Chloe Myrtie was just entering college with a goal of becoming a teacher. Marriage for at least four years was out of the question, and I very much wanted you to realize that." Franklin paused and waited for a reply, but all that Ed could muster was a very weak "yes, sir."

"Well," Franklin proceeded, "Has your situation changed since then…Have you settled on a career or business?"

"No…no, sir"

"Tell me what you have been doing for those years."

Ed dug deep within himself, and found the courage to reply.

"When you sent me away, and gave me money to go back to Vermont, I decided not to go there,. I was walkin' on the docks in Pittsburgh when I was knocked out and left in an alley. A flatboat Cap'n came along and helped me, and then took me to his flatboat and hired me as a cook's helper. Later he made me his first mate an' that's what I did until this year when I went to work as a hired man on the farm of Jason Norton in Nebraska."

Ed hesitated as he tried to estimate Mister Foster's mood. The expression he could read was one of sternness, and his heart sank like a rock in a still pond.

"Go on, young man," Franklin said.

"Like I said I went to Nebraska and worked as a hired man."

For the first time it seemed to Ed that Mister Foster's expression showed mild interest.

"What part of Nebraska?" He asked.

"Central City, sir."

"That's where your mother is. Are you on the same farm?"

"Yes sir."

There was a knock on the door and Mrs Foster asked that they join them in the parlor. The two men rose and silently proceeded to the parlor where Chloe and Cora were seated.

"Papa I hope you haven't been giving Edward the third degree," Chloe said with a sternness that sounded like her father.

"We've been talking about Ed's work since we saw him last."

"Just as I thought," Chloe stated angrily. "Ed and I have not had time to talk to one another. He did come to see me as well as the rest of our family."

The maid announced that dinner was served and the group moved to the dining room. Ed and Franklin, Junior were seated on one side of the table, with Chloe and Cora seated on the other. Franklin senior sat at the head of the table and Myrtie sat in her place. Ed felt that it was no accident that he and Chloe were separated. Table conversation was light banter, which did nothing to relieve Ed's tenseness. At the close of the meal, Franklin firmly stated that he wished to have further discussion with Ed.

"Let the young people enjoy this evening to visit." Mrs Foster stated equally firmly.

"There are things that I want an understanding about."

"Edward will only be here a few days," Myrtie said. "Let the young people enjoy one another this evening."

"If I do not have a conference with Edward this evening, then we will talk another time, but we will have a conference."

Franklin Foster had not achieved his position in the world of commerce by being shy, and he was not going to let his wife take dominance that evening. After the meal, Chloe and Ed found a quiet place in the music room where they planned an agenda for the week. Franklin met them in the hallway as Ed was on his way to the hotel.

"We will have our conference now, Edward," he said.

Ed followed him to the study. Franklin was very direct as they entered his study and sat down.

"Before you leave to go back to Nebraska, I would like to have your word that you will not talk to Chloe about marriage. You are still too young and she is just getting started in her profession. Both of you need time to get your feet on the ground."

"Sir, I know that I can't offer Chloe the kind of life some of her friends can, but she is the kindest most friendly girl I have ever met. I promise you that I will not do anythin' that either she or I will regret."

"Are you promising that you will not ask her to marry you?"

"I will not ask her to marry me at this time," Ed stated.

Ed realized that he had given Franklin only half a promise, and that he had left an opening for later discussion about his future with Chloe. Franklin cleared his thoat to speak just as there was a light tapping on the door. Chloe called to her father.

"May I come in?" She had waited in the hallway while Ed and Franklin were in the study. She decided they had been together long enough, and told them so.

"I think it's time you return to your hotel now." Franklin stated.

He stood with them in the hallway as they shook hands and Ed departed with a mixture of feelings dominated by Franklin's rejection.

While he walked to the hotel, Ed recalled the conversation he had with Chloe when they were alone. Chloe reached for Ed's hand and held it to her cheek, and found it to be calloused and rough.

"You have worked so hard," she said, and Ed sensed deep compassion and understanding in her tone.

"I have worked hard all my life," Ed responded. "Even as a child I was required to work with the older boys."

"I have always had such an easy life," Chloe stated reflectively.

There was a long silence as Chloe tightened her grip on Ed's hand. She changed the subject.

"What is life like in Nebraska?"

"It's a good life, but there's a lot of work to it," Ed replied. "On the farm there is allus somethin' that needs doin."

Do you think I could be a farmer's wife.?"

"Would you give up teaching?"

"Yes I would," Chloe responded without hesitation.

"Your father asked me not to make plans thataway."

"I love my father very much, but there is room in my heart for a husband, and I must make my own decisions about the man with whom I wish to spend my life."

"Have you decided that yet?"

"Almost," she said coquetishly as her grip on Ed's hand tightened and then released.

"Do you mean me?" Ed asked.

"Yes."

"What about your father?" Ed asked.

"I don't worry about my father. He will eventually accept whatever decision I make."

As he walked along, Ed felt more and more blessed that he had met Chloe. Time spent in Chicago flew by for Ed. There were dinners at The Country Club and cotillions where Ed felt out of place because he could not twirl Chloe around the floor as the other young men did. He went to luncheons with Chloe's friends, and evening concerts. These were events that he had never, in his wildest imagination, expected to attend, but to be alone with Chloe surpassed all other events that occurred while he was in Chicago.

"Dearest, I feel like a country bumpkin when I meet your friends," Ed remarked on one occasion when they were alone.

"Nonsense, you are more at home with them than they are with you.," Chloe replied.

"My hands are rough, my talk is diff'rent, and I don't know all the fancy dance steps your friends know. And besides, I got no education at all."

"Foolish man," Chloe said. "Many of these people are one generation away from the farm. They've just been in the city longer than you have, but many of them are still on the farm in their actions."

"I don't even know," Ed grinned, "which fork to use at a fancy dinner, or how to fold my napkin."

"Just remember sweetheart, that knowing all the niceties of life does not make a person nice." Chloe stated. "You have more gentleness in your little finger than most have in their whole body."

They laughed at the thought, and Ed held her close and kissed her full on the mouth.

"I love you," he said.

"I love you more than I can tell," she said.

Seated on a love seat in the music room, their pulses racing, and their breathing rapid, they remained transfixed by this moment of love. They were not aware of the passing of time until Cora came and invited them to afternoon tea. Ed had never been involved with the kind of banter that a session of tea brought forth. Chloe and Cora talked of Corinne Palmer who had married after completing high school. She had two children with a third on the way. Ed noted that there was no bitterness in their voices, but that they did recall events of piano recitals, horseback riding and tennis at the club where Corinne had always tried to be the best by hook or crook. Ed mentally compared their conversations with those he had heard of an entirely different kind. He inwardly smiled to think of the river and farm talk knowing that he could not tell those conversations to Chloe.

The week Ed stayed with the Foster family was pleasant when Chloe was present but, when he was alone with Franklin, he had a vague feeling of deception because he and Chloe had expressed their love to one another against her father's wishes. At the end of the week Ed boarded the train to return to Central City. On the train he dozed and dreamt of every nuance of Chloe's tone and gesture. But more than that, her declaration of love had given him a self confidence he had never known. He knew he was home in the way his mother greeted him when he returned to the farm.

"You go traipsing off to Chicago, and leave Jason with all the work. Dear me, you just don't seem to accept responsibility. Edward, I don't see a bright future for you," she said after a curt greeting.

"Hello, Mother, it's good to see you." Ed stated without rancor. He had decided that anything his mother said would not destroy the sense of self worth he had gained by knowing that Chloe loved him. Winter days passed as Ed shared the farm chores with Jason, and the two men often laid out plans for what needed to be done as they talked of plowing, seeding and field preparation for the next year. One day Jason brought up the subject of Ed's visit to Chicago.

"Ed, since you came back from Chicago there's somethin' diffrent about you. Seems to me you must be in love."

"Jason, for the first time in my life There is someone who loves me," Ed said. "I told her I loved her, and she said she loved me."

"Have you talked about marriage?" Jason asked.

"She asked me if I thought she could be a farmer's wife. I told her it would be a different kind of life, but she could. She promised to write to me and I have already got two letters."

"Have you written to her?"

"Well, yes," Ed hesitated. "But my writin' ain't the greatest so I just write a couple of sentences."

"Mebbe you think she will change her mind when she sees how your writin' is," Jason said with a grin, but Ed was serious.

"No, she remembered me from the first time we met, and she told me she loved me then, and that she still does."

"She sounds like a girl you better hold on to."

"She's the best person I ever met," Ed stated honestly. "We went to socials where there were young men who tried to cut in, and she danced with some of them, but she allus came back to me. She told me they asked for dates, but she told me she wouldn't date them even while she was in Chicago and I was out here."

"Seems to me that you better make plans to marry her as soon as you can," Jason advised. "You know that 'absence makes the heart grow fonder for somebody else.'"

"She will not marry me without her father's blessing."

"Oh, oh, the old man objects to you. Sounds like he thinks you ain't good enough for his pride and joy."

"He made it very clear that he thinks I don't have much to offer. He told me there are young men in business who are already established, and that his lovely daughter could marry any one of them. He said he didn't understand why she had not settled down with one."

"She must be a very special person to give up a life of ease and comfort, and choose a farmer for a husband."

"We ain't married yet," Ed stated wistfully.

Winter yielded its grip on the land, and spring gave way to summer. Fall harvests were in and another winter settled over the land. Mid winter came and Ed took his second trip to Chicago. Chloe had planned an agenda similar to that of the year before. They again pledged their love, and spent every possible moment together. Franklin remained cordial, but was not friendly, while Mrs Foster was neutrally aloof. The evening before their parting Ed proposed marriage, and the lovers ambraced in a long moment of love. Chloe did not give a yes answer immediately.

"I've been waiting years for you to get enough courage to ask," Chloe chided with a smile. "I will marry you as soon as father and mother decide it's the only way for their darling daughter to be happy is with you." Ed then related the following conversation.

"We could go to a Justice of the Peace tomorrow," I stated.

"You have seen how cold father has been to you," Chloe said. "He won't even discuss my future with me. I know you are disappointed, but we must be patient."

"I agreed. The next morning I boarded the train for Nebraska with a heavy heart. For the next year Chloe continued teaching, and you know, I did not return to Chicago. Chloe's letters were warm and expressed her love as were mine to her, but she wrote that there was no change in her father's feelings toward me. Her mother refused to discuss our situation. I began to worry that we would ever marry, but during the summer of 1888, she wrote news that lifted my spirits to the heavens. The rest you know. Here's her letter with good news."

August 2, 1888
Chicago, Illinois

Dearest Edward,

    Father, mother and I had a conference just last evening. It was decided that our marriage was right and that father would give his blessing.

    I would very much like you to come to Chicago as soon as you can so that together we may plan our wedding. If that is not possible at this time, we will make our plans when you are in Chicago in December.

    Ed dearest, I love you more that ever. Eagerly I wait to hear from you.

Your loving bride to be,
Chloe

As Ed and Jason had done each time Ed wrote in reply, they sat together and crafted a letter that expressed his happiness at the prospect of their marriage.

Central City, Nebraska
August 12, 1888

Dearest Chloe,

Dear love, your letter of August 2 made me the happiest man alive. I am sorry I cannot leave for Chicago immediately, but we are putting up hay for the rest of this month. In September we will be harvesting our small grain crops, and then we must help our neighbors with their harvesting. It is customary for neighbors to trade harvest work in this way.

We have waited so long, and there is nothing that I would like better than to be with you, but the earliest I can be with you will be late October or early November.

Plan as much as you can for the wedding before then. I long to see you, but I must stay to help Jason through harvest. I do long to be with you, and I love you more than words can tell.

As ever I am your loving husband to be,
Ed

Chloe's response to Ed's letter was agreement with his schedule. She stated that she would resign from teaching so that she could devote more time to wedding plans. Harvest time did not move fast enough for Ed, and wedding plans kept Chloe wondering how she could ever get everything accomplished. They had not set a date, but she decided that the wedding should take place New Year's day 1889. She hoped that Ed would agree. There was so much to do. The Church, the Minister, the brides maids and their attendants, ushers, decorations, the reception and ballroom reservations, dinners, there was so much to do and so little time.

When Ed arrived in Chicago the last week of November, he and Chloe were together every moment possible. The senior Fosters kept a close watch to see that the rules of propriety were followed by these lovers, but there was no reason to fear for the demanding days of December flew by and their wedding day was soon upon them. There were socialites, laborers, professors, farmers, grain traders, and even Cap'n O'Bryan came to the ceremony. Ed sent him a letter of invitation. Ed was awed by Chloe's beauty, and, he had no reservations about declaring his eternal love for her.

"The most fashionable wedding this season," the <u>Tribune</u> reported. "The bride wore a white silk dress designed by one of Chicago's leading designers and a veil of imported Damask lace. After a honeymoon at Niagra Falls, the young couple will be at home in Central City, Nebraska."

Thus it was that Chloe Myrtie Foster left a settled and secure home in Chicago to become the wife of a hired hand. For her first days on the farm she felt that she had entered another country. Julia and Edith moved from one farm task to another with precision that Chloe could only admire. Without a set schedule they seemed to know what was going to happen next. To Chloe, it seemed they anticipated tasks to be accomplished before the need for any action arose.

"I can never become a farmer's wife," she remarked to Ed after a week on the farm. "I just stand in awe at the way Julia and Edith go about things that need doing."

Ed knew that his words would not make her adjustment easier until she began to realize there was an unwritten method to the tasks they did, and Chloe would fit in when she began to get used to it.

Chapter Ten

In Nebraska Chloe soon learned that farm living was involved with survival more than she had ever realized. She gave much thought to how dependent humanity was on the weather for food, clothing and shelter. It seemed to her that everyone in the Norton household knew how to make the most of circumstances except her. There were few times in her life that she had arisen at four o'clock each morning, and days in Chicago had never begun with the hurry and bustle required on the farm. She marveled at the way Edith Norton and Julia went about doing necessary tasks that placed farm grown food on the table at mealtime. While the men worked the fields to grow food for the family, the women cooked and canned produce as they kept the house and their families in clean clothing. They used a wash board in a tub of water that they often carried to the task in a bucket using soap they had made in their spare time.

To her it seemed that men and women worked under the most difficult circumstances to keep the household supplied with the things needed just to live. She watched as the men carried water for laundry when they had time, and for cooking, and bathing. Chloe was amazed that this must be done in warm weather and cold. Even sleeping in cold winter beds required warm bottles of water, stones or bricks for cold feet. Water seemed to be the key to survival. There was always water heating on the stove. Wood and coal were equally important to keep fires going for cooking and heat. Meals required planning which was centered in the availability of meats and vegetables, milk and flour, and even salt and pepper. There were so many details to being a farm wife that Chloe despaired that she could ever master getting all the things needed and manage the required schedules.

"Dearest, I feel so useless," she confided to Ed when they were alone. "Julia and Edith go about the house doing what needs to be done, and all I can do is stand helplessly by."

"Sweetheart, you can't expect to work the way they do. They grew up on farms and watched the older women. There they learned how to do those things, and that's what you must do."

"Just the same I would feel a lot better if I knew what to do."

"Are mother and Edith impatient with you?" Ed asked.

"No, they are very helpful with me."

"Do they show you how to do what they do?"

"Yes, when they aren't too busy."

"Things will change, you 'll see. Before long you'll be workin' right along with them, and you will be surprised at how much you have learned about doing what they do."

"Something has been bothering me about farm life".

"There're lots of things about it that bother me," Ed said with a grin. "Tell me what's been bothering you."

"Ed, I miss going to church. In Chicago I was always in church on Sunday. Out here everyone treats Sunday as just another day of the week. Why don't farmers go to church?"

"One thing farmers have to do is plow when it's time to plow, and plant when it's time to plant. They must reap and harvest, and Sundays take 52 days away from the work they have to do."

"One day set aside to worship wouldn't delay the growing or harvest seasons, and maybe God would give them better harvests if they thanked Him for their crops."

"Growin' up in Vermont and workin' for Uncle Johnny Roberts taught me that there never was enough time to get the work done."

"Ed, do farmers believe in Divine Providence?" Chloe asked. Ed hesitated and they were both in deep thought before he replied.

"Well, farmers know that the Lord gives and He takes away," Ed replied. "The Lord gives good weather and bad. In good weather farms thrive, and in bad times crops suffer. Farmers can't change that. They just have to work with it."

"Do they believe in the Lord who put life in seeds and provides rain and sunshine to make them come to life."

"Farmers plow an' ready the soil an' plant, but they are at the mercy of Nature. I guess that's what I believe. My God is Nature."

"Ed, I believe in the God who gives us seed time and harvest, summer and winter, and provides us with all things good, and all I ask is that I may be in church on His day for worship."

"I'll have to ask Jason about usin' the buggy on Sundays."

"I very much want you to go with me," Chloe stated.

Ed remained silent and Chloe noted a frown that she felt meant that he would take her, but that he would not go inside the church.

"Sweetheart, do you believe in God?" she asked.

"My life has not proved to me that God ever took care of me." Ed responded. "Most of my life, I have been takin' care of myself. I've had a hard enough time doin' that."

"God has cared for me through all of my days," Chloe stated. "Now I need Him more than ever."

"Why now?" Ed questioned.

"Because we are going to be parents," Chloe replied.

"When?" Ed's surprise caused a sharpness in his tone.

"Probably before the first of December."

Ed drew her close and for a long moment there was silence.

"I love you very much," Ed stated.

"I love you more than ever," Chloe responded, but she knew that she could not force Ed to believe in the God she loved. Later she prayed that he would come to realize his need for faith in God. She was glad he took the time to drive her to Central City each Sunday after that discussion.

It was spring, and by the middle of April a garden had been leveled and gardening time came. The young couple worked side by side establishing rows for corn, beans, radishes, carrots and other vegetables. Ed and Jason had planted tomato, cabbage, and green pepper seeds in a glass covered bed they built to protect them from frost. Soon seeds sprouted and new young plants developed. When the danger of frost passed, these were replanted in rows in the irrigated rich soil. There was always something to do, and Chloe loved watching the plants grow to maturity. Weeding and cultivating lasted all summer while harvesting and canning continued until frost came in the fall. In addition to all the other farm work, maturing plants kept the household busy. To see plants break through the soil and grow to maturity, and to can and preserve their fruits gave Chloe a feeling of accomplishment she had never experienced in Chicago.

On a summer day in July when it rained all day, Ed and Chloe had time to be alone.

"How does mother treat you?" Ed asked.

"She never lets me forget that I am her daughter-in-law."

"Do you want me to say somethin' to her about that?"

"I think it's something that will improve in time," Chloe responded.

"Well if it doesn't, and you think I can help, just say the word."

Chloe agreed that she would. She did not want to be the instigator of a family confrontation so she changed the subject.

"You will be a father, and I will be a mother," she stated dreamily, and there was wonder in her voice, which she saw reflected in Ed's eyes. From that time until their first child, Carrie Marie, was born, there were daily reports on the movement of the baby in her womb. The birth was difficult, and there were many hours in labor with hemorrhaging and pain for Chloe. She came to appreciate Julia who was able to guide her through the difficult days of depression that followed the birth.

"I advise that you wait at least two years before you have another child," Doctor Olson told Ed. "Your wife is healthy enough, but more children may tax her strength more than her body may be able to manage. She will need to rest at least a month, and I recommend six weeks confinement. At any rate I will check on her progress for the next four weeks." He then looked directly at Ed. "After that it's up to you to behave yourself." When the Doctor had gone, Ed and Chloe talked about his directions.

"Ed, I love this baby," Chloe stated seriously, "It was worth all the pain I experienced just to have her. I would not want to limit our love making, because I love you both so very much."

"I wouldn't want anythin' to happen that would take you away from me. My world would come to an end." Ed stated with tears.

"Our fore bearers had larger families than two or three and survived. We will not govern our lives by what might happen."

"Just the same we need to be careful," Ed stated.

"That's another reason I love you. You are concerned for me. I'll be on my feet before you know it."

But Chloe was not on her feet that soon. Hemorrhaging continued into the third week after her delivery, and her temperature remained above normal for a month. When she tried to get out of bed, she became dizzy and often fainted. Doctor Olson knew there was infection, but could only prescribe bed rest and aspirin to control pain.

For the first three months of baby Carrie's life, Chloe was barely able to breast feed Carrie while Julia clothed and bathed the baby daily.

Farm life went on as usual. Jason and Ed went to the fields every day, and housework and meals were on schedule, but there was one major change. Julia saw to Chloe's and Carrie's every need in a way that brought new respect for her to Chloe and Ed. When he tried to thank her, there was no change in her verbal sharpness.

"Ed Foster," She stated. "you men are all alike. You think women were put on this earth to give men all the sexual pleasure they want, but when there is a baby, then they become helpless."

"Just the same, mother, I do appreciate your care."

"It's the least any woman would do, if she had an ounce of concern. Now Ed you go on about your business. You don't know the least thing about how to care for your wife or your little baby."

To continue the conversation would only bring more verbal abuse, but Ed couldn't keep from expressing his feelings.

"Thanks mum," he mumbled almost under his breath as he watched her efficiently bathe Chloe and the baby.

During the days that Chloe was limited in her time out of bed, one of her most relaxing and enjoyable times was playing the pump organ in the Norton's parlor. When she found time to play, the Norton family gathered around and sang. Teaching the Norton girls to play the organ delighted Chloe, and she found them to be good students. She had brought several beginner and advanced student books from Chicago. Edith sat in as many sessions as she could, and the Norton music education program continued as long as Fosters lived there. Edith learned quickly and a new understanding developed between the two women, but Julia remained aloof. She and Ed seldom participated in the family singing. That winter had been most difficult for the Nortons and Fosters, but in the spring Chloe was well enough to work in the garden.

A new air of excitement spread across the country because of advertising in the newspapers and the land offices for settlers to homestead in Colorado. For several years there had been abundant rain in the plains of the west, and the land offices took advantage of it by stating that "there was abundant rain, good soil, a farmer's paradise." Little did they know of the cycles of rain and drought that had kept those areas "unfit for human settlement" as the early explorers termed it. From the 1870s and into the early 1900's thousands of settlers trekked west to find good land and fortune, but a drought cycle had begun in the 1890's which resulted in many tracts abandoned and houses and barns left vacant. Still new settlers came. Grain markets in Chicago reflected the drought and commodity markets collapsed. Even before the major crisis in commodities hit, Franklin Foster was wiped out financially. Chloe and Ed received a letter that outlined his problems.

Chicago, Illinois
October 5, 1891

Dear Chloe and Ed,

You have probably heard of the changes in the commodities markets and my ouster as President of the Chicago Board of Trade. My losses have been great. We have nothing left except our home which we must sell so that we may relocate. We plan to homestead in Colorado. Cora will be staying here where she will be employed as a law firm secretary. Franklin, Junior will be with us.

We are looking forward to seeing our first grandchild and trust that you are well. I urge you young folk to think about homesteading. Owning land is the only security for anyone's future.

I have written a similar letter to Julia and I urged her to join us to file for her 160 acres at the time we do.

We will talk further about this when we arrive later in the month. God be with you.

I remain your devoted father,
Franklin P. Foster

"You are not strong enough to set up the way we would have to in Colorado," Ed stated when Chloe had read the letter to him. "There is too much work for one man on this farm and you can gain strength while we stay here for at least another year."

"Your mother and Edith have been so good to me. I think they have spoiled me," Chloe replied. "I feel I am strong enough."

"Mebbe we can move later on, but I don't see how we can move this year. There are too many things against our moving this year."

When Julia heard the news about homesteading, she was ready to go to Colorado immediately. Chloe and Ed discussed Franklin's letter with her, but had not read the letter Franklin had written to her. One evening she rushed over to begin planning for them to go homestead.

"We could file for adjoining land and possibly farm four hundred acres out there," she enthused.

"How do you figure that?" Ed asked.

"If we each filed for one hundred sixty acres along with Franklin and young Franklin William that would be 320 acres. Add my 160 and yours, and that would be 640 acres," Julia stated.

"You must think of becoming more responsible for your family's future. You could be set up for life with that land. You could become wealthy."

"Chloe is not strong enough to travel in a covered wagon," Ed replied hoping that his mother heard him.

"The railroad still runs and you could drive out with what you need in a wagon," Julia stated angrily. "It just makes me tired how you put things off that would make a better life for your family."

"I am thinkin' of my family," Ed replied. "Chloe is still too weak to have to put up with the way homesteaders have to live. She's not strong enough to have to carry water from a spring or well, an' we have no idea how the winters are out there."

To Ed's surprise, his mother agreed with him.

A short time after that Chloe chose to discuss Julia with Ed.

"I think your mother basically has a kind heart," she said.

"She certainly covers it up with her blustery temper," Ed responded. "She has always managed to make me feel like I interfered with her life. I think it's the other way around. She has always given me more trouble than I asked for."

"You need to look at what she does and not what she says."

"Mebbe we're too much alike," Ed conceded. "When she tells me how worthless I am, an' how I need to learn responsibilities, it makes me mad."

"I hope you can look beyond what she says, and look at what she does for other people. She has been very kind to me."

"Well, I do have to give credit where it's due," Ed stated, and Chloe knew that she could say no more at the time.

The Chicago Fosters arrived on schedule. They stayed in Central City as long as it took them to put together things they considered necessities, and left for Colorado within the week. Their entourage included Franklin, Myrtie, young Franklin William and Julia. Chloe and Ed talked about their spirit of adventure as they departed.

"You have to admit that their excitement was certainly contagious," Chloe stated. "I almost felt eager to go with them."

"Well," Ed replied slowly, "I want to hear what they have to say when they get back."

When Julia returned a month later, she told of good soil, abundant crops and plenty of rain. The Franklin Fosters had contacted the local land office along with Julia and filed for homesteads in an area of dry land prairie. Their homesteads were adjoined within the section of prairie they had chosen. They told that plowing and planting would yield 'a good' harvest.

"The land office people told of forty bushels per acre of corn and wheat," Franklin reported. "Our land is rich deep brown soil that has never been plowed. It's covered with yucca, sage and prairie grass which shows that it will grow excellent small grain crops. We'll go back to Chicago and sell our home and return to Colorado where a good living waits for us."

"Sir, you will need a good team of horses, and most of the farm equipment we use on this farm," Ed replied. "Mebbe you ought to walk around and take an inventory of machinery we use here."

Franklin reluctantly agreed and, after the tour, made a trip to the land office. He later told Ed the land people had told him that everything he needed could be bought reasonably in Haxtun, Colorado. Ed was skeptical, but remained silent knowing that Franklin had never put his hand on the handles of a walking plow nor had he ever driven a team with the reins around his shoulders to prepare soil for planting. Later that week Franklin and Myrtie returned to Chicago to complete the sale of their house, and to prepare for their settlement in Haxtun, Colorado.

Life on the Norton farm settled into the routine of getting ready for winter. The next spring the Franklin Foster family moved to Haxtun, Colorado, but not to their homestead.

They rented a house in town and hired neighbors to break sod, prepare the soil and plant. That summer Julia made the trip to her homestead site, and when she returned she was more eager than ever for Ed and Chloe to go to Colorado and file for land.

"Now is the best time to take advantage of the law allowing homesteading." She urged. "The way land is being settled there won't be any good plots left by the time you get ready."

"Mother, Chloe is expectin' her second child," Ed stated emphatically, "And we ain't goin' to move yet."

"Ed Foster you ought to be ashamed of yourself. The very idea getting your wife pregnant after she had such a hard time with Carrie."

"I wanted another child more than Ed did. You must know that it takes two," Chloe paused, "and in our case, both of us were willing."

"I'll stay here until the baby comes," Julia's tone changed. "Ed, we must give Chloe the best of care and see that she gets plenty of rest. Both of you should be ashamed of yourselves."

"Don't worry about me," Chloe stated cheerfully. "I feel stronger than I did before Carrie Marie was born and now I know how to take better care of myself."

Julia sighed a long sigh before replying. "I guess we'll have to wait till Chloe will be able to travel before we can consider moving."

When Ed and Chloe were alone, they discussed Julia making decisions for them, and decided that they must stay in Nebraska no matter how much pressure Julia put on them to move to Colorado.

"I can see that a mother's management of their children never ends," Chloe stated. "My mother certainly managed for Cora and I."

"It's our family and we decide what we are goin' tuh do, and my mother has nothin' to say about that." Ed stated.

"She is your mother, Ed," Chloe stated, "and we must be careful not to hurt her feelings. I believe she desires the best for us."

"The last time my mother made a decision for me," Ed stated bitterly, "it damn near killed me. I'll never let her make decisions for me or you or any of my family as long as I live."

"Ed, remember…she is your mother." Chloe replied.

"She hasn't treated me like her child since I was five or six years old." Ed rose and began pacing the floor. "There's only one way I can put her in her place. That's to tell her to her face that she can't run our lives."

Fair days and stormy days on the farm meant that time was passing. It was easy for people who lived from day to day to forget the days of the week and certainly to lose track of the month day and year. Farmers learned to tell time by the season of the year, changes of the moon, the first frost in the fall and the last frost of spring. Planting time, seed time and harvest were indicated by the melting of winter snows, budding of first spring flowers, summer rains and the ripening of crops. In between there was weeding, haying, cultivating and care of livestock. Daily chores included milking one or more cows, feeding and watering animals, tending a garden for household needs and maintaining a family.

Chloe discovered that farming was a busy life, especially caring for the children and monitoring family relationships to keep peace between family members.

Chapter Eleven

The months passed and Kate Ruth Foster was born in mid September,1891. The birth was free of complications and baby Katie was a healthy child. Winter, spring, and summer on the Norton farm brought the usual activities of farm living. Time passed quickly as the days and weeks changed with the seasons. During the spring of 1892, Chloe announced that she was with child, and William Prescott Foster was born November twentieth, 1892. Julia was incensed with Ed and Chloe, and let them know her feeling, making reference to their lack of control for weeks.

"You two are worse than rabbits," she said. "I suppose we'll have to stay here until your child bearing years are over. Ed, you know I can't go to my homestead and build anything, nor can I go out there and plow and plant and put up fences. I guess I'm stuck here until you are an old man and I'll be in my grave."

Ed gave her the same answer he had given the last three years, "mebbe next year." His "next year" proved to be the year of decision for Ed and Chloe. Late one day in the fall Julia came into their quarters in a fury.

"Ed Foster, I have had all I can stand of living here. Jason and Edith have been as good as gold to me, but I can't believe you would give up the chance to be on your own and become a land owner. You treat me worse than you do dogs and horses. I'm getting older and I will need a place to live when I can no longer do farm work, but you don't seem to care." She began sobbing uncontrollably.

Chloe went to her and put her arms around her.

"Ed and I have a great deal of respect for you," she said. "We wouldn't knowingly do anything to hurt you."

Between her tears and sobs Julia said, "you might not but Edward would."

"Has he done something that has you upset?" Chloe asked.

"Yes…yes he has," Julia said slowly, still sobbing.

"What then?" Chloe innocently asked.

"He refuses to even talk to me about moving to Colorado. He selfishly keeps me from having a settled property of my own, and he doesn't care one whit about his mother." Her sobs turned into a wail.

Ed was aware that she wanted him to give her a time when they could locate in Colorado, and he also knew that Chloe would be willing to abide by his decision.

"If all goes well this summer and fall, and we have a good harvest here, we could move this fall after harvest."

Julia's crying stopped miraculously. But Ed's promise did not materialize that spring nor for two more years. It was the fall of 1894, and Chloe Myrtie announced that she was pregnant with their fifth child. She experienced cramps that she knew were unusual, but she said nothing to Ed or Julia. As women have done through the ages, she chose the time and place to share this news with Ed. She knew that Ed would insist that they stay in Nebraska. She waited until they had traveled a day on the trail to Colorado before she told him, and quickly assured him that she would be all right. However, Ed chose to remind her how things would be.

"Out in Colorado we will have to start with nothing," he said. "We will have no house and none of the things that make life easier here. We may have to get water from a spring or haul it from a neighbor. We may not even have a house for a couple of years."

"We are young and in good health," Chloe replied. "Life in Colorado may be more of a challenge, but we'll be living on land that we farm for ourselves."

Even before they began their journey, Ed had been planning on the things he would need to farm in Colorado.

"We'll need horses, a plow, and all the hand tools, such as shovels hoes, and rakes out there," Ed stated. "We best go by covered wagon so we can take as much as we can with us. The way I figger it, it'll take three weeks or longer in the wagon. I'll buy a tarp that Jason and I can rig to the wagon. When the weather is good I can sleep on the ground, and you and the kids can sleep in the wagon.'

"We can make the trip an adventure for the children," Chloe stated. "The wagon cannot travel much faster than the older children can walk, when they tire of riding in the wagon."

A day in the autumn of 1894 became their day of departure. As they moved across western Nebraska, the lush valley watered by the Platte River changed to the brown prairie grass of the great plains with the only greenery in the valley of the Platte. As they drove along Chloe related stories of the Oregon Trail she had read in magazines and newspapers, and thus gave her children lessons in history They passed through Fort Kearney and came to the division of the North Platte and the South Platte near the village of North Platte, Nebraska. Night camping in cottonwood groves provided them with wood for campfires. They found that they were not alone on the trail. Many settlers in covered wagons formed wagon trains, and camped and cooked together. Their greatest hazard came from an unexpected source and at a time they least expected.

Between Ogalala, Nebraska and Julesburg, Colorado on a late afternoon they found an ideal spot to set up camp for the night. The evening meal had been served and the western descent of the sun cast long shadows as Katie and Carrie walked away from camp. Chloe told them to remain close enough so they could be heard "if they needed help." The girls had reached a knoll surrounded by clumps of wild plum and willow thickets. Frost had turned the willow to a light yellow, and the plum contrasted its dark purple with the long rays and shadows of the sun. Carrie and Katie did not notice that water from a cloudburst somewhere upstream was quickly rising until it surrounded the knoll Meanwhile, Ed and Chloe found their campsite flooded as water from the nearby South Platte left its channel and began to wash around the wagon.

"Mama we can't get back to camp," Carrie yelled.

"The water got too deep," Katie hollered.

"Stay where you are," Ed answered, "we'll come and get you."

He raced for the horses where he had tethered them, and found himself wading in yellowish muddy water that sometimes reached his hips as he gathered the horses and hitched them to the wagon. They loaded everything that hadn't floated away in the wagon and in a mad dash Ed drove the wagon in the direction where Carrie and Katie were now screaming that the water was getting higher. The wagon lurched, swayed and splashed as Ed drove pell mell over clumps of grass, willow and plum roots. Katie and Carrie were in water halfway to their knees when Ed reached them. He stopped the very nervous horses and the girls scrambled aboard. He drove to higher ground that night where they slept in the wagon. They awoke the next morning to see grass that had been dry and brown the day before now covered with yellow mud. There were large pools of water here and there. As they drove along they exchanged news with fellow travelers, and learned that a child drowned just a mile from where they camped. Julia had taken the train from Central City to Sedgwick, Colorado, and she met them there nine days later. When they arrived on the land Julia had filed for her homestead, they found only open prairie with no improvements required by the law. When Ed realized that, he was angry.

"It's a wonder you didn't lose the land you filed on," he stated. Julia asked why he would say such a thing he replied. "You filed on this land five years ago and the law requires that you make some improvements that show you intend to live here."

"I never intended to live here alone," she replied. "I only filed on this land to get you to move to Colorado."

For a long moment, Ed stared at her coldly, but said nothing more about it. Julia decided to return to Nebraska, and Ed drove her to the railroad station two days later.

For the first three weeks they were in Colorado, they lived in the covered wagon. The second day on the land their closest neighbors, Tom and Berta Kaschke with their children came and introduced themselves to the Fosters. Tom offered to help Ed with the building of a dugout with one large room that would be the kitchen, living room and bedroom for the family on the side of a low hill. Ed decided that in the meantime they could form a shelter using the tarp from the wagon which provided shade during the day, and freed the wagon for hauling. He placed the tarp on the wagon at night for sleeping until the cabin-dugout could be built. Lumber and nails were purchased in Sedgwick and the dugout began to take the form of a frame building with the dugout as a bedroom for Chloe and Ed. When Ed tried to thank Tom and Berta for their help they answered plainly.

"Neighbors were put on this earth to help neighbors," Tom said. "Other neighbors helped us settle in and now it's our turn to help you folks get a place you can live in."

One evening the Kaschkes came over and Berta asked Chloe what her life had been like before they had moved to Colorado.

"My life in Chicago was so much different from the life we have here that I can't compare the two," Chloe replied.

"How so?" Tom asked.

"In Chicago my father was a well known business man when he worked with the Chicago Board of Trade. In Nebraska our lives were concerned with growing the grains my father bought and sold in Chicago." Chloe paused for a moment.

"Your father was wealthy then?" Berta asked.

"My father wanted his family to have every advantage Chicago offered so we had many comforts that we do not have here, but I'll love it here when we get settled," Chloe stated.

"What about you Ed?" Tom asked.

"For me livin' in Vermont was harder than anywhere else I've lived," Ed replied. "I don't have good memories about livin' there. My father died when I was two or three, and my mother and I lived on my Grandfather's farm. I was put to work as a kid."

"Tell us where you folks are from," Chloe said.

"Both our families were coastal plain South Carolina tobacco farmers," Tom said. "My father was killed at Antietam just months before the war ended. I was born the same year he died."

"How did you come to be out here?" Ed asked.

"After my father died, my mother married another soldier," Tom said. "He had lost his farm while he was fightin' for the South. We moved to a town in Ohio, but they didn't stay there long because there was no place for a 'Johnny Reb' family there. We then moved to Saint Joseph, Missouri where my step father worked in the fur tradin' business. Livin' in Saint Joe was a good place for a boy to grow up. There were all kinds of people there includin' settlers goin' west. There were railroaders, fur traders, and riverboat men bringin' in machinery from the east and furs from the mountains. There were Indians and Mountain men as well. Somethin' was allus happenin' there. There was too much goin' on for a boy to go to school, and so I didn't," he paused, "well I did finish fourth grade."

"Did you see any mean lookin' Indians out here?" Carrie asked.

"Well, there was plenty of mean lookin' mountain men," Tom replied with a chuckle, "But they was allus good to us boys. They'd give us a nickel to fetch stuff for them."

"Even the meanest ones?" John Kaschke asked his father.

"Yes, even the meanest lookin' ones," Tom replied.

"Berta did your family move to Saint Joseph when Tom's did?" Chloe asked Berta.

"No," Berta replied. "Right after the war many southern families felt the need to locate outside the South. Our families met while we were part of a wagon train that left Raliegh, North Carolina and settled in southern Ohio."

"How did Tom and you come to get married?" Ed asked. "Tom never forgot me," Berta chuckled. "And I never forgot him. When Tom got older he came to see me in Ohio where my family lived on their farm."

"I came to see my mother's kinfolk," Tom replied with a wink. "They stayed in Ohio, but my father settled his family in Saint Joe."

There were chuckles around the group after Tom spoke.

"Tom I bin wonderin' if you ever heard of a riverman named O'Bryan?'" Ed asked.

"Was he a big man who bellowed loud enough so's you could hear him for a mile or more?" Tom laughed at the memory.

"That's him alright," Ed also laughed.

"Did you know him?' Tom asked.

"Yeah, I worked for him four years on the river. We stopped in Saint Joe every time we come up the Missouri River," Ed answered.

"Well I'll be dogged," Tom stated. "I prob'ly saw you there at least once or twice. One time when I went to the docks that barge unloaded a bunch of Bohunks in Saint Joe."

"I remember boys watchin' that," Ed replied. "You was prob'ly among 'em. I stayed on the boat there."

"What did you do on the flatboat?" Carrie asked her father.

"At first I was a cook's helper. Then Cap'n O'Bryan made me a part of the crew, and I helped load and unload the barge." Ed answered. "Best four years I ever had, that is until I married the children's mother."

Once again there was laughter around the group. Shades of night had drawn across the evening sky as the sun set. Shadows of light and dark formed ghostly bars and shades of gray, orange-pink, and dark blue across the evening sky. Faces were masked in shadows and light as a sense of peace settled over the small group in the wide expanse of the prairie night. The waning twilight slowly became the darkness of night as stars began to highlight the deep blue tones of the heavenly expanse above them.

"Been nice talkin' to you folks," Tom said as he rose and the unspoken bondedness of neighbors was temporarily interrupted for the small group. "I reckon it's time to find our way home so we can hit the hay. We got to rise up early in the morning."

"Will you be able to find your way home as dark as it is?" Carrie wanted to know. She felt they might get lost.

"If old Nellie don't know the way home by now, we will have to sell her to a glue factory in the mornin." Tom chuckled. "We jist let her go and she finds her way home every time."

Goodnights were said and the Kaschkes and the sound of jingling harness faded into the stillness of the night.

There was a "housewarming" when the dugout was finished the first week of November. The day was bright and there were no clouds, but there was a chill in the air and the wind had shifted to the northeast. Ed and Tom talked about the weather as they surveyed their handiwork in building.

"We couldn't have asked for better weather while we were buildin" Ed stated.

"Winter's comin,'" Tom replied. "You surely can expect snow and cold when the wind turns to the northeast. Ed, it don't make sense for you to try to stay in that dugout when winter really sets in. We get blizzards here with drifts over the tops of your windows. You could have a hard time gittin' out, especially since your door faces south an' east. Berta and me would be glad to put you up for as long as you need when the storms come."

"Tom," Ed replied, "I grew up in northern Vermont where we got two to four feet of snow every winter. Can't be much worse out here than it was there. We'll be all right come what may." Chloe was listening as Tom and Ed talked.

"We appreciate your offer, and we may decide to do as you say, but I agree with Ed." She tried to keep the doubt from her voice as she spoke, "we'll stay here," she added.

"You folks just don't know how bad it can git out here. A nice day like this can turn into a blizzard by nighttime. There's nothin' between the North Pole and here but a bob wire fence, an' it don't stop much wind. When we git a blizzard there may not be much snow on the level ground, but the wind can pile it up as high as a windmill, an' behind a low hill like this you can expect five to eight foot drifts in the front of your house. There can be ground blizzards so bad you can't see and you can barely git your breath."

"We'll be just fine," Ed stated with the bravado of a greenhorn to the western plains.

"Just remember our door's allus open when you need us." Tom stated as he waited for his family to board the wagon for home.

Chapter Twelve

Fall weather had been mild until early in December when a series of three day blizzards caused a white out of blowing snow that limited vision to a few feet and made breathing difficult. The temperature dropped to near zero, and water froze in the spring. As a result there was no water for the Foster household or their livestock, so they had to use melted snow for their needs. A drift of about four feet blocked the door until Ed shoveled a pathway out. Windows frosted on the inside and were blocked by snow on the outside. A freezing wind swept down from the north which drove through all the layers of clothing the family could put on. The lean-to shelter Ed had built for the livestock was not sufficient to keep the animals' noses from frost bite, and the cow ceased to give milk.

On a day when the wind subsided, Ed and Chloe gathered blankets pots and pans and the children and herded the cow with them to the Kaschkes. As they moved across the three miles of prairie, Chloe was amazed at the harshness of the wind. There was very little snow on the open ground, but the valleys were filled. As they drove into the Kaschke yard, children's faces appeared in the frosted windows where they had rubbed the frost away enough to see.

"Welcome," Tom hollered as he walked from the corral, "we're glad you folks decided to come over. Berta and I worried that you might freeze. There's nothin' as cold as a damp dugout"

Chloe and the children stiffly got down from the wagon and were greeted by Berta while Ed and Tom tended to the team.

"Ed thought it best that we come," Chloe said apologetically. "We're pleased to have you," Berta stated. "Come in and get warm by the stove while I set the table for a cup of coffee." The children were glad to be inside and settled around the pot-bellied stove to get warm. Chloe and Berta sat at the table with two cups of steaming coffee.

"We had no idea how a storm could be out here," Chloe stated.

"We've been here eight years," Berta said. "It usually isn't this bad this early, but we do have one or two blizzards during the winter.

Nearly every winter we hear of people who freeze to death when they lose their way in the blowing snow."

Shyness that kept the children quiet was soon overcome and the noise of children playing filled the house. Berta and Chloe watched with the interest of mothers as their children became acquainted. Ed and Tom came in and shook the snow off their clothing as they stamped their feet to remove snow from their boots.

"I never saw anything like this in Vermont," Ed stated. "Back there we had lots more snow, but without the terrible wind."

"Don't you folks even think about goin' back to your diggin's until warm weather. You just never know when a blizzard can come roarin' across the prairie without much warnin'." Tom stated.

"Winters in Chicago were cold and blustery with lots of wind," Chloe stated. "Especially on the North Shore where we lived."

Within a few days the two families had established a routine. Chloe and Berta shared duties of the household while Ed and Tom took care of the outside chores. When the weather permitted, the men took the wagon to the South Platte where they gathered wood from the cottonwoods along the river. At times when they started home, they became confused by the blowing snow and had to let the horses find their way home. Interest in their homes and children brought Berta and Chloe to a friendship that permitted them to share their deepest secrets.

"Are you in a family way?" Berta asked Chloe one day.

"Yes I'm in my fourth month, I'm beginning to show aren't I?"

"I would have known anyway," Berta replied. "You have that motherly look that pregnant women get. You look worried along with that. Is there anything you need help with?"

"The birth of Carrie was very difficult for me, and Doctor Olson advised Ed and me not to have more than two children." Chloe stated. "This one will be my fourth."

"Have you been having trouble?" Berta asked.

"Well," Chloe said hesitantly, "I have been having some spotting and cramps even before we left Nebraska, but I have been alright." There was a tremor of doubt in her voice.

"In the spring when you get back to your dugout, and need help in any way, just send for me." Berta said sincerely. "Send Ed or Carrie over any time you need help."

Chloe recognized the genuineness in Berta's voice and gave her a hug of appreciation.

Cold wintry days kept the children inside the Kaschke home, but there were occasional days when the sun warmed and there were no storm clouds. Such days were bright with sunshine that sparkled on new fallen snow as it melted on rooftops that produced icicles on the eaves where the water froze. Temperatures on such days rarely rose above freezing. The children could go outside and play, but on the coldest days Chloe kept them busy with crafts and games. When they were not busy, the children became irritable. The four Kaschke children and the three Foster children were prone to argue when they had to stay inside several days. One day Berta brought up the subject of education for her children.

"All the time we have lived here my children have had no schooling. We need a school," she stated.

"I had been teaching my children before these winter storms changed our plans," Chloe said. "I have books and writing materials, but they are over at the dugout. We didn't have time to bring them."

"If you could get them, would you teach my children along with yours?" Berta asked.

"Indeed I would. Ed could bring the things I need, and we can have school here. If you could take care of my William, he's going on two as is your George. I would be happy to teach the others."

The home schooling began the next week. Chloe was glad for the opportunity to teach, and the children were eager to learn.

"Have your children had religious training?" Chloe asked Berta.

"I have read to them from the Bible, but that's about all."

"Do you mind if I include stories from the Bible?"

"I'd be glad if you would." Berta stated.

After that conversation, tales of Richard the Lion Hearted, and Julius Ceasar were regularly taught along with stories of Moses and King David. The children listened raptly to both kinds of stories.

That winter the days were especially cold and windy with just enough snow to form drifts behind any obstacle, even yucca and sagebrush had small drifts, and small valleys were filled with snow. Livestock could not graze so Ed and Tom went to the farms along the South Platte to buy hay without money. They promised days of work in the spring and summer for each load they hauled. Some of the chickens, froze in the nest, and the survivors had frozen combs that turned black. Eggs became scarce, and many were cracked and frozen, but they could be thawed and were still usable. Finally, April came with cloudy days and cold nights. Warmer days late that month gave a promise that it was spring, but late frosts kept farmers from planting as early as usual.

"Well, Tom, looks like me an' my family can be movin' back to our dugout," Ed remarked one evening.

"Chloe an' me talked it over. "We'll pack up and go next week."

"You've been a good help to me, Ed. Two men can do twice as much as one, and I really like havin' you here. Out here there ain't no fence high enough to keep good neighbors apart," Tom said extending his hand to Ed. They shook hands and the next Monday morning goodbyes were said with "promises to come over anytime."

In an aside to Chloe, Berta whispered "especially if you have any trouble. Send Ed or Carrie if you need me."

Arriving at the dugout, the Fosters found there was frost around the inside of the walls where water had seeped in, and in the center of the floor there was a large section of soft mud. There was alkali mould on all the sod walls, and there were water puddles all around where snow had melted and dripped through the sod roof. Boards under the sod above had begun to sag and a few had long cracks in them. A damp odor of mould clung to the cold moist air inside the cabin. The children turned their noses up in disgust.

"We'll need to git a fire goin' to heat the place up," Ed stated. "Carrie git wood while I git the stove ready, take out the ashes and make some shavin's to start the fire," Ed directed Carrie.

"Mother, you stay wrapped up in the blankets. We'll soon have the cabin nice and warm."

After the fire was going, a closer inspection indicated that it would take more than a few days and nights to dry out the cabin. Ed took the children and Chloe back to the Kaschkes, and stayed in the dugout three weeks before he judged it was livable. The second week, portions of the sod roof crashed to the floor. Ed had to drive to Haxtun to get new boards, and he and Tom were able to repair the roof, but two days were required. After that Ed used a trowel on the walls to reduce seepage and smooth them up, and he packed dry dirt on the floor and smoothed it into the muddy floor until it was hard packed. The third week of April the family resettled in the repaired house. When they had been in the dugout three days, Chloe shared a concern she had not wanted to bring to Ed's attention.

"Ed, I'm worried about this baby," she said. "It is not as active as our other babies were, my cramps have become longer and more painful, and the spotting has increased."

"We best go to the doctor," Ed stated. "I'll hitch up in the morning and we'll go to Sedgwick."

They drove to Sedgwick the next day.

"Ed, Chloe needs all the rest she can get," Doctor Davis said when he came out of the office with Chloe. "Her time is very close and her body has had a great deal of stress, keep her in bed if you can, at least keep her off her feet until the baby comes."

"What else did the doctor tell you?" Ed asked Chloe when they were driving home.

"He gave me laudanum for pain, and told me to get lots of rest, in bed preferably," she replied. "He said my delivery time was near."

"I think it would be best to ask Tom to let Berta come over when she can." Ed stated. "I would feel more at ease if there was a woman in the house. I'll ride over and ask Tom this evenin."

Berta came the next afternoon. Three days later she decided to stay the night. Shortly after midnight, everyone was awakened by low moaning. Ed had risen and was trying to comfort his wife. Berta joined him, and began massaging Chloe's cold arms.

Suddenly there was a loud hoarse scream, Chloe rose to a sitting position and fell back on the pillow barely breathing. "Ed, go to Sedgwick and bring the doctor as soon as you can," Berta directed. "This baby may be here before you get back."

Ed left the dugout and soon the sound of a horse galloping faded away. Almost at the same time, the baby entered the world. Very weak and exhausted, Chloe lay gasping for breath.

"Is…it…a…boy…or…girl?" she asked.

"It's a boy," Berta said. "Now rest while I make you as comfortable as possible."

The Foster children had risen and were standing inside the room in their night clothes.

"Carrie, stir up the fire. Katie, help Carrie get more water on the stove to warm it when we need it. Carrie, when you finish that come and help me bathe the baby. Katie, keep water warm on the stove."

By the time Doctor Davis arrived in mid morning, Chloe and the baby had been bathed and there were clean sheets on the bed.

The doctor looked around and then commented. "There isn't much I can do. Berta you did a fine job tying the umbilical cord. You'd make a fine nurse," he added.

Berta smiled as she replied. "Most prairie women have had lots of baby experience…"

Chloe muttered something that no one understood. Berta leaned close as Chloe spoke again.

"Ed…where's my Ed?"

"Dearest sweetheart, I'm right here." Ed took her hand in his as she opened her eyes, and seemed to be searching each face.

"How's…our little boy?" She smiled wanly at Ed.

"He's doing fine," Doctor Davis answered.

"Is he strong?" Chloe asked.

"He's a bit small, an ounce under five pounds." The doctor replied hesitantly.

"I can't hear him cry," Chloe murmured.

"He's not a loud crier," Berta stated.

"What name shall I put on the birth certificate?"

"His name is Franklin Prescott Foster," Chloe and Ed replied.

Within the first three days of Franklin's life, Chloe discovered that she did not have enough milk for Franklin. During the first week they learned that cow's milk did not agree with him. Ed remembered that the Crow family had a nanny goat. He rode over and they gave him a supply of goat's milk. Franklin seemed to accept that milk, but could only take an ounce at a feeding, and by his third week he had lost six ounces. Breathing for Franklin had been difficult from his birth, and it seemed to Chloe that all his strength was required just to breath. She was deeply saddened when his breathing stopped and he could not be revived. The doctor was summoned that night, and completed the death certificate.

A pall of dismal depression descended on the Foster home.

While Franklin had lost his struggle for survival, Chloe had slowly gained strength. She knew she was not strong enough to travel the eighteen miles to the Sedgwick Cemetery for a funeral ceremony.

"I was present for his birth and I want to be present for his funeral," she said. "Could we have the minister here for the service?"

"I don't know how we could do that seein' that we don't have a cemetery nearer than Sedgwick," Ed replied.

"Could we bury him on this property?" Chloe asked. Ed thought for a time and replied that he guessed they could.

"Could we have a minister for the burial?" Chloe asked.

"It's still early enough in the day for me to drive to Sedgwick," Ed stated. "I'll leave for town right away, an' ask Reverend Ford."

In Sedgwick that afternoon, Ed went to the lumber yard. The carpenter there built a small coffin of pine wood which they loaded in the wagon. It was late that night when Ed returned to the homestead. The next day Franklin was placed in the coffin with his blankets and an embroidered lace pillow. Ed had chosen a site beside the cabin for the grave, and he and Tom prepared it. Reverend Ford prayed for the family and read a text from Psalm twenty three. The neighbors who had come, quietly offered their condolences. Tom and Ed lowered the small casket into the grave, and the funeral ended when the coffin was neatly covered with dirt.

Following the death of Franklin, Chloe found that she had trouble making her body obey her mind. In the early hours of the day she would awaken and find her legs and arms heavy and slow to respond. When she rose, she felt tired as though she had already worked all day. She did not see joy in her surroundings as she had, and even the bright sun that had always given her pleasure seemed dull. Household care for her family was drudgery to her. No one told her she was experiencing depression, but she knew it.

The mound of dirt beside the cabin, and the crude cross with Franklin's name on it became a kind of shrine for the family. No longer did the children play on the south side of the cabin near the grave. Chloe often stood immobile for long periods of time simply staring at the cross and the grave. When the children and Ed found her there, they also stood with heads bowed as their hearts embraced the solitary sadness evidenced by Chloe. A month of this kind of mourning brought Chloe to realize that there must be an end to it, so she resolved that she must demonstrate to her family that life was worth living.

"Death is a temporary stop in the normal process of life and survival," she remarked to herself. That thought awakened her to the despondency she and the family had made a daily habit. When she tried to express her feelings to Ed, she found that he was bitter and angry at a "God who would let this happen." Ed transferred his anger to the prairie climate, but most of all, to events over which he had no control. Chloe realized that he was deeply depressed over the death of Franklin in his bitter outpouring of invective to the God she trusted. To his wife Ed reviewed flaws of prairie life he had heard from others.

"Out here you can't raise chickens without losing a few to coyotes. Skunks and weasels sneak into the hen houses and suck the insides out of eggs. Cattle hooves and tits freeze when the temperatures drop below zero. Horses eat loco weed and go crazy. Crops fail in drought, and corn gets smut that spoils harvests. Rabbits eat garden plants and there ain't enough to can for the winter. Prairie dogs cause distemper in good domestic animals. Rattlesnakes come into our yards, and make them unsafe for the kids to play. Things were a helluva lot better in Nebraska an' I think we should go back," Ed concluded bitterly.

"I'm as discouraged as you are," Chloe responded, "but I think our future is here and we must trust that better times are ahead. You told me times would be hard out here, and now we must learn to cope with bad times and misfortunes as they come."

Chloe knew no other way to stir her family out of this "slough of despond" than to rouse them to do the activities of life with energy and gusto. She knew she must demonstrate a positive attitude in herself even when she felt otherwise. Early one morning two months after Franklin's death, she rose before sunup and deliberately made as much noise as possible. She surprised the family by singing a "song of the prairie."

"It's time to stop our mourning.
Life is not a vale of tears, vale of tears,
We rise early every morning.
We are hardy pioneers, pioneers.
Life is waiting and we must live it
When there's need for kindness, we must give it,
It's time to stop our mourning."

Sleepily the family rose one by one, and they stood and stared in awe at this changed wife and mother. Chloe knew that they were waiting for an explanation, and she was ready.

"We cannot go on in a state of mourning for Franklin the rest of our lives," she stated. "There are bad and good things that happen throughout life, and we must go about meeting whatever comes our way…always looking for the good in every situation. We must make the best of the bad things, and go about looking for the good even when things look dismal."

As soon as she said that, she realized she had repeated the words her mother had told her at the piano recital when she was twelve, and at that moment she was thankful that her mother had given her positive attitudes toward life. She knew that she must now do the same for her family. Ever one to see beauty and wonder in God's handiwork, Chloe had made it a life goal to give that sense of awe to everyone she met. As a teacher in Chicago she made every effort to accomplish that by directing her pupils to appreciate the world around them. Even in these hard times, that sense of God's presence never left her.

On another day Chloe was seeing the beauty of the prairie in the early morning sun. She had seen the harshness of blizzards, drought and even death in her family. But her faith was strengthened when she saw the cottonwood leaves shimmering in the sun after a late frost had turned new leaves black. Now new leaves were pushing the frost blackened ones aside. That sense of the renewal of life returned to her once again as the scent of wildflower, primrose, prairie lilies, and new leafing cottonwoods swirled around her. She saw new life springing from the prairie as once brown grass was beginning to show the greening of spring and she knew once more that she felt at home with God and with nature.

"The grass has turned green from its winter brownness," she whispered to herself. "My life became just as barren as this prairie when Franklin died, and it can blossom again just as prairie life does." She paused, "I couldn't have survived without my faith in God, and good neighbors, and the renewal that is spring on the prairie."

Sun up shadows began to fade as Chloe walked away from the cabin on this morning when the sun shone brightly and the meadow larks were singing their "oh see me I'm a pretty bird." greetings. Prairie larks added their song as they flitted away in flocks of four or five. Chloe's gaze drifted from the unbroken eastern horizon to the north where she could see the distant tree line of cottonwoods along the South Platte River. Beyond that and across the valley there were low hills that she knew reached into western Nebraska. She walked a short distance to the northwest where her vision swept across the outline of Twin Buttes. To the south the horizon was broken by the Kaschkes' house and beyond that was a wide expanse of unfenced prairie that fell away to low hills as far as she could see.

"God's good earth," she said aloud. "My life will be good again just as the earth is given new life in spring."

At that moment her thoughts were interrupted by the plaintive wailing of her youngest child, Willie, and her borrowed time of peace and quiet ended as it always has for mothers.

"Mama, where are you?"

"I'm coming, Willie," she called.

While she walked to the cabin, she silently gave a prayer of thanks for her children and family. Silently she asked that God continue to protect them even as He had in the past. One by one each child voiced the same theme that Willie had spoken.

"Mama I'm hungry." Chloe was brought back to the reality of family living on the prairie. As generations of prairie mothers had done she busied herself seeing to her families needs.

After breakfast, the children settled into their normal playing under the warm blue sky of a prairie day with the confidence and faith they saw in their mother. Following her example, they knew they could meet whatever experiences were ahead for all of them.

Chapter Thirteen

Excitedly, Carrie and Katie burst into the cabin followed by Willie. Quickly they circled around their mother.

"There's somebody comin," they shouted in unison. "We could see dust along the trail to the south," Carrie stated.

"Yeh, mama, then we could see three people on horses riding as fast as they could this way," excited Katie said loudly.

"Yeh, comin' this way," Willie repeated.

"Will they eat lunch with us?" Katie asked.

Before Chloe could answer three riders dressed as cowboys rode into the yard and dismounted. One tall slender rider approached the cabin. Chloe had opened the door and the children stood there with her while the young man took off his hat.

"Mornin' Ma'am," he said. "I'm Hank Robbins an' thet feller with the black horse is Bart Jackson, an' thet other feller on the bay is Pete Smith. We'd like to water our horses at your spring and git a drink for ourselves."

Chloe acknowledged the greeting and nodded to each young man as he was introduced. Each cowboy removed his hat as his name was called. Chloe gave them permission to help themselves to the water. The horses were impatient to get to the trough, and seemed to pull the cowboys along. These young men shared the dipper while their horses drank from the same trough. Chloe remained in the doorway, but the children stepped into the yard and stood outside the cabin. When their thirst had been quenched, the young men tethered their horses to corral posts, and came to the cabin.

"Ma'am, we bin ridin' since early mornin,'" Hank stated. "We surely would like a time to set a spell and have a bite to eat. We bin livin' on hardtack and salt pork, and a slice of home made bread with a cup of coffee sure would hit the spot, if you can spare it."

"We have biscuits and gravy that I was fixing for my children. Would you care for that?"

The cowboys nodded eagerly in unison.

"You may wash up with water in the basin outside on the bench. Carrie and Katie will bring towels and soap. Carrie will get you more water," she added, "when you need it."

Quickly the young men washed their hands and doused water on their faces. Shy Willie followed every move they made.

"Are you cowboys?" he asked.

"Yes, son, yes we are," Bart answered. "Would you like to be a cowboy and ride a horse like I do?"

"Boy," Willie said with wonderment in his voice.

"Might be you could ride my horse after while," Hank said. "You ever bin on a horse before?"

"Papa rides wif me on Dusty sometimes," Willie answered.

"Is thet Dusty in the corral?" Hank asked. Willie nodded.

"He's a fine lookin' horse," Pete stated.

The cowboys finished their wash up and were invited inside where they were directed to sit around the table.

"Would you like coffee?" Chloe asked.

"Yes ma'am," Hank exclaimed, and the other two nodded approval. Chloe judged that the oldest was not over twenty two.

Enamel cups, plates and utensils were placed on the table.

The children were seated in their places around the table and a plateful of warmed over biscuits was set on the table. Chloe then placed a bowl of warm gravy before the hungry young men. The cowboys ate as though they had not had a sit down home cooked meal for a long time.

"My husband will be home before sunset," Chloe stated. "He went to town for farm equipment and supplies."

"Was he in a grain wagon with one bay horse and a black?" Pete asked. Chloe nodded wishing that she had not told them Ed was gone.

"We met him on the trail from Haxtun." Pete replied.

Chloe was not afraid, but she was aware of the leering glances Bart was giving her. Her worries mounted as the cowboys asked Carrie if there were boys around to tease her, but the leering glances of Bart worried her more than the teasing. After they had eaten, Chloe served more coffee and sat down at the table.

"Ma'am you are too pretty to be left alone in this god forsaken place. You should be in a fine hotel where there's music and lots of company," Bart stated.

"Ol' Bart thinks everybody should live in Abilene or Dodge…or Fort Worth or someplace like that." Pete said. "We've been in all those towns and he likes the dance hall girls."

"You spent as much time with the ladies as I did," Bart said defensively. He directed his next comments to Chloe.

"I meant no offense Ma'am, but a woman shouldn't be left alone on this prairie. You have a way of speakin' thet I never heard in Texas. Where are yuh from?"

Chloe paused before she spoke feeling that she had already revealed too much about herself and she knew she must protect her children whatever was to occur.

"I was born and grew up in Chicago. My husband grew up in Vermont. We married in Chicago nearly six years ago."

"You are both damn Yankees," Bart stated. "Excuse my French, but a southern man looks after his women better than any damn Yankee ever could."

"Ma'am, Bart speaks his mind too much," Hank stated. "Excuse his swearin. He don't mean nuthin' by it'"

There was silence for a time as Chloe began clearing the dishes. When she reached for Bart's utensils, he grasped her hand in a tight grip. Anger blazed from her eyes, and her body stiffened, but she said nothing as she pulled her hand out of his grasp. She and Carrie began washing and drying the dishes. The sounds of silverware and of plates put away with the slosh of dishwater were all that was heard for a brief time. More coffee was poured as Chloe asked where they were going as she joined them at the table, careful to sit as far away from Bart as she possibly could without being rude.

"We jus' finished drivin' a herd of longhorns to a rancher south of here. He's fixin' to start a herd down there." Pete replied. "We heard of the Cottonwood Ranch near here and thought we might ride out there. Do you know how to git to the Cottonwood from here?"

"My husband will be home soon and he will be able to tell you. Your horses look worn out and you boys could use rest. You're welcome to turn your horses into our corral and rest for as long as you are here. Ed will know the way to the Cottonwood."

"This is a hard kinda life for a woman. If I had a woman like you, I'd see that she had silks an' satins and a house in town." Bart seemed intent on being outspoken with Chloe.

Hank and Pete shook their heads in disapproval at Bart's actions.

"A cowboy ain't got nothin' to offer a woman except his horse an' ridin' from one place to another. Most cowboys have a dream of a spread of their own," Hank stated. "As long as they are on the trail, they got nothin' to offer a woman."

When he finished, he glared at Bart.

"Yeh, a cowboy gits used to livin' out an' drinkin' from any place there's water. He may wear the same clothes for a couple of weeks without washin' 'em, and then he may just jump in any water deep enough an' wash them while he's still in 'em." There was laughter around the circle as Pete finished, but Pete seemed embarrassed.

"Ain't much time for bein' clean for a cowboy. 'Course you folks have a spring an' I saw a clothes line. I reckon you find time to keep your family clean." Hank said.

"We manage," Chloe replied. "Down in the draw past the corral there is a small pond. If you want to bathe, we have towels and soap. You could clean up there."

"Come on, Bart we've got to look after our horses before you spoil our welcome," Pete said as he went outside.

Hank and Bart followed. Chloe heard them arguing as they headed for the corral.

"Bart, if we play our cards right we may be able to stay the night" The voice was Hank's, but Chloe could not really tell as they walked away.

"Yeh, why the hell did you want to insult anybody?" That voice was Pete's, and he sounded angry.

"Aw, I didn't mean nuthin,' Didn't you gents see how pretty she is? A man would have to be blind not to notice." Chloe guessed that was Bart.

Their voices faded out of hearing as they walked away. They unsaddled their horses and turned them into the corral. Chloe watched the new horses as they caused a stir among the other animals.

Ed's saddle horse and a colt were quick to move to the new arrivals and sniff them front and rear. There was squealing and kicking as horses chased around the corral. It soon subsided to animal indifference as the horses adjusted to one another. The cowboys' horses were looking for places to roll after saddles had been removed.

Carrie and Katie had gone to the corral under careful instruction from their mother.

"You may go, but keep your distance from the cowboys. Don't let any one of them get you alone. Be polite when they talk to you. I will call you to the cabin if they get too friendly."

The two girls stood apart from the strangers, but they could hear their conversation. As they watched the black rolled once and shook the dust it had gathered from it's hide, and began coughing. The roan rolled over once and then seemed to enjoy the feel of the ground and stayed on its back with its feet in the air and flexed head and tail back and forth. The bay did not choose to roll.

"Your horse is tryin' to git rid of the feel of the saddle and your weight on her back," Pete told Bart.

"That bay of your'n didn't even roll which shows he ain't worth a damn." Bart said.

"You yahoos forgit thet he rolled three times yestaday," Hank said with mock hurt pride.

"Thet horse of your'n has the heaves," Pete chided Bart as the black lustily coughed.

"She just got dust in her nose when she rolled." Bart replied.

Chloe called the girls to come to the cabin, and the cowboys began looking for shade where they could lie down away from the hot sun. For the cowboys there wasn't a whole lot to see around the settlement, and they were inclined to get on their horses and ride to anything over a half mile away rather than walk that half mile, which meant they would rather sleep than go to the pond to bathe. They found a place of shade behind the livestock shed and soon were sound asleep. They had been asleep for a couple of hours when the sound of a wagon rolling into the yard with steel rimmed wheels striking stones, and the clinking of harness chains was enough to awaken them.

Ed stopped at the cabin door and Carrie came out to hold the team while the groceries Ed had purchased were unloaded.

"Ed we have company," Chloe stated.

"Yeh, I saw their horses in the corral," Ed replied.

Roused from sleep the cowboys walked around the shed. Introductions were made and Ed drove the wagon to its place beside the shed. The cowboys followed along and unhitched and removed the harness of the team while Ed directed them to the place he usually hung the harness. Hank and Pete carried the harnesses to the shed while Bart and Ed turned the horses into the corral. The three of them helped Ed with the evening chores all the while with good natured banter. The ritual of horse greeting horse was repeated when Ed's team entered the corral. The sun had lowered and early night was blending with a slight haze in the air that caused the distant northeastern hills to reflect the purpling shades of night.

"Too late to ride tonight," Ed stated. "We ain't got a lot of room in the house, but you boys are welcome to stay the night. Looks like it will be a clear night. You're welcome to throw hay out where you were this afternoon and put your bedrolls there. Alls you may git fer supper is sowbelly an' beans. My wife makes good biscuits and bread and we'd be glad to share what we have."

"Mister Foster don"t worry about where we'll sleep, we're like prairie mavericks, we can bed down anywhere." Bart and Hank grinned and nodded approval as Pete spoke.

"Time and tide, and milkin' the cows wait for no one," was an expression Ed had learned in his youth. He had taught his family well, and so it was that Carrie was sent to the barn with a pail and instructions to stay with her father while he did the milking. Before she left the cabin, she was given instructions about the cowboys.

"Be polite. Answer questions briefly. Do not be unfriendly, but be careful about being alone with any cowboy. Stay close to your father, and let him talk to the cowboys."

The banter and good natured teasing of the cowboys was a new experience for Carrie. Ed listened as he milked the cow, and saw nothing amiss in what was said. Carrie followed her mother's instructions, which made her seem shy and caused the cowboys to tease her even more. When the milking was finished, the small group made its way to the cabin. Chloe had baked bread that afternoon, while Katie and Willie had taken turns with the butter churn. Supper of sowbelly flavored beans was served along with fresh bread, butter and cinnamon rolls that had been baked along with the bread. There followed a time of entertainment that centered around the cowboys telling stories about trail-herding cattle from Texas to points north, and they sang songs of the trail. Many of their songs were hymns, and Chloe joined the singing. She was surprised that her voice harmonized well with the voices of the cowboys.

Night settled over the prairie, and a large moon swathed silver across sage and yucca. As the three young men left the cabin to spread their bedrolls, a coyote yelped short barks that carried across the evening enchanted prairie air.

"Must be chasin' a jackrabbit," Hank muttered.

An answering long drawn howl seemed to hang in the cooling air of night for a moment.

"Must be its mate," Bart speculated.

"They'll eat tonight." Pete added.

These three young men were wise to the ways of the prairie, and settled in for a peaceful night circling their bedrolls with their lariats to keep away prairie rattlers. Ed and Chloe discussed their visitors.

"I'm worried about the one they call Bart," Chloe stated.

"Why? Did he do somethin' that upset you?" There was worry along with anger in Ed's tone.

"In a way yes. He took hold of my hand when I served him at noon. He didn't seem to want to let go…" Chloe was hesitant to say more. She was not sure of Ed's reaction.

"Did he say or do somethin' else?" Ed asked.

"When I was cleaning up, he came and told me he'd take me to see the bright lights, and said he could give me jewelry, silk dresses and a good time."

Ed was furious and began pacing the floor.

"He prob'ly hain't been around a pretty woman fer a long time," Ed speculated. "You're the prettiest woman for miles. I'll be around all day tomorrow. Things'll look diff'rent in the mornin.'

"Just the same we need to be careful tonight."

There was a long silence and Chloe realized that Ed was asleep. She heard every squeak and creak in the cabin all night, and felt she hadn't slept a wink when morning came.

At sunrise Ed went out to do the morning chores and found the cowboys with their horses saddled.

"You boys ridin' out now?" He asked.

"Sure looks like a good day fer ridin,'" Pete stated.

"Boys, we'd be glad to have you fer breakfast. My wife will have biscuits an' gravy an' hot coffee."

"We surely do appreciate your kindness, but we want to get an early start before it gits hot" Pete said.

"We have hardtack an' coffee so we can git by," Hank said.

"How do we git to the Cottonwood Ranch?" Bart asked.

"Ride north to the South Platte, go east three miles and you come to Cottonwood Crik, go north till you come to the ranch."

"Take good care of that pretty wife of yours," Bart winked at Ed as he mounted, Texas style.

"Just you remember who's wife she is," Ed stated.

Bart laughed, waved and rode away north.

"We sure do thank you folks for your hospitality, Pete said. "We'll ride herd on Bart so he don't come back alone."

Hank nodded that he agreed and the two riders galloped away and soon there was nothing to be seen of them but a dust trail going north toward the river.

"Those boys need to settle down somewhere," Ed muttered to himself. When he returned to the dugout after finishing the chores, he was surprised to hear the children singing.

"What's that all about?" He asked Chloe.

"Carrie found a letter from Central City Grandma in one of the boxes of groceries," she replied. "Carrie read that she's coming for a visit, and they're happy."

"Yeh, I guess I forgot about the letter. What does it say?"

"Grandma's comin' to visit. Grandma's comin' to visit," the children sang happily.

"Well, that's somethin' to think about," Ed mumbled.

Chloe heard Ed's comment, but there was no opportunity to talk about it for several days.

Chapter Fourteen

Two days of hot sultry weather came, and there was an oppressive quality in the air. Chloe and the children spent those days with Berta and her children while Ed and Tom hauled hay. The second afternoon while Ed stayed at the homestead to stack hay, the darkest cloud Ed had ever seen rose in the west. As it neared the homestead some areas of the cloud seemed greenish and of lighter color than the blue-black along the far horizons. As the cloud neared there were broad white bands that blended with the gray-green streaks, and a constant rumble of thunder became a deafening roar as lightening seemed to flash from pole to pole of the narrowing horizon. Dust and debris of all things movable preceded the rain and hail. Ed raced toward the dugout as a twisting swirling funnel swept past the dugout and sped southeast across the plains.

The storm did not directly hit the buildings and lasted less than an hour, but the force of the wind caused the barn to lean southeast as though pointing in the direction the storm had gone. Ed emerged from the dugout just as Tom Kaschke rode into the yard. The two men stood silently looking around at the damage left in the storm's path. The horses and the cow had been driven to the corral fence where they stood with their backs covered with hail. The whitened ground sloshed two to three inches of melting hail when the animals moved away from the fence.

"Don't look like you have any crop left," Tom stated.

"Tom, I don't know what to make of this prairie," Ed said slowly, "looks like it don't want settlers to live on it"

"That storm was a bad one," Tom replied, "an' it surely caught you folks at a bad time. You just gittin' started an' all. Looks like it blew away the hay we just hauled. I'll help y'all git more hay and feed, right now let's hitch up your team and we'll go to our place."

Without a word Ed followed Tom's lead. He sat quietly on the wagon seat, and mumbled short answers to Tom's questions. Once again the Fosters found themselves as guests in the Kaschke home. Every morning Ed returned to the cabin to do the necessary chores. A day later Chloe accompanied him, and they entered the dugout to estimate what needed to be done there. It was disheartening to see water trails on the walls where melting hail had left them. Mud had washed as far as the center of the floor, and there were mud drippings where water had seeped through the sod walls and roof. Ed swore and Chloe cried, but she knew she must encourage Ed.

"We can clean it up in no time," Chloe stated brightly.

"What's the use," Ed replied. "It'll not do much good and I'm beginning to hate this damn place. Did you look at our field?"

"All I saw were little short stubs," Chloe said with honesty.

"The wind stripped the stalks of leaves an' the hail beat the ears that had formed into the ground. There's nothin' left worth a damn. Nobody can figger this country, if early frosts don't blight your crop, a cyclone comes along an' ruins it. How can anybody live in this god forsaken place?" There was a plaintive note of confusion in Ed's voice that was heavy with discouragement.

Chloe remained silent as Ed's depression transferred to her. Instinctively she knew that she must be the strong member of the family, but at the moment she did not know what to say or do. She went into the dugout and gathered water and mud soaked garments for laundry later. As she did so she noted there was slight damage to the cabin where the rear wall joined the dugout, but the rest of the cabin was muddy, but not damaged. As she worked she sensed Ed's feelings, but kept her thoughts to herself for fear of making his depression deeper. She put as many things as she could in a burlap bag, and they returned to the Kaschkes.

Nine days had passed since the cyclone, and Ed and Chloe spent those days cleaning and repairing the dugout and cabin. Chloe had forgotten the letter from Central City Grandma. She found it as she was putting clothing in the burlap bag, and decided to read it to Ed.

"I had forgotten about it until I was gathering clothing at the cabin. I will read it now, if you like." Chloe stated. Ed nodded and sat with head bowed, and silently listened.

Central City, Nebraska
June 12, 1895

Dear Edward and Family,

The news of your letter of May first concerning the death of Franklin was most disturbing to me. That you decided to bury him beside the dugout was barbaric to say the least.

I am sorry I could not come to offer my help at that time. Edith Norton was ill and I felt that I should stay and care for this family.

Since I have not heard from you since May first, I have taken pen in hand to let you know that I will be coming to Sedgwick and will arrive on the twenty first of August.

All in Jason's family are now well. Cousin Clarence Norton was helping throw hay to the animals and fell from the loft. No bones were broken, but he suffered severe bruises along his right side. Jason's work load has doubled since you left Nebraska. As a result of Clarence's injuries Jason had to hire a man.

Please write and confirm the twenty first. I will stay with you two or three weeks.

With kind regards I remain your mother,
Julia Foster

That evening after the children were in bed, Ed and Chloe went outside to enjoy the cool evening air. It was then that Ed expressed his feelings about his mother.

"'With kind regards,...' I suppose she thinks I'll be glad to see her." The bitterness Ed had harbored for many years was in his voice.

"I don't understand your feelings Ed..."

"Understand, hell, from the time I was four years old that woman gave me nothin' but grief and misery." He lapsed into silence, and Chloe placed her arms around his shoulders. For a time Ed laid his head upon her breast and wept bitter tears.

"I never knew how a mother ought to treat her children until I saw you bein' a mother to our children," Ed raised his head and they embraced in tender love and concern for one another.

"Thank the good Lord I met you. I love you more than you can ever know," Chloe stated.

Ed listened as Chloe uttered a brief prayer of praise to the Lord for bringing her to this man. Their time of tenderness was brought to an end by the sound of a child crying.

"This ain't no time to feel sorry about the past," Ed stated.

Chloe settled the child for the night, and in the deepness of love, they renewed their awareness of the other's presence in tender embrace. In the morning Ed was in a better mood, and Carrie read the letter to the children. They danced and sang their joy about their grandmother's visit.

"What a happy time we will have," Carrie shouted when the morning chores were finished.

"It will be good to see Grandma again," Chloe stated. "Children, think of ways you can help us get ready for her visit."

"We can help you cook and clean," Carrie stated.

"We can help papa more," Katie said.

"I can help papa," Willie yelled.

That evening the children told Ed how they were going to help get ready for grandma's visit. Days passed quickly as the children were kept busy doing the tasks they had set for themselves. When the day for the trip to Sedgwick came, the wagon was loaded with all the supplies they would need for a picnic along with blankets and things the children had chosen to keep themselves occupied. The train was to arrive at noon, and the trip to the homestead would take about five hours so the family left the homestead at sunrise. The train arrived on time and, after greetings at the depot, they had a picnic at the water tower where there were newly planted Russian olive trees and green grass. With the help of the children, Chloe spread their lunch on a blanket, while grandma talked to Ed.

"Edward I hope you are aware of the responsibilities you have taken on as a family man," she said. Ed nodded, but said nothing, and repeating her comment she added, "A family needs a responsible father more than I ever knew."

"Ed has been a good husband and he's a fine father to his children," Chloe stated with obvious defensiveness.

"Well, he certainly needed to learn responsibility," Grandma responded. "Are your children healthy? Willie looks a bit pale to me." "The children love the prairie, and Willie is stronger here in Colorado than he was in Nebraska," Chloe stated firmly. "He loves the prairie, and the climate agrees with him."

Things Grandma said she needed and a supply of household items were purchased at the general store, and the children settled in the wagon. Getting Grandma in her place was a different matter. Ed wanted to make his mother as comfortable as possible, and asked her to ride on the spring seat with him. He had forgotten that she was short and a great deal overweight. The usual way to mount a wagon was to step on the hub of the front wheel, grasp the side of the spring seat and then step on the top of the wheel. After that, step on the top of the wagon box still holding the steel frame of the seat and move to the spring seat. For Grandma there was the problem of getting over the side of the wagon. With Ed on one side and Chloe on the other, they tried to help her accomplish this feat. Chloe later wondered if her disposition for the rest of her stay was the result of her anger at the method Ed had chosen, or the comments of bystanders.

They attempted to steady her by placing their hands on her rear to lift as she used her hands and feet cooperatively. That did not happen. Grandma stiffened her back and refused to move a muscle.

A group of rowdy cowboys along the false front store building on Main Street began shouting advice on how to accomplish the task.

"Get a hoist, Ed," one shouted.

One wag stated that he would go for a step ladder.

"Say the word an' we'll give you a hand," another said.

"I've never been so humiliated in my life," Grandma shouted.

Ed decided that it would be best to lower the tailgate and place it as a ramp at the back of the wagon. He and Chloe helpfully held grandma's arms as she struggled up that ramp and into the wagon.

"It wouldn't have been so humiliating had those ne'er-do-wells not stood and made catcalls," Grandma said later. "I am thankful that none of them offered their help. I would have been mortified to tears had any one of them put a hand on me."

Ed turned his head so she could not see the smile on his face, but he couldn't keep his shoulders from shaking as he laughed within himself, nor could he keep a titter or two silent.

"Ed Foster, you're just as crude as they were," Grandma accused. "Couldn't you have borrowed a buggy? That I can manage very well. The very idea making me climb over the wagon wheel."

For almost a mile there was silence in the wagon.

"There's nothing beautiful about this country," Grandma said. "I don't know what got into me to file for land out here. How can you stand to live where there are no trees?"

"There are trees along the South Platte," Ed stated.

"How far from your settlement is that?"

"About six or seven miles to the north," Ed replied.

"For heaven's sake, those trees must be so far away you cloudn't see them with a telescope."

"We can see a green line where the river is," Ed stated.

"Where do you get water?" Grandma asked.

"We have a good spring," Ed stated.

"How far from your settlement is that?"

"We built the cabin close enough," Ed answered.

Most of the trip from Sedgwick was over the Haxtun to Sedgwick trail, but the last three miles were across open prairie. The wagon bumped along over sage and yucca, and Grandma jounced and bounced as Ed drove. The children let their voices hold a note which caused a chorus of unharmonious noise. Grandma tried to hush them, but they were having too much fun to be silenced. When they arrived at the cabin and she had her feet on the ground, she let them know what she thought of the settlement.

"What a desolate forsaken place this is. Eighteen miles from anywhere, and three to the nearest neighbor with no trees between, at least the farmers in Nebraska have plowed out roads and keep them smoother." She looked around disgustedly.

"This is the land you were granted for your homestead," Ed stated. "Your name is on the survey report."

"Yes, but we didn't stay long enough for me to really know what it was like," she replied. She turned her gaze to the dugout cabin with an expression of disgust.

"Edward, I should think that you could have built a more comfortable home for your family. There's hardly room enough for all of us to sleep, and it doesn't look like it's fit for humans."

"We'll fix a bed for you in the room where the children sleep," Chloe said. Though she felt otherwise she knew she must be patient.

"For heaven's sake, how can I have any privacy in a room with three children?" Grandma demanded obviously disgruntled, disagreeable, disgusted and disappointed.

"We'll try that for tonight," Ed replied. "If that ain't good enough we'll see if we can arrange something better."

That a confrontation with his mother was bound to happen, Ed knew, but he preferred to set the time and place. He was trying his best to keep the bitterness and malice out of his voice when he talked to her, but he knew he couldn't hold his feelings in for very long. During her visit he spent his time "helping the neighbors," or walking around the cornfield, or "seeing to the livestock." To keep himself busy outside, he hoed corn, weeded the garden, gathered wood from the South Platte, or groomed his horses. On the last day of her visit he finished the morning chores and remained in the dugout for the purpose of confronting her.

"Mother, there were many things wrong for me when I was a kid," Ed stated with so much coldness that she responded defensively.

"You are the same now as you were when you were a child," Julia said. "I haven't forgiven you for running away from your apprenticeship. You could have become a shoemaker and had a trade that would make a living for your family, but no, you ran away. Uncle Johnny should have sent you right back to the shoemaker instead of letting you stay with him."

"Uncle Johnny and his wife were the most decent people I ever met. They were the first people who made me feel that I was more than a slave. I learned what I know about farming from him and Jason Norton. I hated that old son-of-a-bitch in that shoe shop. If I

125

had stayed there, he would have beat me to death or worked me for free without ever feeding me enough."

Ed momentarily lost control. "Damn that old bastard."

"Ed Foster, you will go to hell for swearing like that in my presence. Think of your wife and children," Grandma said indignantly.

"You never taught me to swear like that," Ed stated with feeling. "What you taught me was that a Christian family could work a child to death and stay pious while doin' it. Your family taught me that a kid could be put to work liftin' rocks that were too heavy, and carryin' milk pails that were too full. That hard work caused me a rupture that I still have trouble with. I'll never forgive them for that."

"You have no right to talk to me like that..." Julia began to cry. "After all," she continued between sobs, "I am your mother...you owe me respect." She began to cry uncontrollably.

"What I owe you is the right to visit your grandchildren. I owe your family for a rupture that still bothers me when I do heavy work. I do not owe you the right to tell me, my wife or my children what we have done wrong. I will always be your son, and you are always welcome here as the kids grandma, but you have got to have the decency to treat me and my family with the same respect you expect from us. Talk about respect..." Ed's voice trailed off into anger.

In cold fury Grandma stopped crying.

"Edward," she said with wounded dignity, "I'll be ready to leave, first thing tomorrow."

There was no conversation between Ed and his mother for the rest of that day. That night Chloe convinced Ed that he must make his treatment of Julia as considerate as possible on the return to Sedgwick.

"After all, she is grandmother to our children," Chloe said.

"They need to have the best possible memory of her."

"That's more than I have," Ed replied sadly. "I can't forgive her for abandonin' me when I was a child. I don't hate her, but I won't forgive her"

"Forgiveness will free you from your upset with her," Chloe stated. "We can't change the past, but we can make the present a time for our children to gladly remember."

Ed did not reply.

On the return trip to Sedgwick, Ed was civil but not overly communicative with his mother. She rode in the wagon with the children, and remained silent with reddened eyes and an occassional sob. The children quietly played a thumbs up game, but Carrie, Katie and Willie often hugged her and told her everything would be alright.

Goodbyes at the Sedgwick depot were civil for Ed, and he stood by as Chloe and the children expressed their love with hugs and kisses as Grandma boarded the train. Ed was the last to say goodbye. He held out his hand and Julia shook it while they both peered directly at one another.

"For my wife and family's sake, I'm goin' to try to forgive you." Ed stated with a degree of sadness.

"You will never know the sorrow and lack of understanding my life has given me," she replied. "Your wife and children have given me more pleasure than I have ever known. All I ask is that I visit them as often as my remaining years will permit."

"As I said before, you are the children's grandma, and you will always be welcome to visit my home." With that Ed released her hand, turned and walked out of the train station.

Back at the cabin Ed went about his chores as though he were an automaton. When he returned to the cabin, he sat with shoulders drooped and his head bowed. After two days of that kind of behavior, Chloe decided that she needed to confront him, and told him that it would be best for him and the family if he could talk about his feelings.

In anguish of soul he told her about a home where there was little love shown to him among the eighteen children who lived there. He related that children were put to work at an early age and seldom received encouragement for anything they did. Punishments were usually swift and severe. He told of being apprenticed to a shoemaker and the life he had there until he was fourteen when he ran away to the farm of Uncle Johnny Roberts. As he related this, he faced Chloe several times and stated that he had fallen in love with her when he first met her. He said that he had learned how a mother could love her husband and her children from her. He stated that he would love her forever.

"I was closer to suicide after my mother left than I have ever been," he said. "You understand that my mother never told me the truth about my father, and let her family convince me that he was a rascal. Uncle Johnny told me that he had died a hero in the war between the states. No one knows the loneliness I felt when I was placed in the shoe shop with Old Man Alberts. I learned to tough it out, and I learned that it was up to me to change my life. That's why I ran away, and anyways that old man never taught me anythin' about makin' shoes." Ed paused in reflection. "The best thing that ever happened to me was meeting you," he stated.

"It was best for me too," Chloe said.

"By givin' me your love and support, you have taught me how to be a father to our children. Comin' to this homestead has taught me how fine a person you are. My mother complained about everything and found fault with everything, but I have put you through things that are harder than anythin' she ever had, and you have not complained."

A closeness that only those who are deeply in love know drew them to one another into a prolonged embrace. Before they entered the cabin they continued their love making as only lovers do when they discover the depth of true love.

Morning found the Foster family going about the tasks of survival, and in their accomplishment they gained self sufficiency and confidence in one another. Gathering eggs, doing the milking, washing dishes, feeding the livestock, sweeping the cabin and making beds gave the children feelings of security as a family that they remembered all their lives. Through the activities of daily living, they learned the meaning of their own lives.

Chapter Fifteen

Prairie settlers shared a common experience in that broad expanse known as America's desert land. Most had moved away from familiar surroundings and had gone through family loss, drought in summer and freezing winters. The hardiest stayed with the land in good years and bad, and most knew there was no other life that gave them the sense of independence and freedom found on a homestead. To return to their former lives meant they would leave with nothing but "the shirts on our backs," and begin over again without resources. Even in the midst of despair, they willed themselves to stay in hope that the future would be better than the past. There was a camaraderie among them, and a silent contract of mutual help that gave them hope for a better life. The Fosters knew that survival living in a dugout on the prairie was temporary, and that "things had to get better."

Chloe had come from a secure life, but she was willing to endure prairie living, and continue to hope just as their friends and neighbors hoped for better times. Springtime planting always brought new hope, for there was a freshness and expectancy in planting that brought new life from the barren ground as seeds sprouted and new plants appeared. On this early spring day Tom Kaschke had driven a team over with the planter Ed had asked to borrow, and as farmers do, they talked about the weather, rainfall, and expected harvest in the fall.

"Your field looks good," Tom said. "You're a bit late plantin,' but if it rains enough you'll have a good crop."

"That's a pretty big 'if,'" Ed replied. "Almost anythin' can happen between now an' harvest."

"You're right about that, but a farmer is the biggest hoper I know. He hopes it won't rain too much when he's plantin,' an' he hopes it will rain enough durin' the summer so he will have a good harvest in the fall. I've never seen the beat of it."

Both men chuckled at that idea "In Nebraska there was a good balance between the two," Ed stated. "There was more rain in summer than here, crops were better."

"How was it in Vermont?" Tom asked.

"It was about the same for rain as Central Nebraska. In Vermont there was more snow in winter which set the ground up for spring plantin.' When it's dry out here a farmer plants anyway, an' hopes there will be enough rain for the crop to yield a good harvest."

"In South Carolina we had a good balance, and besides that we had a longer growin' season than you do out here."

"Good talkin' to yuh, I got to git back to my hoein'" Tom said as he turned his team toward his farm. Ed waved as he drove away.

The next morning, Ed drove to the field, and began planting. On just ten acres he could not hope to have a large harvest, and he knew that he would have to earn enough to feed his family by working for his neighbors during the summer. It was a hot day, and dust raised by the planter had covered his face and clothing by ten o'clock. He was grateful when Chloe and the children brought drinking water to him.

"I don't know why they call that a walkin' planter," he said with a twinkle in his eye. "It hain't walked anywhere that I didn't make it go, and I'm the one who did the walkin.'"

Sweat had streaked the dust on his face with muddy droplets, and he used his bandana to clear it from around his eyes.

"Some of the larger farms use Rumley steam engines that pull three planters," Chloe said.

"I know," Ed replied, "and they can plant a field like this in less than a day. "Followin' this planter has got to be the hardest work I've ever done. Lettin' the planter blades get too deep puts the seeds on hard pan, an'keepin' it even is almost impossible. When a furrow is too deep, it makes large clods that are hard to break up, and when it's too shallow, the grass ain't turned, and grows right back crowdin' out the new plants when they come up."

"Papa we watched you walk behind the planter with the reins around your shoulders, and your hands busy with the handles, and we could tell it wasn't easy," Carrie said.

"I try to make the rows as straight as I can," Ed stated. "But along with guidin' the team, I have to use both hands to set the depth of the furrow. At the same time I have to turn the team right or left when they git off the furrow path."

"Your team has never been used this way before," Chloe said. "I remember your first day in the field. I never saw you so frustrated.

Your first furrows seemed to start somewhere and end up nowhere. I'm glad the children and I couldn't hear you, because there was a blue cloud of swear words as you vented your anger at the sod, the planter, the team and especially yourself for not doing a better job. Early in the afternoon you stopped in disgust, and brought the planter in, and put the team in the barn. I remember what you said as you stood by the corral and looked out at the hodge podge rows."

"Chloe I can't git things workin' right to make furrows as straight as they ought to be."

"Could I help?" I asked.

"Well, I don't know what you could do. This damn team has a mind of its own. If I can't git them straightened out my field will look like hell's half acre, and I sure as the devil won't be proud of it."

"Perhaps I could lead the team till they get used to making straight rows," I said. "You agreed, and I sent the children to the dugout to play."

"Yeh, that was three weeks ago when I was plowin' the field," Ed remembered. "I told you it would be best for you to walk on the left side of the team where the sod hadn't been turned. I thought it would be smoother there, and that's the way we started. I hollered giddup to the team, an' we made a furrow in a half circle to the left."

They laughed at the memory.

"Dammit," I said, "you've got to pick a target at the end of the row and head for that, when we turn around you've got to pick another target and head for that."

They had made two furrows across the field in a semi-straight line. They decided that method needed some improvement.

"Mebbe you could drive the team and I could work the plow," Ed then said. "That way you would only have to hold the lines and I could guide the plow. You would still have to aim at a target."

That method had worked well, but there was too much sage and yucca on the left side of the plow and too many lumps of sod on the right side. Chloe suggested that they would have to clear the field of sage and yucca before they could plow straight.

"We're already late with our plantin," Ed stated.

"Ed, no one could walk a straight line the way that field is now. It has got to be cleared." Chloe emphatically stated.

"It'll take two or three days or more to do that."

Chloe noted a tone of defeat in Ed's voice. They both stood and silently surveyed the field in its virgin state of yucca and sage.

"With the help of the children we can do it in less time," Chloe stated. Ed reluctantly agreed and they decided to get shovels, hoes and a rake to begin the task.

They found that yucca roots were protected by the spines of the yucca, and that many spines were more than a foot and a half long. To chop out the roots required clearing away the spines so the roots could be reached. Neither Chloe nor the children were able to perform that task, and even Ed had trouble chopping out the roots. Rabbits, mice and an occasional prairie rattlesnake found shelter under those spines which posed a danger to anyone attacking their nests. On that first day Ed found rattlesnake nests under two of the yucca plants.

"Looks to me like I will have to poke around each one of these bushes before we try to chop them out," he told his family.

"The children and I can remove the debris while you do that."

Work proceeded slowly for two days, and by evening of the second day they had only cleared a quarter of an acre.

"It'll take us forty days to clear this field if we can't do better than that," Ed stated.

"Let's see if we can develop a system that will be faster."

"We have only one pick ax and one shovel," Ed said. "We can't go faster than our tools will allow. Mebbe we'll have to clear the field this year and plant next year, and besides that this kind of work is too hard for you and the children."

"Just the same it has to be done," Chloe replied. "Do you suppose we could put fire to the base of each plant?"

"Fire might drive out the snakes and other varmints," Ed speculated. "I see that the yucca plants have dead spines around their bases. It just might work. We'd have to control it so it didn't set the whole prairie afire."

"If we did that we would have to be careful to keep the fires we set under control," Chloe agreed. "I could use the pitchfork to carry a small fire from bush to bush. We'd have to work in the early part of the day when the winds are not as strong as in the afternoons."

That method was tried the next morning, and Ed noticed that Chloe used the pitchfork as a weapon whenever she came upon a snake. He also discovered that yucca plants have wide root tops and getting at the tap roots required using the shovel to dig around each plant. Using the same method on the sage plants, they were able to clear about half an acre that day. That evening the family looked like walking zombies with their soot covered faces and clothing. Water was taken from the warming tank, and everyone did a cursory clean up of themselves in an area that had been screened for bathing. While the children bathed, Chloe prepared the evening meal. After the meal Chloe gave directions to the children "Carrie you and Katie please do the dishes and straighten up while your father and I go bathe at the spring," Chloe directed.

She gathered clean clothing, towels and soap while Ed filled two buckets with warm water from the warming tank on the side of the stove. Half an hour later a refreshed Chloe returned to the cabin.

"I might as well take care of the animals and do the chores while I'm at it," Ed stated.

"Now you look like mama," Katie stated, "but you still smell like burning sage or yucca."

"Katie please take this pail to your father so he can milk the cow," Chloe directed. Katie obeyed her mother and fifteen minutes later Ed and Katie returned to the cabin with a half pail of milk.

As each day passed the family worked together clearing the field, and their adeptness improved as time passed. By sunset of the sixth day they had cleared the field of sage and yucca. Ed had been able to begin plowing for spring planting on the seventh day. After another week the field had been cleared of roots and brush and plowed. The following week Ed harrowed and leveled the field. When the field was ready for planting, Ed decided to borrow the planter from Tom.

That summer there was enough rain to bring forth a good crop, and for the next year winds and rains were favorable. Ed was able to harvest good crops, but the third year there was very little rain and no crop. Day after day he watched for a cloud that might bring rain, but there was none. Corn plants that should have been waist high by the fourth of July were less than twelve inches tall, and their leaves curled and crackled in the dry winds. There was barely enough water from the spring to supply the livestock, but Ed had to haul water from neighbors for family needs. Somehow Chloe was able to keep the garden growing, and she was able to can enough vegetables for their winter needs. The sky remained brazen even into the days of late fall, and there were no corn ears large enough to feed the livestock for long.

With bitterness Ed remembered the posters he had seen in the Central City, Nebraska post office concerning homesteading in Colorado. "Twenty five inches of rain a year. Verdant fields of grassland waiting to be tilled for planting. Farm on land of your own, file your claim now. Rich soil, ideal climate. A farmer's paradise."

"Plenty of rain, good harvests, a farmer's paradise," Ed remembered with sarcasm. "A farmer's hell," he mumbled to himself.

Early in August when the bright sun spread a haze of heat waves over the prairie, Ed walked to the cornfield and felt the parched corn leaves. He picked up a handful of dust, and let it sift through his fingers as the hot wind carried it away. Whirlwind driven dust devils swirled along the dry rows as the corn leaves rattled with a sound that mocked his dismal thoughts. Even the buffalo grass crackled with dryness as he walked across it, and there was no greenness for the livestock in the pasture. Only the sword like yucca and sage seemed alive. Water in the spring, that usually had a good flow, ebbed to a trickle. When Ed brought water from the river for the livestock, they fought one another until they were able to get to the water trough. Day after day Chloe recognized Ed's dejection as he walked around the field. For a time neither spoke of the future, should the drought continue, but the day came when Ed felt he had to vent his feelings.

"What a damn fool I was to believe those posters," he said. "Looks like whatever corn there is won't be worth much. There won't be enough to feed the livestock this winter. I can't see any way we can stay on this land."

"We can work together as we always have," Chloe said quietly. "You can trade your labor next summer for hay this winter. Berta will share her garden stuff with us, and I will do my best to can tomatoes and vegetables. I know we will be able to get by this winter."

"The other farmers are as bad off as we are," Ed stated. The tone of his voice carried his months of frustration with the drought. There was silence between them as they surveyed the withering corn stalks that were less than waist high at harvest. Corn ears on the dwarf plants were nubbins with few mature kernels.

"Ed, I can always teach," Chloe stated with a gentleness that she hoped would not offend.

"Well," Ed was calmer as he spoke, "I don't want you to unless worst comes to worst."

"While we were in Sedgwick, I heard that a teacher was needed in West Sedgwick School. For me to get started I would need to take my credentials to the President of the School Board, John Crow. If I am hired, we will have a sure income."

"Your place is here taking care of the children," Ed stated, "I don't want my wife workin' away from home."

For several days and many discussions later, they arrived at the same impasse, and after each discussion, Ed repeated the ritual of going to the field and scanning the sky for rain, but he knew it was too late for a crop that year. He came back to the cabin discouraged.

"I've got to do somethin' that will change things for us," he stated after two weeks, "I asked Tom if he knew of anythin' I could do to earn a little money."

"Did he know of anything?" Chloe asked.

"Tom told me there are potato harvests going on west of here, and they need workers. If I go there, mebbe I can make enough to get us through the winter. I don't like the idea of leavin' you alone with the children, but I don't see any other way."

"Ed we are a family," Chloe reminded, "and what we must do to survive we must do. When would you have to leave?"

"I could take the wagon, an' leave tomorrow." There was urgency in Ed's voice. "I don't want to leave you here alone with the children, but it's the only thing I see where we can git by."

"We'll be fine," Chloe replied with what she hoped was assurance. "Carrie is a good rider, and she could ride Dusty for help if we needed it. We'll be fine. You do what you feel you must."

That night Ed packed a loaf of bread, a slab of sow belly and a frying pan, and left early the next morning. When he arrived at the potato fields near Greeley, he learned that it was customary for farmers to give itinerant laborers a noon meal and a dollar a day for work from sunup to sunset. Most of the itinerants slept in barns, haystacks, or wagons just as Ed was doing. When the farmer needed an extra team to haul potatoes to the potato docks, wages were a dollar and a half and the noon meal. To be fair owners rotated the job of driving among those who had brought a team and wagon, and Ed was hired occasionally as a driver. After six weeks of harvesting potatoes, Ed returned home with forty dollars.

"Looks like we'll have flour and beans this winter," he proudly announced to his family. "We will even be able to buy grain to feed our selves and the livestock."

"Ed, if next year is as dry as this one, we'll be just as bad off as we are now," Chloe stated. "I feel we must go to see John Crow."

She was more firm than she had been earlier. "It is no shame for a woman to teach, and I can earn enough for our living." If the weather stays as dry next year, we will be on the edge of survival. I might as well use my education to help the family."

After a long silence and much heavy sighing Ed stated that he would like to try to stay on the homestead one more year. Chloe agreed to wait until summer before going to the School Board, and the problem was temporarily settled.

An average winter with light snow and no blizzards passed, and in the spring Ed was able to plant on time. By mid June the new plants stood halfway to Ed's knees, and there had been enough early rain to give him hope that there would be a crop.

"Looks like we'll be able to make it out here, if we can survive this summer," Ed stated to his family at the end of June. "A few years of good crops and mebbe we can build a house. We won't be rich, but we'll be able to have a better life."

"Ed, I'm pleased that the children seem to have adjusted to life on the prairie and I'm feeling stronger every day," Chloe replied. "But I know how drought can come just when you think the year will be good. From June to September we could have weeks of drought, and no crop by harvest time."

It was not Chloe's nature to be pessimistic, but she remembered that dry years had started the same with early growth and then drought that withered the corn and blighted the ears on the stalk. For a moment Ed sobered, and then invited Chloe out to see the field.

"All we need," he stated, "is two good rains before harvest."

Chapter Sixteen

The rains did not come that summer. Drought enveloped the whole area of the dry land from Wyoming and Nebraska to Colorado, Kansas, Oklahoma, and Northern Texas. Many dry landers lost faith that rains would ever come and abandoned their farms leaving empty houses and outbuildings to sit as stark reminders that their builders could not survive dry years. By the end of July with no rain since June, Ed began to despair that there would be a crop that year, and the prospect caused him to doubt that they could survive.

"I can't stand by and watch the corn dry up because we haven't had rain," Ed said one day. "There is wheat harvest goin' on in Oklahoma and Kansas. This year I'll follow the wheat harvesters. Wheat harvest begins about the middle of the summer."

"You do what you think best," Chloe replied.

For the first time since they had left Nebraska, Ed and Chloe began talking about the lives they had lived before their marriage.

"Do you miss the life you had in Chicago?" Ed asked.

"No dearest, my life is here with you and the children," Chloe responded. "I wouldn't want to be anywhere without you and the children. Sometimes I do miss my family."

"Even living in a dugout like prairie dogs and rabbits?" Ed asked with a twinkle in his eye.

"Even with rattlesnakes and gophers," Chloe answered as she gave Ed a hug. There was a solemnity even in their humor.

The children had been sent to gather buffalo chips, and Chloe had poured a cup of coffee as she and Ed were discussing their situation. They had barely had time to taste the coffee when the sound of an excited child roused them to rush outside.

"Mama, Papa, come quick," Katie yelled as she ran toward them. "Willie has a snake bite. A rattlesnake bit him."

"Where is he?" They asked in unison.

"Over there," Katie hollered pointing wildly. "Just over that hill. Hurry! I'll show you. Hurry! Come on and hurry!"

Katie turned and started running in the direction she had pointed. Chloe and Ed followed her to the top of the hill, but Carrie and Willie were nowhere in sight.

"Katie if this is one of your tricks, I'll give you a good thrashin,'" Ed yelled as Katie dashed down the hill.

"It's not a trick, papa. We were gathering chips just like mama told us. Willie didn't see the snake an' it bit him right here." She indicated a place on her left leg halfway between her ankle and knee.

"I believe her." Chloe stated and added, "hurry we've got to find him." She tried to speak calmly, but there was fear in her voice.

Without another word Katie ran to the crest of the next hill. When Ed and Chloe arrived, they could see Carrie and Willie opposite in a low valley. Willie seemed to be lying against Carrie who appeared to be sitting calmly. As they approached, they could not tell whether Willie was conscious. When they drew nearer they could see that Willie's eyes were closed and that his face was very pale.

"Willie…Willie wake up," Ed yelled as he knelt beside the boy and began patting his cheeks.

Willie roused and lifted his head looking around. It seemed to Chloe that he did not recognize the faces above him.

"He's alright, papa, I knew what to do," Carrie said. "I did what you told us when somebody has a snakebite. I found the two holes the fangs made, and I sucked the poison out."

"Honey, did you swallow any of the venom?" Chloe asked.

"No, mama, I spit it out just like you told us."

"Where is that damn snake?" Ed asked.

"It got away," Katie answered.

"Git up son," Ed ordered. He was anxious to leave this spot as soon as possible.

"We'll let him rest until he feels strong enough to walk back to the dugout." Chloe stated.

After an hour Willie was able to walk, and the family slowly made its way back to the dugout. Within a week Willie was running and playing as he had before. The Foster family returned to its normal lifestyle of observing the sky for relief from the drought hoping to see an indication that it might rain. In spite of the hardships of drought, storm and snakebite the family had endured, Chloe felt at peace with God and her fellowman.

The next day she was mixing ingredients to make dough for baking bread and cinnamon rolls. As she worked she often thought of a verse in the Bible that promised the kind of peace she felt. "Great peace have they who love thy law, nothing shall offend them." Even at midday in this non sacred place, she sang a verse of a hymn as she worked, and she felt at peace.

> "What a friend we have in Jesus,
> "All our sins and grief to bear.
> "What a privilege to carry
> "Everything to God in Prayer."

She returned to working dough for the rolls and had sprinkled them with butter, sugar and, cinnamon and prepared two loaves in pans as the children played outside. As she watched her busy children she breathed a silent prayer for their safety. While the dough was rising, she started a buffalo chip fire to heat the oven. She placed the rolls and loaves in the oven when the thermometer in the center of the oven door indicated it had reached the desired heat. Carrie had been sent to the Kaschkes to borrow sugar. The children had gone outside to play when Katie and Willie burst into the house.

"Mama, there's a funny looking cloud comin'" Katie said.

"We can't see Twin Buttes," Willie added. "It's over that way," Willie said pointing toward the west, "and it's movin' this way."

Outside Chloe examined the sky and saw that there was an unusual yellowish cloud swirling low to the ground coming rapidly toward the cabin. Her first thought was that another tornado was coming, but as she stood facing the west she could see a line of fire at the base of the cloud and realized it was a prairie fire coming straight toward their cabin. There was a blast of hot soot laden air which caused a chill of fear to course through her very soul. The thought of Carrie caught in the raging fire as she rode home brought chills that made her body tremble.

"Come quickly children," She directed. "We must hurry into the dugout. It's the only safe place we have"

Inside the cabin she drew the children around her and prayed for safety as she asked the Lord to protect them all. As she prayed a crackling hissing roar along with the neighing of a horse, the lowing of the cow and the squawking of chickens overpowered her quiet supplication. The cabin filled with choking smoke, and Chloe knew that the wooden structure of the cabin was burning. She directed the children into the dugout, and put a blanket over the doorway to keep most of the smoke of the burning cabin out. The forefront of the fire passed quickly, but in its wake there were charred and burning ruins. Even the door frame holding the blanket and the blanket were smoldering. When the sound of burning subsided, there were live ashes that were not safe to walk through in every grass clump and yucca plant in the yard. By that time friends and neighbors had arrived and formed a bucket brigade. Soon there was a safe path that Chloe and the children could use to exit the smoking and smoldering timbers of the cabin. When Chloe surveyed the extent of the damage, she was overcome and wept bitterly. The children gathered around her and wailed even as they were directing their mother not to cry.

Corral fence posts were smoldering, and in places there were still flames in grass and field. The chickens that were still alive were singed and some of their feathers were burned off so that seared flesh was visible. Dusty, the saddle horse had singed spots on his sides and back. Where the barn had stood there was a pile of smoldering ashes. The haystack was now a mass of glowing red orange with flickering flashes of flame.

"Don't cry mama," Katie comforted. "We'll be alright. You prayed and the Lord protected us."

"I am very thankful we had the dugout," Chloe said.

Tom and Berta Kaschke with Carrie between them drove into the yard leading Dusty behind the wagon.

"Thank God. Oh thank God," Chloe murmured. Carrie joined them and she drew each one close in a tender hug.

"I wish papa was here," Willie stated.

"Me too," Katie responded.

"Papa went to work at the Townes," Carrie said.

The rolling boiling cloud of yellowish blue and black along the southern horizon told Ed that a fire had swept across the prairie in the vicinity of the homestead. He forced his team to gallop and dashed pell mell over clumps of sage and yucca as the wagon careened and bounced along.

"God, keep my family safe," he pleaded silently. "Keep Chloe and the children safe," he repeated aloud.

He slid from side to side on the spring seat as the wagon careened and bounced over clumps of sage and yucca. When he was closer to the homestead, he could see that the fire had traveled on a swath one to two miles wide, and the homestead buildings were in the middle of it. He could see that the barn was no longer standing and that the cabin part of the dugout was a mass of fallen and twisted timbers of burning wood. The sod roof of the dugout had smoldering clumps of burning grass. There were neighbors with buckets splashing water into the embers of the cabin. The scene of devastation made him heartsick, and he wildly searched each group of people for a sight of Chloe and the children. He leaped from the wagon almost before it stopped, and started for the dugout. Chloe and the children stepped out of the crowd.

"Ed," Chloe yelled.

He whirled around and ran to the place where she and the children were standing. He drew them all into his embrace weeping, laughing and praying all at the same time.

"Bless God you're alright. You're alright." he repeated. "Bless God you're alright."

He continued to hug each one and seemed to be examining them to see that they were indeed, "alright." All were grimy with soot and their clothing was sooty and water splotched.

"How bad was it?" Ed asked.

"We were safe in the dugout," Chloe solemnly stated.

"The smoke made us choke and cough," Willie said.

"How did you get so grimy?" Ed asked.

"I did the best I could to keep the fire away from us," Chloe answered. "I put a blanket over the dugout doorway, but that didn't keep all the soot and smoke out of it. Anyway we were in smoke and soot as the fire swept across the prairie before we came into the dugout. Thank the Lord we had the dugout."

"What are we gonna do now? Why in hell would God let this happen?" Ed centered his frustration on the God he had just blessed.

As he spoke Tom and Berta Kaschke joined them. Tom and Ed stared at one another silently, and turned to survey the path of the fire. Their gaze shifted to the people who were splashing buckets of water on the smoldering ruins of what had been their home.

"Ed," Tom stated, "it's a damn shame. I've heard of prairie fires, but I've never seen one this close."

"Looks like the fire has beat us." Ed stated dejectedly, "if we go back to Nebraska, I can git work as a hired man. We can't be much worse off than we are here."

Again there was silence between the two men as they began a walking tour of the corral. Both men nodded silently as neighbors shook their heads or in other ways showed understanding. The cow was lowing mournfully as she stood in the center of the corral. Surviving chickens were running here and there flapping their charred wings and squawking. Ed looked at them sadly.

"There ain't a one of them worth a damn," he said. "We're through here. We can't stay and let this country beat us at every turn. We can't survive tornados, hail and prairie fire."

"Ed, you're not in a position to make up your mind about what to do. Chloe told Berta she is expecting, and you best not travel just yet." Tom said. "We'll help all we can."

"Right now we can't just pack up and leave," Ed stated. "But there ain't much ahead for us here."

"Give yourself some time," Tom said. "You know you're welcome to stay with us until you can figger out what you and Chloe want to do. You still have your land, and now you've got to think about what's best for your family, but first you need a place to stay."

"Tom, we can't ask you folks to do more for us than you have"

"Out here neighbors is the only thing any of us have. You know Berta and I will do everything we can to help you git on your feet. Now we need to take care of your team, your cow…and your family."

Ed realized Tom was right. The Foster family had nowhere to go. His team was still hitched to the wagon, and Ed dazedly went into the corral where he examined the cow. He noted that her udder had been seared and that her hide was badly singed. Even her nose and ears had been made raw from the heat of the fire.

"She won't be givin' milk for a while," he said to himself.

"Load up your family and come on over," Tom invited. "Berta will see that Chloe and the kids git cleaned up. I'll herd the cow along and, when we git home, we'll put your animals in with ours, we'll do the chores and then we'll have supper."

Quietly Ed followed Tom's directions as though he had lost the ability to direct himself. Chloe agreed as Ed told her of Tom's invitation. The children were subdued as Chloe and Ed settled them in the wagon. Berta had gone ahead, and when they arrived at the Kaschkes, the greetings of Berta and the children were quiet, but happy to see them.

"You folks are having your share of bad times," Berta said. "Tom and I watched as the fire swept between our place and yours. We could see it move past your buildings."

"It didn't move past," Chloe stated wearily, "Thank the Lord we had the dugout. We were safe inside, but the poor chickens…"

There were tears as her voice failed. Berta hugged her until her sobbing stopped.

"Come in and we'll get you and the children cleaned up. You are about my size and can wear my clothes until Ed can bring yours that survived in the dugout."

That evening after chores were done and the children were settled for the night, the four adults sat at the table and talked.

"Ed the most important thing for you is Chloe's condition now." Berta knew she was about to voice an opinion that Ed might not like.

"What do you mean?"

There was an absence of feeling in Ed's tone that Berta did not know how to interpret, but she decided to tell him her concern for his wife even if he were to become angry with her.

"Since your family has been living in the dugout, she has been through about as much as any woman can stand," Berta said as she turned to Chloe. "My dear, how do you feel?"

"Right now I'm very, very tired, but I'm feeling alright."

"Chloe, how do you really feel?" Berta insisted she answer.

"This pregnancy has been the easiest I've had, but from the very beginning I've been so tired I can hardly get anything done."

"Now what does that tell you?" Berta asked Ed.

"I suppose it means she needs to rest as much as she can."

"And the best place for her to rest is right here until the baby is born, you best not even think of moving to Nebraska or any place else at this time." Berta was emphatic and mildly angry because she did not see the concern she desired. Ed became more alert in his response.

"Chloe can stay till she gits her feet on the ground, but my place is at the homestead."

There was a finality in Ed's answer. Berta knew the conversation had ended, and each couple went to bed.

While Chloe remained with the Kaschkes, Florence Bell Foster became the fourth living child in the Foster family. The birth was without difficulty. Ed and Chloe rejoiced that both the baby and she were healthy. Ed now set a priority on going to the homestead daily to make it ready for occupancy, but he and Chloe realized that four children and two adults living in a one room dugout was neither satisfactory nor desirable.

In the field where Ed had planted corn, there were only charred stalks. Every day Ed returned to the Kaschkes silent and morose, and no one could cheer him up. After two months with the Kaschkes, the Fosters returned to the dugout, and a despair descended upon Ed that made him almost unable to perform his chores. He seemed to have lost interest in his surroundings, and they both avoided the field where they had spent so much labor.

"Even the garden was ruined by the fire," Chloe stated sadly.

"No way can we get through this winter." There was a finality of defeat in Ed's voice. "We can't stay here and we can't move anyplace else."

Carrie thought to cheer them up by singing a song she had learned about Nebraska. As she sang Katie joined the song.

> "Oh Nebraska land, sweet Nebraska land,
> Upon the highest hill I stand.
> I look away across the plains,
> And wonder why it never rains.
> Then Gabriel blows his trumpet sound,
> And says the rain has gone around."

"Carrie and Katie" Chloe impatiently admonished. "We're trying to decide what we need to do and we don't need to be reminded about rain and drought in Nebraska. We've had enough of that here."

"Mama you can teach at West Sedgwick School just like Mrs Kaschke said," Carrie stated.

"Ed, Berta told me that West Sedgwick School still needs a teacher, and she said John Crow asked her about me teaching there," Chloe stated. "I'm willing and able, but we would need to make some arrangement for the children."

"I don't want you to teach," Ed stated emphatically.

"Ed, I know how you feel, but if I can help us stay here I think I should. You said we would decide if worst came to worst."

There was a long period of silence as Ed sat with his shoulders hunched and his head bowed. He finally raised his eyes to Chloe, nodded a silent agreement, and made his way out of the dugout and to the field where he sobbed in silent defeat, knowing that Chloe was right. They could not survive the winter unless Chloe taught.

The next morning the children rose to see a mother who had wakened them early, fed them and told them to gather things they would need for a three day trip to see John Crow. Ed had placed the stays over the wagon bed and had stretched the tarp over it just as he had when they moved to Colorado. Chloe and the children placed blankets and food supplies they would need along with toys and pillows in the wagon. When all things were loaded in the wagon, off across the prairie they went. When they reached the South Platte, Ed drove along the south side of the river until he came to a place where his team and wagon could ford the stream. There was very little water flowing in the river, and the wagon jounced and bounced down the steep bank and into a meadow close to the water on the other side.

Late that afternoon they were near the Crow farm when they decided to locate in this reasonably placed spot of grass and cottonwoods. They made their camp and Ed tethered the horses close enough to the water so they could quench their thirst. He dug a deep place in the river sand near the flowing water and watched as water seeped in and the silt settled. He was satisfied that the water would supply their needs for cooking and drinking. Chloe and the children had gathered wood for a small fire and a fire pit with stones was fashioned so they could boil water and cook. After their meager meal, beds were made in the wagon and the Fosters settled snugly for the night. Next morning Chloe met with John Crow.

Chapter Seventeen

"Yes, we need a teacher in our school" John stated after greetings. "If you have credentials and are qualified we will consider you for the job."

"I taught three and a half years in South Side High School in Chicago, and I have several letters of recommendation." Chloe stated as she handed a sheaf of papers across the table.

"Will I need Colorado Certification?" She asked.

"We can grant you an interim certificate after we review your credentials," John stated. "As President of the School Board, I will need to contact George Homan and Frank Pafford. It will take me a couple of days to do that. Your homestead is too far south for you to travel back and forth every day. There is a small house you can rent near the school. The salary is fifteen dollars a month. It is the teacher's responsibility to keep the school house in order and to see that it is warm in bad weather."

Chloe and Ed agreed to return after three days for the decision of the School Board. Directions to the school and to the house they could rent were given and the Foster children were excited to go and see this place that might be their new home. They drove to the Pafford farm and secured the key to the house. Frank Pafford told them they could stay in the house for a few days since Chloe was considering the teaching position. They thanked him, said good bye, and drove to the school, and then to the house. At the school the children saw the swings and slide and were eager to go there and play, but Chloe told them to stay in the wagon while they went to inspect the house that was a part of the contract.

They found the house to be a well constructed frame with three rooms. Inside there was a large living room and kitchen area where there were rough hewn cupboards and shelves in one corner. There was space for a cooking range which would also serve as their heat, and there was a pitcher pump with a sink beside the stove. A previous occupant had left an iron framed day bed in the living room that folded to make a settee. In one room there was a regular sized iron bed frame with no slats or mattress. All the rooms were dusty as though they had not been occupied for some time. A small corral a short distance from the house had a shed for animals, and there was a windmill with a round metal water tank where the animals could get water. The yard was fenced to keep wandering cattle out.

The excited children ran everywhere exploring every corner of the schoolyard in anticipation that this would be their new home. Ed drove the team to the corral and unhitched and removed harnesses, and turned the team into the corral. He found pegs in the shed where he could hang the harness, and then threw the hay that had served as their bedding into the corral for the horses.

"This is a very nice house," Chloe stated as Ed entered. "I like it already. It will be so nice to live in a real house for a change."

"I like it better than that old dugout," Katie stated.

"Can we stay here?" Willie asked.

"We must wait to see what the School Board decides," Chloe said. "Do you like this house?"

"Yes," Willie answered. "I even like the cows outside."

There was a herd of grazing cattle beyond the fenced yard, and several of the curious animals had gathered to inspect the new occupants. After the family had eaten a meal of cold chicken and bread with butter, Ed and Chloe walked around the house with the children. The young cattle at the fence panicked and withdrew a few yards away where they whirled and watched these strangers.

"We won't have any trouble findin' cow chips here," Willie stated. There were nods of agreement from the other children.

"But we may have trouble finding wood," Carrie responded.

The family looked around and saw that the closest trees were in a valley between hills more than a mile away, and that those proved to be more shrubbery than trees.

"We'll have to bring wood from the river," Ed stated.

"We must spend the day cleaning, and preparing for our stay here," Chloe stated as though she knew that this would be their new home. She organized a cleaning brigade and the day passed in the busy activity of cleaning.

Evening clouds they had hardly noticed began to reflect the rays of the waning sun as it etched them in silver. The deepening sunset brought forth flecks of gold which began as a faint glow that widened along the broad horizon. Clouds above took on a faint pink and purple set in the darkening gray velvet of the approaching night. A lonely coyote spoke to the descending night with a mournful song which ended in a series of complaining yips. Quiet settled over the prairie.

A bed was made for Willie on the day bed. Carrie and Katie were put to bed on the floor of the living room. Ed and Chloe settled in the third room where they had made a bed for Florence and one for themselves on the floor.

The next morning the children wanted to explore the hills around the school. The family walked slowly up the hill nearest the house where grazing cattle moved away and kept their distance as the family walked. On top of the hill they could look west and see Twin Buttes which were about three miles distant. Turning east they could see a trail that led to the Cottonwood Ranch and then on to Sedgwick which was more than seven miles in that direction. There were trails that led to farmhouses in the valley, and the town of Sedgwick. The school was eight miles closer to Sedgwick than their homestead.

Chloe and Ed decided they would take the teaching assignment if the School Board offered it to Chloe. They returned to John Crow three days later. John told them the Board had approved her assignment as teacher for one year, and Chloe requested that she keep her children with her in the class room. John stated that he would ask the Board to approve that. A part of the contract included renting the house for five dollars a month. When Chloe informed her children there was whooping and shouting for joy. She and Ed decided to move into the house as soon as her contract was signed.

Drought that summer made many dry land farmers decide to leave their homesteads, some made arrangements with those who stayed to farm the land, but others abandoned their houses and lands. Many turned their cattle out to roam free, and small herds of wild cattle were soon roaming the prairie. The livestock of homesteaders became thin and gaunt from lack of grass on pasture lands. Grass, which was usually harvested from the bottom lands along the river and was used for hay, produced only one meager cutting. Farmers took a dim view of survival for that year with dismal hope for next year, but those who had remained on the prairie kept the resolve to stay where they had settled. Ranchers who had large tracts of land under their control knew they could survive, and reduced their herds by sending unneeded livestock to market. Beef prices dropped, and those with the best resources were able to make it through this drought.

The move to the new house was made two days after Chloe accepted the teaching position at West Sedgwick School. When the family was settled, Ed returned to the dugout. Tom came over and lent his hands to clearing away the debris of the burned out cabin. Hoping to lift Ed's spirit as best he could, Tom related the problems of making a living on dry land.

"Ed every neighbor out here knows what this country can do to a man and his family," he said. "We've all been through hard times, but none as bad as the last couple of years for you. We know it's twice as hard when you're just gittin' started. Neighbors try to help neighbors by helpin' to build again when there is loss."

"Tom, even if we could build a house on the homestead," Ed replied, "the question of whether or not we could survive all that has happened these last two years, and what may happen next year has us licked. Chloe has taken the teachin' job at West Sedgwick School, and it looks like I'll be workin' for farmers wherever I can find work. I'll work the homestead land as best I can."

As the two men talked they gathered the charred lumber from the house that had not completely burned, and threw it in a pile and set fire to it. Chickens that remained at the homestead were gathered up, and the yard around the entrance to the dugout was raked. New sod replaced the old where needed for the roof, and a door was made and placed for a dugout entrance. The burned out stove was still intact enough for cooking and for heat, and a pipe hole was repaired in the dugout roof for a smoke stack.

The hot winds of August gave way to the warm winds of September and West Sedgwick School was opened in mid September. Two Homan girls were of high school age, there were three Taylors, a boy in fourth grade, a girl in second grade and the other boy in sixth grade. Kaschkes managed to board their children with the Towne family, and they were placed in first, third and sixth grades. Townes had young Rufus who was in sixth grade.

Chloe adapted the materials she had used in Chicago for the children in sixth grade and above, but she lacked materials for the younger children. Her first lessons were based on materials from Bible lessons she had taught, but she knew she could not continue to use them indefinitely. With Chloe's help the School Board decided to order material for first through sixth grades from Denver. Ed had been able to find work with farmers near the school, and the family felt settled and more secure than they had ever felt since they had arrived in Colorado. After a days work on the Crow farm Ed came home with good news from their new neighbors.

"The Crows would like to get better acquainted with the new School Ma'am," Ed stated that evening.

"That would be nice," Chloe replied. "Have they asked you what would be a good time for them?"

"Today after we finished repairin' corral fences, Mrs. Crow came and asked that we come over Satidday for supper and stay over until Sunday afternoon. She thought their four children and ours could get better acquainted."

"Tell them that we accept their kind invitation when you go to their place in the morning." Chloe said adding, "I'm pleased with their invitation. We need to get to know people in this neighborhood."

Ed changed the subject. "There's talk that the irrigation company will start work on the resevoy in the spring. John thinks they will build where the school now sits. He says they will build ditches halfway to Julesburg. That will open up thousands of acres for irrigation, and give jobs to quite a few men."

"Did John say anything about what will happen to West Sedgwick School?" Chloe asked.

"He thinks they may move it further west. He said others think they will leave it right where it is and put the resevoy further east. Most people agree that they want to git the resevoy built as soon as possible. That will change the farming in the whole valley."

"Perhaps, it becomes a matter of priorities," Chloe stated. "Water from the reservoir will benefit the whole valley, but so will the education of the valley's children."

"Well," Ed spoke slowly, "I didn't listen very well when we lived on the homestead and the Crows talked about it, but now we're right in the middle of it."

"Do you think it will mean no school for a year or so?" Chloe asked with a worried tone.

"No, there's talk that the new school will be built about two miles west of where it is."

Evening had settled over the land as they made their way to the house. At dusk a stillness descended as shadows lengthened and blended into the gathering night. Evening bands of the setting sun stretched from the western sky to the eastern horizon. Overhead the sky held the appearance of a giant weaving of cloud and sun rays to form a patterned basket. Night bird sounds joined cricket chirps in a prairie serenade. In great contentment Ed and Chloe joined hands and enjoyed the quiet peace of knowing the depth of their love.

The month of October dawned bright and clear, and by mid month frost dominated the early mornings. A frozen hardness during colder nights now stayed in the ground until mid morning. All along the river the line of cottonwoods turned brilliant yellow mixed with the red of woodbine and deep purple of wild plum. Toward the end of the month the leaves had turned brown and gusts of wind drove them from the branches that became starkly bare against the azure sky. Last summer's bird nests that had been concealed by leaves, were now a part of the skeletal trees. Crows that had nested there could now be seen grouping and regrouping in search of daily food, and their caws seemed louder and more raucous as the days passed.

In the schoolyard where grass had been, paths appeared where children played, and bare areas formed patterns of the games they played. Boys set up a ball field for a game they called one-o'-cat, and girls set up an area for jump rope and tag. The Taylor boys brought a bat they had received as a Christmas present along with a ball they had made out of string The children played these games before school, at recess and during lunch time.

Each child carried lunch from home, and on warm days they ate outside, but in cold, rainy or snowy weather they stayed at their desks and played indoor games. For many children home baked bread and strips of bacon or sowbelly, fried to crispness, formed sandwiches.

Cakes and cookies were brought for desserts, and occasionally a child would have an apple or an orange. Such fruits were seldom seen, but home canned pickles were common. Carrots and turnips were vegetables that could be kept in root cellars and peeled for a child's lunch. Drinks were usually water or a glass jar of milk.

A plea for books for all levels of reading went out from Mrs. Foster, and the community responded sending books for all grade levels. Chloe loaned the school her copies of Plato and Dickens, and she spent a part of each day reading to the whole school. As soon as books were read by one grade they were passed on to the next. Even first and second grades were exposed to reading beyond their grades. Recitations were scheduled for all classes with the help of the Homan girls who assisted with the younger children. Each school day was begun by a student reading from the Bible.

An event in November brought a large measure of togetherness to the community. The Homan family loaned the school a pump organ in good condition, and Mrs. Foster added music to the curriculum. At the November meeting of the School Board, Chloe recommended that a community sing be held every Sunday afternoon at the school, and the Board agreed.

Within a short time Sundays became a time of caravans of buggies, wagons, walkers and riders coming to the school to enjoy the fun and fellowship. Chloe prepared an agenda of songs such as "The Little Brown Church in the Wildwood," "When you and I Were Young, Maggie," and "The Old Oaken Bucket." A time of requests from the crowd brought forth hymns that the people knew and included "What a Friend We have in Jesus" and "Work For the Night Is Coming." There were children's songs that expressed themes including "Jesus Wants Me for a Sunbeam," and "Jesus Loves Me." Many community families requested that a Church service should be held, and the School Board agreed.

An itinerant preacher was contacted, and came to preach for the community twice a month. Chloe became the organist for these services, and when she was unable to play Mrs. Homan took her place at the organ. A time when Chloe could not be present occurred sooner than she expected in October.

On a Thursday morning she rose and seemed disoriented and could not get the children fed or dressed. She came to the kitchen at the usual hour, but could not get her thoughts organized enough to see that her children did the chores necessary for eating and getting ready for school. Carrie helped her manage to get through the needed activities so that she presented herself to the classroom at the usual time, but while she was teaching in mid morning, she fainted. Mrs Crow had come to assist with teaching the high school children in home making and sewing. Chloe revived, but Amy Crow decided that she was too weak to teach. The children were sent to the playground where they stood in whispering groups.

After a brief time, Amy Crow called the children in and sent Carrie and her mother home. A short time later Katie, who had complained of not feeling well, was sent to the Foster home with Clara Homan. Mrs Crow sent Bessie Homan to Sedgwick with a message asking Doctor Davis to call on the Fosters. He arrived about the time Ed returned home from his days work. The Doctor examined both sick people and reported his diagnosis to Ed.

"Ed, your wife is suffering from exhaustion and must rest in bed for at least two days. Katie has scarlet fever and I'm going to have to quarantine the house. No one is to go beyond your yard for two weeks. Scarlet fever can lead to rheumatic fever which can affect the heart so Katie must remain quiet at home for at least six weeks. If she doesn't have a temperature after two days, the rest of your family can leave the house, but the children can't go to school during the quarantine. Chloe has a temperature which means she has an infection, and I will leave a small amount of laudanum for her pain and quinine to reduce her fever. Katie should take a dose of quinine or aspirin at least twice every twenty four hours to keep her temperature under control. I will stop by tomorrow and see how they are doing."

The doctor gave Ed the two prescriptions and left. He returned the next day, and found Chloe and Katie resting well. Chloe slept the better part of the next two days and her temperature was normal the third day. She was able to assume her household chores, but Katie's temperature held for the full week. The following Monday Doctor Davis was pleased with their progress, but gave further instructions.

"Ed, since you work outside, you can go back to work. Chloe should not return to school for at least a week. Your school children cannot go back to the classroom for another three weeks. All bedding must be thoroughly washed with strong soap and allowed to air outside before your children go back to school. If another case of scarlet fever happens in the school, I will have to quarantine the school. Looks like we may be in for a siege before the school is safe."

During the quarantine of the Fosters, Ed had been very restless, and spent his time walking from the house to the barn and from the barn to the house until he had worn quite a path. When he was able to go back to the Crow's to work, he was informed that the Townes and Crows had children who had scarlet fever and that the school would be closed until there were no more cases of the disease. Before the epidemic stopped, every family in the school had one or more children who had been ill. It was April before classes could resume.

It was the practice in farming communities to dismiss school in late April or Early May so that older children could help with the spring farm work, but this year the School Board voted to have the children return to school the last two weeks of April so they could take tests to decide their grade placement when school started again in September. It was Amy Crow's and Chloe's task to devise the tests and they chose to complete the testing the last two weeks in April with questions in math, history, reading, and English from lessons the children had in the past.

Chapter Eighteen

Monday and Tuesday the testing went so well the two women decided they would not need two weeks to finish testing. Wednesday had begun bright and clear with a warm spring breeze that carried the promise of warmer days and happy times for the school, but by ten o'clock there were low ominous clouds in the northwest, and the breeze had become chill with biting sharpness. By eleven the clouds had filled the sky and snow began to flurry around the school. By one thirty drifts began to form and visibility became limited. The children became restless and stated that they should be going home, and the younger ones began to cry. Amy comforted the younger children while Chloe spoke assurances to the older children. Chloe had been instructed that she was not to let the children go home in a severe snow storm unless their parents came to get them, and today Amy Crow agreed. She had lived through many such unpredictable storms.

"Let's all work together," Chloe stated. "We have plenty of fuel to keep us warm for several days. If the storm becomes severe, we will be cozy and warm right here."

"Last year I was lost in the snow," Rufus Towne stated. "If my horse didn't know the way home, I never would have made it. My horse, Old Charlie, I just let him find his way, and boy was I glad when I got home. I think Charlie was too."

Chloe and Amy held a quick conference and afterward Amy spoke to the children.

"We think that today no child should leave the school until an older person comes to get them."

As the afternoon progressed, the wind rose to a howling banshee wail. At dismissal time it was snowing so heavily that the outbuildings could not be seen from the school windows.

Foresighted farmers had stored wood in a shed attached to the schoolhouse. Chloe and Amy organized the students with the older boys given the chore of keeping wood inside and keeping the fire going in the pot bellied stove. Girls were given the task of moving desks and chairs to the rear of the room The force of the wind was driving snow in around the windows, and it became necessary to seal them with cleaning rags. Boys and girls were given that chore.

Sleeping areas were arranged for the boys near the door while girls were given space nearest the stove at the front of the room. Amy Crow was placed in charge of the girls for toileting and Chloe chose Forrest Towne to be in charge of the boys. Schedules were set up for each group. Darkness came and kerosene lamps were lit.

"It will be necessary to keep the fire going through the night," Chloe stated. "Girls will be in charge till midnight and boys will take over for the rest of the night. Boys will be in charge during the day. We will ration our food, and share what we have."

A table was set up for the children to put as much food as they had left over from lunch on it, but there were only a few slices of bread, an apple or two and several cookies with three pieces of cake.

"We will have enough bread to give each child a small square, and there are enough pieces of cake and cookies left so that we can have a piece of cookie or a piece of cake for our evening meal. The pump is outside and we will need to keep water in the pails. When one pail is empty, two of the older boys will go together to the pump for more water. We have tea or coffee which I have brought for my use, but we can share that. We will sleep in our clothes." Mrs Foster turned to Mrs Crow, "Do you have anything to add?"

"Only that your families will be worried about you, and your fathers will come to see about you as soon as it's safe," she said. "There is no reason for you to worry, and it's better to be here where you'll be warm than for you to try to get home and freeze."

"What do we do when we get hungry?" first grader Addy Taylor asked in six year old innocence.

"We will be brave and remember that our fathers will come for us the first chance they get," Mrs Foster said.

The storm began on Wednesday, and for two days the children were reasonably comfortable. Saturday dawned with the sun shining, but there was a cold translucent haze in the morning air and a ground level white out driven by a whetted knife wind that drove the temperature well below zero. In many places only the tops of fence posts were visible and landmarks were obliterated. At noon Rufus Towne, John Crow and Ed Foster arrived at the school. The children laughed to see them for Rufus had a large snow filled beard and Ed and John had the appearance of walking snowmen. Scarves and eyebrows were solid white, and only their eyes were visible. Each man carried a pack, and the children cheered as they began putting food on the table. Most of the bread loaves were frozen, and were placed near the stove to thaw. Boxes of cocoa and bags of sugar were quickly made into a warm drink using hot water. Bread was sliced and cheese sandwiches were made. The children received their first food since the storm began two days before.

"Hey, this is a winter picnic," young Rufus Towne shouted, and the children caught the spirit and cheered as they ate or stood in line waiting to be served.

"Mrs Foster we are certainly grateful to you for keeping the children here," John Crow stated. "This is the worst spring blizzard any of us can remember this late in the year. We came to drifts that were over our heads and we had to go around them. A child caught out for more than two hours would have frozen to death no matter how they were dressed."

"There was wind with the storm we had last year, but not like this," Rufus Towne said.

"As soon as the kids have had enough to eat, we'd best be on our way home," John stated. "We've got to get home before it gets dark. One good thing, we'll have the wind at our backs," he added. Rufus and John Crow busied themselves getting their own children and the Taylor, Homan, Kaschke, and Smith children ready to leave the school.

"We have an agreement with our neighbors that when there is a storm, they come to our house for their children," John stated.

"Before we leave the school, children," Amy Crow said, "we will all hold to the knotted rope which John brought. Each child will have a space between knots. If any child falls, those closest will help until they are able to get back on their feet. No one will try to go faster than the whole group. I know it will be cold, and we must keep going even when we think our hands and feet are frozen. John will lead us and Rufus will be the last person. The wind is blowing too hard to talk. John and Rufus will get us home."

When they were ready, that group left the building.

"We had best leave now," Ed stated.

"I don't want to go." Katie said. "It's too cold and windy."

"We must see to our house," Chloe stated. "There hasn't been anyone there since the blizzard began."

"Did anybody take care of the cow and horses?" Willie asked.

"No," Ed replied. "I couldn't leave the Crows, and your mother had to stay with you at school. The cow and horses will need water and hay."

"Your father is right," Chloe said. "No one was at our house to take care of things. We must take care of our animals who have had no food or water for two days. We will hold on to the coat of the person in front. I will be the last person and your father will lead. We will stop when anyone needs help. We will be fine, and the Lord will guide us to our house."

The children caught the determination that Chloe imparted and busily put on their coats and scarves. Their path was at an angle that caused them to partially face into the wind, and their vision was no more than eight feet ahead. There were gusts that reduced that to less than three feet. The children tended to drift away from the path in the direction the wind forced them to go. A single strand of wire fence had been placed between the house and the school which Ed followed for a short distance before he realized they were separated. He was barely able to hear Chloe and the children above the howling gale. He found them twenty feet from the trail.

For a few moments they huddled together, and the children clung to each other with Chloe and Ed on the perimeter as though to say they could go no further. Chloe took her scarf and yelled at the top of her voice for each child to hold on to it, while Ed turned in the direction that he thought would lead him to the strand of wire. Within a few minutes he realized they were lost. Keeping his fears to himself he pushed on making a path for the family to follow. By chance he felt a lessening of the wind and realized they must be in the shelter of their house. He turned toward the lessened wind and soon found himself almost against the front door. The wind and cold had coated that side of the house with snow so that it blended with the swirling drifts. Inside, the house was dark and very cold. Drifts had piled snow over windows on the lee side of the house.

Snow had blown through the cracks of the windows on the north side where the wind had forced it in. Chloe lit the lamp and Ed busied himself starting the fire. Katie and Willie were crying that their hands and feet hurt. Florence had frost bitten ears, but there were no frozen hands or feet. The fire Ed had started blended the crackling of burning wood with the sound of smoke and heat in the chimney and the wild sound from outside. Wet clothing was thrown over the inside clothesline along one wall and the children drew chairs up to the stove for warmth. Soon the house had partially warmed and the children began drawing pictures on the frosted windows.

"Must have been more that two feet of snow," Ed stated "The way the wind's blowin' I might have trouble gittin' out to see to the animals."

"Can you see how they are doing from here?" Chloe asked.

"There's too much blowin' snow to see much," Ed replied while he put on his sheepskin coat and got ready to go outside. "I can barely see the top of the barn. Guess I'll have to go see if they are all right, and see that they have water and hay."

It took him almost half an hour to get to the corral because of drifts, and blowing snow. At the corral he forked hay from the snow covered stack, and when he reached the water tank, he found it frozen over and almost hidden under snow. He took the shovel and cleared the snow away and punched a hole through the ice. He went to the pump and found it frozen so that he could not pump water.

"Guess I'll have to see if I can thaw it out later," he muttered. He looked around at the horses and saw that they were huddled together in the shelter of the barn. He noted that they seemed to be all right. He couldn't find any chickens. The cow had stayed in her stall and was the most protected of the animals. He put grain in her feed box, and then decided that he best get the milk pail and milk her. She had not been milked for three days. He was able to return to the house where he brushed and stamped snow off his clothes.

"Good thing there was a light I could see," he said. "There's more snow than I thought, an' with the snow blowin' the way it is I could barely see the house. The wind and the cold suck your breath away. Sure wouldn't be hard to get lost out there."

"I certainly hope the Townes and Crows got home all right with the children," Chloe worried.

"All we can do is hope for the best," Ed replied. "A man's a damn fool to go out and hunt anybody in this kind of weather."

"We can pray for their safety," Chloe stated.

Ed did not reply as he took the milk pail and a pail of water for the cow and went out and milked. Supper was ready when he returned to the house, and the evening meal was served. Chloe followed her usual practice of reading from the Bible, and prayed for the families of the school. She led the family in singing songs and hymns they liked. Even Ed seemed to enjoy the evening.

All that night the wind swirled and whipped around the small house with mounting and falling wails and sounds seldom heard. Before day break Ed rose to find there was no warmth in the stove and that water had frozen in the teakettle. At the window facing the barn, he rubbed a place large enough so that he could see, but there was nothing but whiteness. He went to the leeward side of the house, and found that snow had settled as high as the middle of the window, Chloe asked how the weather looked outside.

"I think we're snowbound for sure,' he dejectedly replied. "I'm not sure I can get to the wood pile. It'll git pretty cold in here if we ain't got wood. I should have brought wood in last night."

"Have you tried to open the door?" she asked.

Ed shook his head, and opened the door only to discover that the snow had drifted to his eye level. He pushed his foot against the drift and a cascade of snow entered the room. Chloe could tell he was silently cursing as he dressed to go outside.

"Well," he said, "the snow ain't hard frozen yet"

He took the broom and began pushing snow back away form the doorway until he had cleared a pathway large enough so that he could reach the shovel beside the door. Wind propelled snow filled the path almost as soon as he shoveled it away. After an hour of shoveling he had reached the wood stacked against that side of the house. Chloe went to the pump to draw water and discovered that the pump needed priming. Water in the pail they kept for drinking had frozen and the bottom was bulged by the expanding ice. Ed returned with several snow covered cottonwood stove length branches, and put them in the firebox beside the stove where he cleared the snow from them. Chloe told him about the pump.

"I'll have a fire goin' in just a few shakes," he said. "You keep the children in bed until I get things warmed up a little. We can melt snow to get water to prime the pump."

He set about making kindling of one of the branches, and soon had a fire going so that he could put larger lengths of wood in the stove. The children crowded as close as they could to get warm.

"We'll have to put pans of snow on the stove for water until the pump thaws out," he said.

By continuing to shovel and carry wood, he brought in enough to last for the rest of that day and night. One by one Chloe and the children rose and gathered around the stove with blankets around their shoulders as the inside temperature was still near freezing. Chloe began getting breakfast while Ed went out to do the chores. She fed the children who huddled around the table.

"Where's papa," Carrie asked as they ate.

"He's out taking care of the animals," Chloe replied.

In good weather he could do what he had to do in twenty minutes to half an hour. He had been outside for an hour. Chloe had visions of him lying in the snow freezing to death, but she said nothing to the children. After an hour and a half she decided to put on warm clothing and go see if she could find him. When she opened the door, she stepped out into the fury of wind blown snow. The path Ed had made in the drifts had largely filled over. Chloe tried to move ahead and found herself floundering. By chance she located the shovel and began pushing snow aside the best she could. She tired quickly, and decided to call out.

"Ed can you hear me?" she shouted.

There was no response, and she felt that the noise of the wind and its coldness mocked her words. She tried pushing snow for another four or five minutes and yelled again. This time she thought she heard a faint answer. Another five minutes of shoveling brought the two together. Through the haze she saw him struggling to force his way through waist deep snow. They made their way to one another and hugged briefly.

"Thank God you're alright," she said not knowing whether or not he could hear her.

He took the shovel and together they worked their way back to the house. Inside they stood for a few minutes catching their breath before either of them were able to speak.

"You took quite a chance. We both could have been lost between the house and the barn," Ed stated when he had warmed enough to speak.

"I had no idea how bad the storm was," Chloe said. "Do you suppose the Townes, Taylors and Crows were able to get home alright? After going out in this storm it makes me wonder."

"All we can do is hope for the best. Anybody's a fool to go out to look for them today," Ed replied, and they laughed briefly as they remembered that conversation of a day ago.

During that day Ed only left the house to get wood and pans of snow. By evening the wind had lessened, and Ed was able to get to the corral without problems. When the evening meal was served, the dishes done, and the family gathered around in a half circle, Chloe read from the Bible and offered a special prayer for her family and the neighbors. About ten that night the wind rose again to its blizzard force. In the morning Ed found that the below zero cold had hardened most of the snow. He was able to do the chores with no problems and returned to the house. By noon there were small patches of blue sky with low hanging wind driven clouds scudding swiftly toward the southeast. Frost in the air caused the horizon to appear hazy. That afternoon there was a knock on their door. Seth Parker, the closest neighbor to the school, shook the snow off and was given a cup of warm coffee.

"We was kinda worried for you folks," he said. "I thought it best I come to see if everything was alright. I had quite a time gittin' through the drifts, but worst of all the wind drives the cold right through your clothes. Must be twenty five below."

While Seth was speaking Rufus Towne knocked and came in. He reported that all the children had gotten home safely. The conversation turned farmers to talking about their livestock and the effect the storm would have on that year's crops. Coffee was served and the men rose quickly and put on their heavy coats and mittens.

"We'd best be getting' home," Rufus stated and Seth nodded.

"Seems to get dark earlier on these stormy days," he said.

Goodbyes followed and the men left. That night Chloe said a special prayer of thanks for the safety of the school children. Within a week a most welcome spring came and the school was again the center of focus for valley people. The April Board meeting decided that school would stay in session until the end of June because of all the days missed due to illness and weather. At the Board meeting in early May, a representative of the irrigation company recommended that the school should move two miles west to make room for the reservoir. Rufus Towne formed a resolution to that effect, which was passed unanimously. The question of the house where the Fosters lived was raised, and John Crow formed a resolution that it be moved to a site nearer the school. It passed unanimously.

That night Chloe asked Ed where the house was to be located.

"They didn't decide that," he stated. "I guess we"ll just have to wait until the next board meeting to find out."

Chapter Nineteen

During the spring and summer excitement reigned in West Sedgwick, and the community was abuzz with rumors about moving the school. When neighbors met there were new rumors and new questions for Mrs Foster, but she did not know the answers.

"Where are they gonna put the new school?"

"What about your house?"

"How can just plain farmers move the schoolhouse?"

For every question Chloe Foster answered with Ed's statement.

"We will just have to wait and see."

At a special May Board meeting, the Board arrived at the decision that land three miles west of the present school site on higher ground would be traded for land needed for the reservoir. At the board meeting there was heated discussion concerning paying the men who would have the work of seeing that the move was completed in good order. It was decided that each landowner would contribute one hundred dollars to the community fund. Those who did not have the money could work their share at four dollars a day, which meant they would give twenty five days of labor to the move.

"Where are we gonna find men who know how to do a job like that?" Rufus Towne asked.

"We'll scout around the towns nearest and see if we can locate men who know a little about building," John Crow said. "And anyways most of us have had to do some buildin' to get settled. We have put up houses and barns with the help of neighbors, and we'll prob'ly be able to find men in the community when we need them."

"Why couldn't we hire a steam engine and a movin' company. None of us has worked on a job that big." Ed Foster said.

"We'd have to have money to do that," John stated. "We'd best git somebody from the county to help us work out a plan."

"How much time do we have to get the job done?" Tom Kaschke asked.

There was a long pause in discussion as the people tried to estimate a time frame for the work.

"It would be best if we didn't try to have school until the move is completed," Elmer Taylor stated.

After long debate, the decision was made that school would be suspended for one year, but that the Fosters could remain in the house until it had to be moved to the new site.

"If we ain't gonna have school, we won't need to pay Mrs. Foster," Seth Parker stated.

There were noes and yaes to that suggestion. It was decided that the Fosters would not pay rent, and that they could remain in the house during the move.

"Maybe we could talk to the irrigation company about gittin' them to help," Rufus Towne said. "They might even lend us an engineer to draw up plans and guide the work."

A vote was taken and it was agreed that John Crow and Rufus Towne would talk to the irrigation company management as soon as possible. Another special meeting was called five days later and John Crow reported to the School Board.

"The irrigation company will lend us beams and house jacks. Joe Kellog, their engineer, will survey the ground for the house and the school. He will also draw up plans which will detail what must be done and how to do it. The irrigation company will provide cement and gravel for new foundations. They will also provide lumber for forming foundations for the buildings. We have to furnish wagons and men to haul all they are willin' to give us to the new site. Four or five wagons should be all we need, and we can prob'ly get it all to where we need it in one or two days. The hardest work we'll have is raisin' the school off its foundation with jacks and gittin' the foundations away from under it. Buildin' the foundation on the new site should be done within a week after we git started on it. Joe Kellog will help us with the jacks, and with settin' the foundations for the school."

"When will Joe have the sites set up?" Flora Taylor asked.

"We should have his report this week." John answered.

"Where is the new site,?" Chloe asked.

"It will be three miles west on higher ground where the road crosses Plum Crik," John replied. "The house where the Fosters live will be just east of the school. We don't have Kellog's report yet so I don't know the exact place the buildings will be."

"Will it still be in Sedgwick County?" Elmer Taylor asked.

"There may be a question about that, but it doesn't make any difference. School district boundaries don't have to be in the same county or even in the same state."

"Maybe not," Elmer persisted, "but each county has it's own superintendent. If the new school is in Logan County, we may lose our superintendent and our teacher."

"Not if the buildings are controlled by West Sedgwick School District," John replied, "and it is. Kellog's men will survey and we'll put the buildings where the survey plans them to be. Our Board will still have charge of the school."

Impatience mounted in the community as the prospect of the move was becoming reality. Joe Kellog presented a blue print for the site of both buildings which showed them to be where he had surveyed on the Plum Creek road. John Crow and Joe decided that Joe would be the superintendent, with the agreement of the Board, and the work began on Monday three weeks after school was out for the summer. Men from the community were given the work of setting the foundations for the new buildings at the new location, while a crew from the irrigation company raised the school building with jacks and readied the large beams that would be placed under the building when the time came to lift it off its foundation. Meanwhile work on forming the foundations at the new site proceeded.

Amy Crow organized the community women to provide a noon meal for the working men. The women were used to preparing meals for haying crews and thrashing crews, but it became a task for them to provide a meal everyday for workers that would number as many as twenty men. Food was brought to the Foster house and prepared there. There was much banter between the community ladies and the workers. Most of the irrigation company men were young and single, and the ladies had homes and families. Comments usually stayed within the bounds of good manners, but Flora Taylor was one of the ladies who enjoyed the repartee, and the young men soon learned that she would let them know when they were too fresh.

"Hey Flora, when's the last time you flirted with a guy my age?" one young man asked her.

"I've got two boys at home about your age," Flora replied. "I keep them in line, and I let them know how to treat a lady."

"I never saw no 'lady' wearin' an apron. When I was a drover with the 101 ranch cattle, I saw lots of 'ladies,' but I never saw one prettier than you with thet pretty blue apron."

Chloe recognized Bart Jackson, but decided for the moment to say nothing to Ed for fear that he might try to attack the younger Bart.

"Oh, go along with you," Flora answered. "You have three things to worry about here. One is your boss, the other is my husband, and the third is me. Right now you best worry about your boss."

"Bart, these women have been feedin' us too well for you to mess things up," Joe Kellog stated. "We owe them thanks for bein' so good to us. Get back to your job and keep your thoughts to yourself."

Bart gave the usual excuse that 'he didn't mean nothin' by what he said, and Joe replied that they had work to do and he didn't want to hear anymore of that kind of talk. Joe left to inspect the work they had done that morning, and the other workmen began razzing Bart.

"Boy, you sure did git yer come uppance," one said.

"The boss told you how the cow ate the cabbage," another said.

"Any one of you yahoos could have said the same thing to Flora," Bart replied. "Anyways I don't see nothin' wrong with what I said. I've heard everyone of you say just as much as I said to Flora."

Chloe tried to avoid Bart, but knew that she could not. The confrontation occurred the next day. Ed had joined the work crew after the noon meal, but Bart did not. He stationed himself where he had observed Chloe, and when she walked by, he stepped forward and grasped her arm, whirling her around so that she was facing him. He attempted to put his arms around her and kiss her, but she struggled free with obvious anger.

"Leave me alone," she said.

"You know I can take you away from all this," he said. "I've wanted to keep my promise to you for a long time."

Chloe turned without another word and ran to Ed who had seen Bart waylay Chloe. Ed leaped toward Bart and the two men fell to the ground. They were wrestling when Joe came and pulled them apart.

"Bart follow me to the time keeper," Joe said between clenched teeth. Bart followed like a naughty school boy who had been caught. Ed was furious and swore that he would kill Bart if he didn't leave Chloe alone.

Several farmers surrounded Bart and one called for a rope. Joe Kellog intervened and told the crews to go to their places of work. Bart started to join them, but Joe told him to leave the job.

"Gather your things and git off this job," Joe yelled. "Go to the company office and draw your time. I don't want to see you hangin' around town after this. Now git goin'."

Sullenly Bart left the job and was not seen in Sedgwick again.

Joe Kellog returned to the men. "Boys we done real good this mornin,' but we best git back to work placin' the timbers where they'll be ready when we need them. You farmers will need to go about gittin' three four horse teams together. When we can git under the house with the foundation out and the beams in place on the wagon frames we'll lower the house to the beams. My men will rig a system of log chains so we can hitch the teams to the chains and pull the schoolhouse out of where it is now and to the new site."

By mid September the building had been raised as high as Joe recommended. A problem arose when they found the ground under the building damp and in some places muddy. When the house was lowered, the wagon wheels sank to their hubs which caused the building to lurch sideways where it teetered nearly sliding off the beams and trapping several workmen under its weight.

"Too wet to pull those wagons out," Joe stated. "We'll have to use the jacks again to raise the buildin.' I'll have to pull my crew and wait till it dries out enough. If that doesn't work we'll have to build a platform big enough for the wagons to roll onto it."

Later he talked to John Crow and Rufus Towne.

"You boys have done a good job puttin' in the foundations at the other site. It'll take a week to ten days for the ground under the buildin' to dry enough. Like I say, we may have to build a solid ramp to roll the wagons onto before we can lower the buildin'. When it's dry enough we can begin work again, possibly in ten days to two weeks."

"Is there anything we can do in the meantime.?" Rufus asked.

"Best you clear the brush and sage away from the path we'll have to follow when we're ready to move the school," Joe said. "This is September, we'll be back around October first. We'll leave everything in its place under the school building until we return."

The West Sedgwick men watched as Joe and his men loaded a few things in their wagons and left. They were accustomed to clearing land of sage brush and yucca, and decided they would begin work early the next day. The farmers had finished their work of clearing a roadway from the school to the new site in three days. John and Rufus asked the farmers what they thought they could do next. It was decided that they best smooth the trail they had made. When the irrigation company men returned, they were pleased to see a cleared and leveled roadway from the school site to the new location of the school and the house.

"It's dry enough," Joe stated when he had inspected the ground under the building. "Let's begin puttin' in the jacks. When we git the building raised high enough, we'll have to shore up the under side of the floorin' with six by sixes accordin' to plan. We'll pair up you farmers with my men, and half will work on the floor while the other half git the Jacks in place. We'll use planks for a base. We may have to nail two together to git enough strength for the jacks to hold the weight of the school, and so the jacks don't sink too deep."

The crawl space under the school was three and a half feet from the base to the floor studding. When the building was raised there was clearance enough so the men had room to work, but most of them had to hunch their shoulders forward to keep from bumping their heads. Beams had been placed on the wagon frames so that there was space enough above the top of the wheels to allow them to turn freely as long as the surface they moved over was smooth. There could be no dips in the roadway more than two or three inches deep, nor could there be ruts longer than a foot or two on either side. The school house had to be evenly balanced to keep it from tipping, and sliding off the beams as it was pulled over the roadway.

After a week of hard work under the school, Joe decided the building was ready to move, and again the wagons were moved into position. Ordinarily two men could easily push and pull a wagon wherever they wanted it to go, but the heavy beams on the wagons and the difficulty of pulling them under the school required all the men of both crews to move each wagon. That work done, the men cheered when both wagons were in position. After inspection, Joe decided that four cross beams would need to be placed to better balance the load, two for each wagon, one at the front and one over the rear wheels. There was barely room between the floor of the building and the four beams to rest upon when the men placed them. Joe had the crew put a system of log chains in place with the rear wagon chained to the first using the tongue of the second wagon to allow proper spacing between the two wagons. The building was lowered, and it came to rest just as Joe had planned. The under structure provided balance designed to steady the swaying of the building as much as possible as it moved along the trail the farmers had made. The next major job for the farmers was hitching the teams to the chains in the front of the building and to the wagons under the building.

"When we broke up the sod on our place, we used four horses abreast to pull the plow," Tom Kaschke stated. "Looks like we ought to have two three horse hitches, three in front and three in back."

"I think we'd best string them out two and two," Ed Foster said. "You guys don't know nothin' about getting' the most out of your team. The only way to do it is to set two in front and four in the rear." Elmer Taylor stated with an air of finality.

Joe Kellog settled the issue.

"I've looked the roadway over, and we'll hitch the horses in pairs," he directed. "There ain't room enough on the roadway for three or four abreast so we'll use a six horse hitch. Once we git the building rollin,' we'll keep goin' until we reach the new site."

Ropes were attached to the middle of the building and along the eaves at each corner. Four men were assigned to each set of ropes so that a total of twenty four men were given the task of steadying the building against the possibility that it would slide off the wagon frames. All things were in place to Joe's satisfaction, and he gave the next order.

"Move out."

At first the building creaked and groaned as though in protest, but barely moved. Farmer teamsters were aware that horses needed a first attempt to move a heavy load, and let them get their wind. On the second command to the teams to "pull," with great effort the teams moved the building to the edge of the ramp. The soil under the building was more uneven than Joe had realized and the first wagon stopped at a skewed position to the left. The men on the right side were straining every muscle to hold the building in place while the men on the left were holding slack ropes. Beams to keep the building from sliding too far to the left were quickly placed under the left side, and Joe called for a conference.

"Men, we can either hire a steam engine to pull the building' out of the spot we're in, or we can get more horses and take our chances on gittin' it out," he stated.

"Gittin' more horses ain't a problem for us," Rufus Towne said.

"How many more do we need?" John Crow asked.

"We'll need at least two more teams," Joe stated.

"We can have them here tomorrow," John said, and several men nodded their agreement.

"The more teams we add the harder it is to git each team to pull their share," Tom Kaschke said, and several agreed with him.

"Let's give it a try in the mornin,'" John said. He arranged for four additional teams by asking each man who had work horses to bring them in the morning. The men went home for the night, and the next morning the new teams were ready for work.

"Our biggest problem is to lift the building high enough so we can place beams under the wagon wheels that will lift the left side." Joe stated before they began work. "We will build up the jacks enough, but keepin' the buildin' steady for the horses to pull it out is another matter. This is a dangerous job. I'll need six men and myself to git under the buildin' to jack it up. If it slides off the frame underneath, it could cause real trouble. My crew is used to workin' in these situations so we'll see what we can do."

He named five men to get under the building along with himself, and they began placing the jacks along the left wall of the building. As the jacks began to do their work a beam used to shore the building up suddenly gave way, and caught Joe Morgan's leg between beams. There was a helpless yell of pain, and a flurry of activity under the building. Joe Kellog and another man were able to lift the beam enough to get Morgan out from under it. Above them the building groaned and creaked as it swayed dangerously toward the left side They were able to get the injured man out and a team and wagon took him to Doctor Davis. There was no more work for that day. Without further incident but with great effort for men and horses, the building was moved to the new site.

Joe had designed a system of beams and wagon wheels that allowed the workmen to slide the building onto the new foundation as smoothly as it was possible to do it. The house where the Fosters lived was moved with the same system, and both buildings were ready for occupancy by November tenth. There were repairs to cracks in the walls and ceilings and a new coat of paint was added to the inside and outside of the buildings. A community celebration was held at Thanksgiving and School began the first of December several months ahead of schedule.

Chapter Twenty

For years the West Sedgwick women had discussed forming a club that would provide meals, sewing, and guidance for the community. A formal meeting was scheduled at the home of Amy Crow for the last week of August. Fifteen women attended, and an election was held. Amy Crow was chosen president, and was given freedom to ask any woman she chose to chair each meeting.

"What shall we name our club?" Flora Taylor asked.

"Why not the West Sedgwick Ladies Sewing Circle?" Berta Kaschke asked.

"That's a good name," Amy replied, "and we will keep it in mind. Are there other names anyone would suggest?"

"I've been reading about a club called the Royal Neighbors," Chloe said. "They do just about everything we have discussed."

No other names were suggested and a vote was taken. The West Sedgwick Sewing Circle received one vote and the Royal Neighbors Society received fourteen.

"Our name will be The West Sedgwick Royal Neighbors Society," Amy announced.

Chloe was happy they had chosen that name, but she could not foresee how much her family would need the Royal Neighbors in the future. Most of the community men agreed that a club for women was a good idea 'so long as it don't interfere with gittin' meals and takin' care of the kids.'"

For the first meeting, Amy had invited Maude Smith as the speaker. Maude was the first child born to homesteaders in Sedgwick County, and remembered the early days when the nearest neighbor was four miles east of the Crow farm. She presented a comparison of homesteaders "Then and Now."

"Prairie settlers are a breed apart from any other section of the country," Maude stated "We have chosen to settle on raw land where our men had to break sod by plowing, and then we had to work the soil into land we could farm. Many of us found that we could not make a living on a homestead in the dry land areas, so we were able to move into the valley and carve out an irrigation system by building ditches along the South Platte that made twenty thousand acres good for farming. Many dry-landers either quit their farms or moved to the South Platte Valley so they could survive. We have all seen blizzards, tornados, and prairie fires along with hail and drought that destroyed crops. Those who settled around West Sedgwick School have proven they are survivors. We have all gone through hard times and have established a fine community."

"If anyone had asked us how we endured such 'hardships' we would have replied, 'hardships, that's just the way it is out here.' We have learned that good times follow bad and bad times are followed by better times, but we got used to that and we just kept on livin'. When we accepted the conditions of homesteading, it turned out to be good livin.' We have raised families and we know the Good Lord has blessed us, and some are seeing their grandchildren grow up."

When Chloe told Ed about those words, he replied that their family had certainly found what Maude said to be true.

"You've made things better for me and the kids than most families," Ed stated. "I watch and listen and I'm amazed at the care and love you show to all of us, and you make things fun for the children."

To Ed it seemed that whatever a task required, Chloe was able to bring enjoyment to it. On one occasion he remembered watching as she planted a garden beside the new school. She had a song that made a game of planting which made the work seem like play for the children and himself.

> "This is the way we measure the rows,
> measure the rows, measure the rows,
> This is the way we measure the rows,
> in our prairie garden.
>
> We plant, and water and hope it grows,
> hope it grows, hope it grows,
> We plant and water and hope it grows,
> And that's our prairie garden."

Each child was given a handful of seeds and instructed when and where to plant. Green beans, carrots, and radishes were planted in neat rows. Pumpkin, squash, and melon seeds were planted in hills. Most of these seeds could be planted as soon as the frost left the ground. Chloe's planting song made the work fly, even for Ed as he worked with them.

> "We plant the seeds into the ground,
> into the ground, into the ground.
> We plant the seeds into the ground
> in our prairie garden.
>
> We plant in hills all around,
> all around, all around.
> We plant in hills all around,
> That is our prairie garden."

The next summer was enjoyed by the Foster family more than any they had spent in Colorado. In the fall they picked wild grapes from vines in the brush along the South Platte River. That fall there was an abundance of grapes, and Amy Crow planned a "grapeing" day for Chloe and the children. No sooner had they arrived at a good location than Katie and Willie jumped out of the buggy and began exploring vines for wild grapes.

"You must be careful to stay out of the poison ivy," Amy Crow called after them, but it was too late for Katie and Willie.

Amy called the group together and instructed them on how to recognize poison ivy. She then told them her remedy for lessening the effects of the vine.

"I have brought bicarbonate of soda so we can wash the places in strong soda water. Then we make a soda paste and put it on the places that have the ivy. We let that dry, and it gradually flakes off. That doesn't stop the itching, but it lessens it, and best of all, it gets some of the poison off. Before we go grape picking we need to set up camp," she continued. "Does anyone know how to get good clear water for our horses?"

"I do," Katie yelled.

"Alright, Katie and Carrie will fix a place for the horses to get water," Amy stated. "Now we need wood." She appointed her son John to search for wood with the help of Willie. "Chloe, you take charge of seeing to our lunch, with my help," she added.

Thus assigned everyone began to form a camp. All things were soon accomplished, lunch was served, and Amy made a point of cleaning up after their lunch.

"Now we can get our containers and go pick grapes, but first be careful not to mistake places where poison ivy is mixed in with grape vines," Amy instructed. "Don't try to pick grapes there, no matter how good they might look. Besides we need to leave some for small animals and birds. When you take a bunch of grapes from the vine be careful not to spoil the vines. We come here every year and we want to find grapes every time."

The families quickly filled all the containers they brought, and were ready to go home. Amy gave a welcome invitation.

"Bring your family and your grapes over tomorrow after morning chores and we'll make jams and jellies."

The next day the Fosters arrived at the Crows after morning chores, and the work of preparing the grapes began. First, the grapes were thoroughly washed and strained through cheese cloth so that pulp and pure juice remained. Second, jars and glasses were prepared for the finished product. When the work was finished, Chloe had twenty one half pints of jelly and ten of jam.

"Have you ever made hominy?" Amy asked.

"No I never have," Chloe answered.

"When the men harvest corn this fall, come over and we'll spend a day making hominy," Amy said.

"Amy Crow is a very good neighbor," Carrie told her mother on the way home. "It's good that she can show us how to make things from wild plants and things we grow in our garden."

"Amy has been a good neighbor," Chloe answered. "This whole community has been very good to us. We will have jam and jelly to last at least half the winter. When we learn how to make hominy, we can get corn anytime during the winter or summer and make hominy."

Chloe learned how to make hominy that fall during corn picking time. The Royal Neighbors Club exchanged recipes for various dishes that included ways to cook hominy, and it became a staple for many meals at the Foster home. Amy gave instructions to the club.

"First, we soak the kernels in lye water for twenty four hours to soften the outer shell. This makes the kernels swell and bleaches some of the color out of yellow corn. You don't have to worry about that with white corn, but it also must be soaked. There isn't much white corn grown in this valley.

My husband brought me a pan of corn which I soaked in lye yesterday morning. Now we must let them soak in clear water to remove the lye. We then rinse them at least three times to make sure the lye is gone. We can spread the kernels to dry on a clean dry surface. When they are dry, we use flour sacks to store them.

After the club had dismissed, Chloe and Amy talked further.

"How much lye do you use?" Chloe asked.

"I'll give you my recipe, but not more than half a cup for a large pan of corn." Amy said. "By the way, I"ll be canning tomatoes tomorrow. If you come and help me I'll share what we can with you."

Amy was silent a moment. "Yes, and when John butchers a beef, you can help me can that, and I'll share that with you."

"You are the most thoughtful neighbor I've ever had," Chloe stated. "I can't thank you enough for all you have done and are doing for us." There were tears in Chloe's eyes as she spoke and the two women hugged.

"We'll have lots of food this winter," Katie blurted.

"We can't let our school teacher and her family starve if we can help it," Amy said smiling.

On the way home Chloe taught her children a hymn of thanksgiving. The warm days of September blended with the cooler crisper days of October, and the Fosters' family life settled into the routine of chores, canning, school, and community events. Chloe observed her children growing in capability and assurance as they dealt with prairie life. She had seen Carrie capably take care of Willie when he was bitten by a rattler. Katie and Willie had become self confident, and could take care of most situations they encountered. Chloe knew she had gained a measure of independence by learning how to harness Dusty to the buggy and drive him to places she needed to go. She felt that she had even controlled him when he ran away across the prairie with herself and the children in the buggy.

"Our children have learned so much since we have lived out here," she remarked to Ed one evening.

"How's that?" Ed asked.

"They have gained confidence from having to learn the ways of the prairie," she answered.

"What do you mean?"

"For example, when Willie was bitten by the rattlesnake, Carrie did what you taught her to do. They have been able to go to their friends houses on their pony or in the buggy without escort. They are learning how to make jam and jelly, and Amy Crow has taught them how to can meats and tomatoes. Carrie taught me the way you told her to drive Dusty with the buggy."

"It's been a good summer," Ed stated.

As long as the weather held, Ed was usually away working for a farmer or working on one of the ditch crews helping build the ditches that would carry water for the irrigation of farms in the valley. Many of the farmers he worked for were not able to pay him for his work, but traded hay, vegetables from their gardens, canned goods, and occasionally poultry or livestock for his labor. He was pleased with the excitement when he brought home a small pony Rufus Towne had given him for two weeks work. There was excitement when he presented it to the children.

"What shall we name it?" Chloe asked the children.

"I know, I know," Katie shouted. "We can name him Spot 'cause he has a large brown spot on his side."

"Spot is a name for a dog," Carrie stated with dignity.

"What shall we name him, then? He has one brown eye and one blue eye. Maybe we should call him blue eye." Katie was insistent.

"He needs a horse name. I think we should name him Tom." Carrie said, but the others turned up their noses.

"Tom is Mister Kaschke's name," Katie said with disgust.

"Perhaps, we could each think of a name and put it on a piece of paper. Then I will put the papers in a hat, and Florence will take one out. The one she draws will be the pony's name."

Chloe cut strips of paper and gave one to each child.

One by one the children wrote a name. She placed them in Ed's hat, and eighteen month Florence drew a name.

"Puddin,'" Chloe read.

"Goody, that's the name I chose, and anyway his brown spot looks like puddin'" Willie shouted with joy.

"How can we ride him?" Carrie asked and added "we don't have a bridle or a saddle."

"We'll have to ask papa about that," Chloe answered.

Ed fashioned a bridle from old harness straps, and showed them how to ride without a saddle. Within a couple of days, one of the children rode it everywhere they went. Arguments about whose turn it would be were settled with a schedule of days and children who would ride that day.

Late one night the Foster household was awakened by a terrible racket coming from the hen house and corral. Chickens were squawking, horses were snorting, and there was a yelping going on that Ed thought was a coyote. He threw on his clothes, took his shotgun, and raced to the chicken house in time to see a black and white shadow race toward the brush behind the building. He took a shot in that direction, as he became aware of the pungent odor of skunk, and realized that he had been sprayed. He went to the corral to calm the horses, and as he entered, an animal approached him. He raised his gun and was ready to shoot when the animal whimpered, and he realized it was a dog.

"Git, git outta here," he commanded. He could see the wagging of a tail while the animal licked his boots.

"Oh well, you can stay till mornin'. Then I'll try to find out who you belong to," he said.

He returned to the house and the dog followed him. Before he entered, he told it to stay and the dog lay down. When he entered the house, the strong aroma of skunk spread to every corner of the room.

"Ed Foster, you can't get in this bed as long as you smell like that," he heard in the darkness.

"What do you expect me to do?" he asked.

"You'll have to sleep in the barn, and tomorrow we'll wash your clothes. You'll need to bathe yourself. Take a blanket and sleep in the barn tonight. I'll bring you clean clothes in the morning."

That night he threw his clothes in the horse trough, and hung them on the corral fence to dry. He took water from the horse trough and bathed, and then wrapped himself in the blanket and made his bed in the hay. Next morning wrapped in the blanket, he returned to the house where Chloe gave him a bar of soap and a towel along with her orders for him.

"Go bathe yourself in the spring and come back when you don't smell like a skunk," she said smiling, and added, "please."

When he had finished bathing and had put on clean clothing, he returned to the house and hung the blanket on the clothesline. Through all his activities of the morning, the stray dog followed him everywhere he went. When the children saw the dog they wanted to rush out and pet it, but they were restrained when Ed told them there was a strong odor of skunk about the dog.

"You'll have to bathe it for the same reason you did." Chloe laughed. "Ed, before we let the children do anything with it we best find out if it likes children."

"Is it a boy or a girl?" Willie wanted to know.

"It's a boy," Ed stated.

After breakfast, Chloe prepared a pan of warm soapy water, and Ed took it and some rags, and the dog followed him to the watering trough. While he was soaping and rinsing the dog the children came and stood around, and the dog wagged its tail in friendship. When Ed was finished, he gave the rags to the children and they went to work drying it's fur, which the dog seemed to enjoy. Carrie told her mother that the dog already acted like it belonged to them.

"Now you all need baths," Chloe responded. "You all have the smell of skunk about you."

Later that week Ed learned that a family named Munsey had lost a dog similar to this one. The next Saturday afternoon he prepared the buggy and the family drove to the Munsey farm, and the dog went with them.

"Yes," Carl Munsey said, "that's my dog. He's only a year old, and was part of a litter our dog Belle had last spring. As you can see we still have one brother and one sister of his. My children named him 'Shep.' He is part shepherd."

"That's what we'll call him." Katie said.

"Looks like your children have already adopted him," Carl said. "Well that's alright with me."

He thought a moment and then addressed the children.

"If I let you keep him you must take good care of him. You must keep burrs out of his fur, and feed him every day. I have no patience with people who let a dog run and let it get thin, so you must feed him well, and keep him home as much as possible. If you promise that you will do those things, then you can keep him."

There was a chorus of "we promise" as the children gave the pledge that children have ignored since time began. "We'll take good care of him."

"Ed and I will see that they take care of him," Chloe stated.

"Now we have a dog just like our neighbors do," Katie stated, and Shep was added to the growing Foster menagerie.

Even as good times followed bad times, so it was with joy and sorrow. In the West Sedgwick Community there were accidents, runaway horses, snake bites, and every other kind of crisis that could happen. Chloe never ceased to give thanks to the Lord for keeping her family safe. When a crisis came to her family or the community, she sought the Lord to help them through it, and she always felt confident that prayer and action were a part of neighborliness.

Chapter Twenty One

While blizzards were a winter threat, lack of rain was a major problem in summer. Crops failed when drought settled in for a dry summer. Farmers greeted one another by stating that the prairie was "tinder dry, and it wouldn't take much to set it afire." There were few roads or streams that could serve as fire breaks and a fire, once started, could sweep broadly over the plains. Often the only sign that a fire was moving across the dry land prairie was a column of smoke that swept along with the direction of the wind, stayed close to the ground and traveled rapidly. Just such a fire started late one evening several miles west and south of the West Sedgwick School. When darkness came just after twilight, there was a red-orange glow which was moving southwest in the direction of the Foster homestead.

"Ed do you think that's a prairie fire?" Chloe asked.

"Sure looks like one," he replied.

"Do you think it's going past the Kaschkes or our homestead?"

"Looks to me like it could burn both places." he replied.

"What can we do about it?"

He replied that he didn't think there was much they could do, but wait for news. Few settlers had telephones, but most towns had telephone operators at telephone central. The operator in Holyoke called the operator in Sedgwick who called John Crow. He sent his son to mobilize a crew from the West Sedgwick Community much as Paul Revere had done in history. One by one men gathered at the Crow home with shovels, hay forks, and any other useful tool they thought would help set up a back fire to stop the fire. They boarded wagons and drove at a fast pace in the direction the fire was moving. These homesteaders met wagons filled with other men, and they continued southeast trying to get ahead of the fire. They soon realized their mission was impossible. The fire was moving as fast as they were, and it covered an area at least a mile wide.

Each community group stopped and gathered together to decide the best thing they could do. All knew friends or relatives who lived on the table land south of the river. The news passed from group to group that they best try to locate families living in the path the fire had taken and offer help to them. After visiting several farms in the path of the fire, Ed persuaded those in his wagon to go to the Kaschkes home. As the wagon neared the Kaschke place Ed noted that the fire did not reach his homestead, but it had traveled further south and included the Kaschke farm. He was not surprised to see that the Kaschkes' house and farm buildings were burning heaps of ashes amid the wide expanse of blackened prairie. The Kaschke family was nowhere to be seen.

"Oh, God," Ed muttered to himself, "I hope they got away before the fire hit their house."

These hardy men stood around and silently surveyed the ruined scene. To them tragedy was not new. Finally Rufus Towne spoke.

"It's almost daylight men, there's nothin' we can do here. Might as well git in the wagon and go home."

Silently two or three men nodded agreement and they all boarded the wagon. Men who had lived as far away as six or seven miles began to make comments.

"Tom was a good man," one said.

"He helped me and my family git settled out here," another solemnly stated.

"Without the Kaschkes we couldn't have made it through our first winter." Ed said remembering those days when they built the dugout and the help Tom and Berta had been. He became quiet, and tears filled his eyes as he remembered the death of Franklin and the help Berta had given Chloe.

"We don't know if they made it out of their house or not," John Crow stated. "Let's believe they made it before we mourn for them." He added as he glanced at Ed, "We'll head for home and hope to find them at one of our farms."

Early morning shadows were settling over the land, and each man in the wagon was lost in the shadows of his own thought. At West Sedgwick School they saw that Tom's wagon was beside the house, and his horses were in the corral still harnessed. Chloe, Berta and the children came out of the house and greeted these tired, dirty and frustrated men.

"Where's Tom?" Ed asked.

"He took Dusty and said he was goin' to ride to the fire line and see if he could help get the fire under control," Berta replied.

"How did your family escape the fire?" John Crow asked.

"We saw the smoke and flames coming about a mile from our house. We were right in the center of the worst. Tom had hitched the team to the wagon and we were ready to leave before we realized there was a fire. We loaded the children in the wagon and Tom made the horses race away as fast as he could. Thank God we got away even as our house was already burning." Berta stated calmly. "Men, I think we should ask God to protect the men who are still fighting the fire," Chloe said. "John Crow, would you lead us in a prayer to ask the Lord to help those who were made homeless in this terrible fire?"

"Our God, we humbly ask for Your help and guidance through this difficult time for the homesteaders who were burned out by this fire. Open our hearts to their needs. We want to be good neighbors to those in need, because we know that all of us had to ask for the help of our neighbors in the past. We ask this in Your name, Amen."

There in the yard of the school these men, who were covered with soot and dust, bowed their heads as John prayed, and several added their amen when he finished.

John and the men who had come with him boarded the wagon and left. Ed gathered things he would need to clean up and went to the well while Chloe, Berta and the children began preparation for a quick meal. Tom had not returned, and the worried families were subdued as they ate. An unwritten code in crisis was that mention of a missing person only heightened the anxiety that family members felt. Not so with Berta, she could not contain her worry for Tom, and kept repeating, "I hope Tom is safe. Oh, I hope Tom gets home alright. Lord, please keep Tom safe."

That evening when the children were in bed Berta, Chloe and Ed began a vigil of waiting for news of Tom. At about three in the morning they heard sounds of horses neighing and a single horse answering. They thought a rider had approached so Ed went out to find Dusty at the corral gate, but Tom was not there. There was no joy in the Foster household that morning when the Kaschke children rose to find their father still missing. They dutifully went out to play, but one or another would come in to ask about their father. At ten thirty Doctor Davis drove into the yard, and there was Tom seated in the buggy with bandages on his hands and face. His clothing was black with soot and there were holes burned in his shirt and pants. He eased himself out of the buggy, gingerly walked to the house and greeted Berta, and their children gathered around.

"Tom, oh Tom, are you alright?" Berta sobbed as she put a hand on his shoulder. She was afraid to give him a hug lest she cause him to wince in pain.

"I'll make it," he said with a smile that was half covered with bandages and seemed more like a grimace than a smile.

"His hands should heal in a week," Doctor Davis stated. "He's quite a hero from what I hear. He rescued a mother and her two children when their horse ran away in the aftermath of the fire, and their buggy upset. Tom caught the runaway horse and went back to the buggy which he righted. He got the mother and her two daughters aboard, and rode the horse which he hitched to the buggy out of the path of the fire."

"How did you get so burned?" Berta asked.

"Well, I fell while I was racin' around tryin' to get everybody loaded in the buggy," Tom stated through his bandages. "I tripped over a yucca root or somethin' and fell into a bunch of smolderin' grass. For a time I couldn't get loose and get up"

He was silent for a short time, and then added "I see ole Dusty made it home."

"I surely found out somethin' about a prairie fire." Tom stated. "This one moved fastest in the center, an' it spread slower on its edges. As I rode along, I could hear children screamin,' an' I rode upwind behind the fire until I found the buggy. I guess the mother and children were in a draw that the fire didn't enter. I think they tried to get out after the fire passed."

Doctor Davis finished Tom's story.

"I understand he was riding your horse Ed, and it got away while he was getting everybody in the buggy. It seems that he fell due to smoke inhalation and he passed out briefly."

"How did the woman and her children get away from their house?" Berta asked.

"When they saw the fire comin' to their farm, they hitched a horse to the buggy, and their buildings protected them enough so they could get a start just as the fire caught up with them," Tom said. "I guess they drove into a deep dry-wash and the fire passed over them. The husband was on the fire line further along. He didn't know what had happened."

"He was told about it this mornin,'" Doctor Davis said. "Men came from Sedgwick, Haxtun and Holyoke and formed a backfire line along the Haxtun Sedgwick trail and stopped the fire there."

"Folks, I'm awful tired, and my hands are hurtin.' I need to find some place to git some sleep. Since we ain't got a house, I guess I'll sleep in the haystack." Tom stated.

"We can fix you a bed in the school," Chloe stated. "There's no school until September, and we'll try to keep our children quiet."

It was agreed and the school became a dormitory, not only for Tom, but it included Berta and their children until other arrangements could be made for the unfortunate Kaschkes. John Crow sent word around the school that a meeting would be held for volunteers to help the Kaschkes rebuild. On the scheduled date every family in the community was represented. Community men volunteered for a construction program and voted to build a house and barn on the Kaschkes property. Community women held a meeting of the Royal Neighbors and formed sewing circles for the purpose of making new clothing for the Kaschke children.

"I have nothin' to pay you men and women," Tom stated, and was quickly assured that "that's what neighbors is for." Berta made the same statement and was quickly reminded that she was a member of the Royal neighbors whose motto was "We Royally Help Our Neighbors.'

"It's the work of the club to assist members in times of need. We've all been through times when we were down and out and a helping hand from a neighbor lifted us up, and that's what we will do now," Amy stated.

As the building of the house progressed, furniture was gathered from many households. When the house was ready, it was fully furnished. Corral fences were rebuilt around the new barn and it was stocked with two cows and a flock of chickens. The Royal Neighbors women held sewing and quilting bees, and soon the Kaschkes, who had lost everything, were able to function as they had before the fire. School opened the first of October and community life continued as usual. While these activities were taking place, Platte Valley families faithfully gathered for Community meetings and to trade news about current happenings. Amy Crow and Chloe Foster found themselves talking more often about the direction they perceived the community opportunities for young people were going.

"John thinks this Community will be swallowed up in the politics of the County and the State," she commented to Chloe one day.

"Why does he think that way?" Chloe asked.

"He says as roads improve and people become less tied to their farms, young people will go to the larger communities for education and good jobs," Amy replied.

"You may be right," Chloe responded. "I can't say our young people have a lot to look forward to other than to go on in the footsteps of their fathers and become farmers. Larger towns have so much more to offer young people in education and jobs."

"As more people settle in communities such as ours, there will be some jobs in stores and services for farmers," Amy replied, "and there will be need for hospitals, hotels and other services, John and I want our children to be educated and ready for careers in fields they choose to enter. We are aware that they may leave our Community."

"Ed doesn't see the need for further education at this time," Chloe stated. "He feels that to finish eighth grade is enough education for their future. He says they are going to be farmers anyway, so why do they need more education. I don't openly disagree with him, but secretly I have vowed to make as much education available to our children as we can afford after they finish the education we offer here."

That conversation stated the kind of discussion that was going on in most of the homes in the valley. Women of the Royal Neighbors voted to hold a public discussion designed to involve all the families in the community. A speaker from the County Superintendent's office came and a lively discussion followed. The topic she chose was "Involving Fathers in your Child's Education." A few days later

Amy and Chloe held a conversation about education for their children and the reaction of the community to the meeting.

"What do you feel the families of West Sedgwick thought of our meeting?" Amy asked.

"Ed stated that he could see why boys might need more education, but he felt girls would become housewives and would not need to go past high school."

"What did you think of that?"

"Well, at least it's a step forward for Ed," Chloe replied.

There followed two years of warm summer days and cool nights with enough rain for corn and wheat to grow, and farmers took heart that good times would continue. Winter weather was mild and there was a good feeling among the families of the community, When time permitted many neighbors stopped by one another's homes just to visit. During the 'good years,' living improved for the Foster family. Ed worked for the irrigation company at fifteen dollars a month. He was part of the survey crew that plotted the area for irrigation ditches. Chloe found happiness in leading many community events along with teaching. The Foster children were growing and maturing to become capable helpers for their mother, but the course of prairie living was to be jolted to its very soul by future events.

Social life for homesteaders formed as families blended traditions they had brought from their former communities. Neighborliness grew between families who had not known one another until they settled in community. As families shared experiences, an ethic developed that many called the 'Code of the West.' Help for a neighbor was freely given, but the one getting help had an obligation to return favor when a crisis involved others. Another practice that developed in the Code of the West was that travelers could find shelter from storms or just to rest along the way with families of the community.

As the teacher for West Sedgwick School, Chloe extended the spirit of hospitality to the homes of the community, and with the approval of the School Board, the school continued as the center for community activities. The Royal Neighbor Society held meetings in the school to work on projects for the benefit of those in need.

Projects included making quilts, infant and child clothing, dresses for young ladies and even taking meals to shut ins.

In October 1899 Chloe confirmed that she was expecting an addition to the Foster family. She asked Ed to remain quiet about it until she began to show.

"I will talk to Amy and John Crow and I'm sure he will want to bring it up with the Board, when I am ready," Chloe stated.

Ed agreed, but he could not keep the ladies of the Royal Neighbors from guessing the coming event. At the November meeting projects for making Christmas dolls for girls and new shirts and clothing for boys were assigned, and names of school children were drawn by the ladies who were asked to make a suitable toy for the child whose name they had drawn. Near the end of that meeting Berta surprised the group when she asked Chloe "are you in a family way?" Chloe hesitated longer than Berta had patience.

"You are," Berta laughed.

"How could you tell?" Chloe asked.

"You have the look that women who are expecting get," Berta said, and the ladies of the meeting laughed.

"When is your due date?" Amy asked.

"It has been three months," Chloe answered. "So I think it will be May or June next year."

That will give us time to make nice things for your baby," Helen Buchanan stated. She gaveled the meeting to a close and the ladies gathered around Chloe to express their pleasure that a new infant was to be added to the Community.

"Do you need anything?" several ladies asked at once.

"I have most things I need," Chloe replied, "but I could use more diapers and a layette."

"I'll crochet a blanket," Amy stated, and several ladies said they could make various items for the baby.

One by one the ladies left the meeting talking excitedly about the coming event.

Christmas with Chloe Foster as teacher was a busy time at West Sedgwick School. There were decorations for the children to make and place on windows and walls, songs to learn, a program to rehearse, and a distribution of gifts for every student. Amy Crow and

Beth Homan came and assisted in these activities. Amy took charge of helping the students learn their parts for the Christmas program, and Beth worked with the student decorations. In a small somewhat isolated community Christmas programs were a highlight of the year. Everyone tried their best to make it so at West Sedgwick, but it was hard for Chloe to fully participate in the spirit of the season. She was experiencing spotting with cramps. Her morning sickness began early so that she felt nauseous and faint as early as her second month. By Christmas she was having heavy spotting and the Doctor was worried that she might not be able to carry the baby to term. The fetus was more restless than she had experienced with her other children.

"You must stay off your feet as much as possible. If I had my way you would stay in bed for the duration of this pregnancy," the Doctor seriously stated.

"How can I do that when I'm the only teacher the school has?" Chloe asked with some desperation.

"I'm sure the school would survive," Davis said, "but your health and the baby's are more important than the school."

"Doctor, I would rather keep this information quiet. I know I cannot keep Ed from knowing, but as the only teacher in the community, I feel that I must be present every possible day I am able."

"That's just it," Davis replied. "You must put your health and the health of your baby first. The Community will survive, but your present weakness in health may mean either you or the baby may not."

"Please, Doctor, I must fulfill my duties to the Community."

"All right," the Doctor acquiesced, "but promise me that you will stay in bed as much as possible, and that you will not be as active as I know you have been at school."

Chloe agreed, knowing that keeping her home up, and managing the school were tasks that required more of her energy than she felt she could give.

Chapter Twenty Two

While Chloe knew that her physical and emotional states were at a low ebb, there was no let up in the sense of anticipation or excitement for her children as they brought home patterns of stars and snowflakes, and how to make them that they had learned at school.

"This is fun mama," Katie said as she folded paper to make snowflakes. "We can make chains, and snowflakes, and strings of colored popcorn for our house just like we do at school."

"Yes, we can make our house as nice for Christmas as the school," Chloe replied. "Carrie, I will tell you the way to make flour paste, and you and the children can decorate our house."

Eleven year old Carrie followed her directions, and the children turned every free moment into making the decorations for their Christmas at home. Carrie was very much aware that her mother was resting more than usual, and she recognized that day by day her mother was asking her to manage the household more and more.

It was not possible to hide serious health events long from curious children who used the same outdoor toilets their parents did, and Carrie had seen the evidence of blood spotted clothing when she used the toilet. She knew better than to bring this up when the younger children were present, but she soon learned that Katie had seen them too, and for once Katie did not immediately ask her mother about it. Instead Katie asked her older sister for an explanation. Chloe had informed her daughters about the happenings of a young lady maturing, and Katie knew what to expect as she matured.

"Are you starting to have your monthlies?" Katie asked.

"No. why?" Carrie asked angrily.

"I saw some cloths with blood on them in the toilet," Katie said.

"Mama has been bleeding with this baby," Carrie answered, "and that's why she has to rest so much. We best not bother her any more than we have to, and it would be even better if we didn't talk too much about it."

Katie remained thoughtfully silent. She would remember in later years that this conversation helped her understand events that were soon to happen.

Decorations were put in place and the date for the School Christmas program came and went. People of the Community said it was "the nicest and loveliest program they had seen for a long time." Each grade of the school presented a part of the scripture that told about the birth of Jesus. A very brief version of "A Christmas Carol" was presented by the older children, and refreshments were served with a large Christmas cake that the Royal Neighbors had baked.

A school board meeting was held to discuss Chloe's pregnancy, and it was decided that she could continue teaching and that school would close two weeks early in the spring of 1900. At the March meeting of the Royal Neighbors discussion turned to Chloe's situation.

"Have you and Doctor Davis set a time for the baby's arrival?" Amy Crow asked Chloe.

"We think it will arrive about the mid week of May," Chloe replied "I have usually been on time with my children."

"Do you think you will be able to start the school year in September?" Frances Towne wanted to know.

"We'll have to take that up with the school board later." Amy stated. "Right now we are talking about getting things ready for the new baby. We also want to honor Mrs. Foster when school is out for the summer at our meeting in May. You all know that, as the teacher for West Sedgwick School she has done more than her share to bring enjoyment into the lives of all the children, and she has extended her talents to the whole Community. Since she has been here we have begun church services, we have had Community sings, and Chloe has been more than willing to help with these and other special occasions."

"She hasn't done all that by herself, you know," said Georgia Spafford. "We have all had a part in planning Community events."

"I grant you that," Amy replied, "but what were we doing as a Community before she arrived?"

There was silence for a short time, and Amy continued. "We were not a Community before Mrs Foster came. It seems appropriate to me that we form a committee to plan a day of honor for her before her baby arrives."

A committee was named and the next order of business centered in making things for the new mother and the baby.

The day chosen for honoring Mrs Foster was the Sunday after school had closed for the summer. On that afternoon The County Superintendent was the keynote speaker. She had gathered notes for her speech from former students and members of the community, and had been asked to present a plaque at the conclusion of her talk. A very much pregnant Chloe Foster was asked to come forward and accept the honor. She had known there would be a presentation and had appointed her daughter Carrie to accept in her stead, but the large audience was not going to be satisfied until they heard directly from her. She remained seated in her place at the front of the schoolroom and quietly made her remarks.

"I wish to thank the West Sedgwick School Board for giving me the opportunity and privilege of teaching in this school, but most of all I want to express my appreciation to the students, the mothers, and the men of the Community for their help in making this school a place where the pupils of West Sedgwick could learn. It has been a joy to see the growth and interest this Community has had in the education of its children."

"There are two ideals that a teacher must remember. First, each student has a desire to learn when challenged, and second, each student has a mind that can acquire knowledge. When lessons are presented in this context, both student and teacher can know the joy of learning. I am honored to accept your praises, but I would remind everyone here to keep a goal for the most education possible for the children of West Sedgwick Community. Thank you very much."

The Superintendent presented a plaque amid the cheers and clapping of the audience. In the place of Mrs. Foster, John Crow had been asked to present awards and certificates to the students who had achieved excellent ratings for their diligence in their studies. Ladies of the Community had prepared a reception with cookies and refreshments. The meeting closed with Chloe seated at the head of the reception line to receive the thanks of the Community. That night Chloe and Ed discussed their expectations for the future.

"Doc Davis spoke to me about your health at the meetin'," Ed said. "He thought you were weaker than you should be."

"What did he say?" Chloe asked knowing that the Doctor had told her he was very concerned about her times of hemorrhaging.

"He thought you lost too much blood and that you were anemic. He said that you barely had strength to deliver a baby. All along he said you needed a build up of iron in your system."

"Yes, I know," Chloe stated. "He has told me that I have lost too much blood and that I needed more red beets and other vegetables with our meals. Amy Crow and others of the Community have been supplying me with red beets and other vegetables they canned."

"No wonder we've been havin' so much of that," Ed replied. "Did Davis say anythin' about how healthy he thought you and the baby might be?"

Chloe was silent a long time before she replied and she spoke slowly. "He wouldn't say what might happen at the birth. The only thing he would say was that he thought I was in a very weakened condition and that he hoped I and the baby survived."

Ed sighed deeply and Chloe knew that he was not satisfied with her answer. She had come to depend on her children to keep the household in order, and had followed the Doctor's orders to stay in bed, to reduce the time she must spend on her feet. She was amazed that the children had prepared meals and for the care they had given her. She knew that she must reassure Ed that she was not afraid of the future for herself or her family.

"I understand the Doctor's concerns." she stated. "I would like for you and the children to accept what God has for our future. After the baby is born, I'll be able to teach just as before."

"We can be glad Carrie and Katie are old enough to help you." Ed stated after a moment of quiet.

"Willie does fine helping you with the outside chores," she reminded Ed. "Florence is just as demanding for attention as any normal two year old. We'll be just fine."

Ed nodded, but said nothing.

"How are you doing with your diet?" the Doctor asked on his next visit. "Have you rested as I told you to?"

"I feel very weak and I tire easily, but otherwise I feel fine," Chloe responded. "I haven't been so at peace in years. Ed is worried, but he needn't be as worried as he is."

"Ed's a good man, but he's exactly that," Davis stated. "Like most men he does not understand the needs of a pregnant woman. You must make him understand that you need special care and attention at this time."

After the Doctor had talked to Chloe, he went to the corral and talked to Ed.

"Ed, your wife's situation is very serious. She is not a strong woman, and she could lose this baby or, if worst came to worst, she could die in childbirth. I think it best you understand that, because you must not make demands for her to wait on you, and you must see that the children follow your example."

"I'll do my best to make her as comfortable as I can," Ed stated.

When the Doctor had gone Ed found a time to talk with Chloe.

"I'm glad we're havin' another child," he said.

Chloe read deep concern in his voice and expression.

"There is nothing anyone can do to change the course of nature," she said. "Women have been having babies since the beginning of time. I have a strong belief that God is in control of our lives, and whatever happens, He is in control. "Do you believe in God?"

There was the same reluctance to answer that Ed had shown in times past, and there was a long silence before Ed replied.

"I believe there is a God. He lets things happen and He can make things happen. I can't believe that a God of love would take the life of a child like Franklin before he had a chance to grow up. A God who loves would not have made life the hell on earth it is, but I do believe that God brought you into my life."

Chloe carefully considered a reply. "The God I know understands all things. I believe human life is more than a struggle to provide the things we eat and the things we wear. To me people are his creation and are not just 'beasts of the field.' God gave man his soul so that he could respond to others and to the God who made him. He gave man a spirit so that man could communicate with Him in prayer, and so man could feel his love as He cares for us. He gave us His love in the person of His Son"

"I love you more than I can ever tell, and I love our children. To me love is a person that I can see and talk to face to face. I can't love anythin' I can't see. God is real to you and I love you for that, but my life had very little love in it before I met you. I guess I don't disbelieve, but I don't feel the personal presence of God like you do."

Chloe was not depressed by Ed's statement, but deep within she wished that he could believe that God did love him, even when he found survival on this prairie to be most difficult. She knew that she could not convince him by argument, and for that reason she did not wish to continue a conversation that he had not responded to in the past. In silent prayer she asked God to 'have His way in Ed's life.'

April passed and the Foster family tried to bring the presence of blossoming flowers and spring to Chloe who was now spending most of her days in bed. Nearly every day the children brought her bouquets of primrose, wallflower and pussy willow buds. For every show of love for their mother, Chloe was thankful, and expressed love for their thoughtfulness. She pointed them to the God who made such a beautiful world.

Before dawn May twenty third, Chloe knew that the baby was going to arrive. Her contractions were hard, often and painful and her bed was soaked in blood. Unconsciously she moaned in pain with each recurring spasm and contraction.

"Ed...you best...go for the...Doctor. Send Carrie...for Amy Crow." Ed tried to comfort her but realized she was in labor.

"Hurry." Chloe was panting for breath and moaning.

Ed dressed and hurried to awaken the children. He told Carrie to dress quickly while he went to saddle the horse and prepare the buggy. He then directed Carrie to ride to the Crow's for Amy. and an hour later Amy and Carrie arrived to find Chloe semiconscious with three frightened children standing by her bed.

"Katie and Willie, take Florence and see that there is a fire in the stove. Put on a kettle of water to heat. The Doctor will be here soon and we must have hot water," Amy directed as she set about bathing Chloe and cleaning the bed. While she was doing this she became aware that Chloe was silent. She felt her pulse and found it very weak. Amy and Carrie began massaging her arms and legs hoping to improve circulation.

About ten thirty Doctor Davis arrived and took charge. He produced a bottle of a brown liquid and poured some in a glass. He raised Chloe's head and put it to her lips. She revived enough to drink it, and shortly afterward seemed slightly more alert.

"Chloe, if we bring this baby into the world, you must help all you can," Davis said. He felt her pulse and found a medium strong response. Chloe opened her eyes and saw the Doctor. Doctor…I'm…glad…you're…here." She had trouble getting her breath between words.

"It's going to take all the strength you have to get this baby born. Do you understand?"

Chloe nodded weakly.

"You've got to breathe and push. I will say breathe and then push, and you must do as I say. Do you understand.?"

Again Chloe nodded and the Doctor started a regular rhythm of saying breathe and push. The Doctor realized that he must let her rest for short intervals. A half hour passed. The children tried to enter the bedroom, and the Doctor ordered Ed to keep them out. Amy went to the opposite side of the bed, and she and the Doctor rubbed Chloe's arms and legs. Chloe gave a loud cry and the head of the baby appeared. The Doctor continued his voice commands and within a few minutes a baby girl was born. The umbilical cord was severed and tied and the Doctor handed the new born to Amy for its cleaning. At first he thought that Chloe had fainted, and tried all he knew to revive her. He worked with her for more than an hour, but could get no pulse or breathing response. Ed had replaced Amy at the bedside rubbing Chloe's arms. He knew that Chloe was making no response.

"For the love of God, Doc, keep trying," His voice was hoarse with emotion, and panic.

"I'm doing all I know to do," Davis replied.

Finally the Doctor rose to his feet, looked at Ed while shaking his head, and left the bedroom. Ed lay beside his inert wife, held her hand and began sobbing and babbling a kind of sing song mixture of love words for his wife and invective against her God who let her die.

Amy had cleaned the baby and soon everyone within hearing knew baby Myrtie was blessed with a voice.

Warm water was poured into the wash basin and the Doctor washed up. He then went to the bed and put his hand on Ed's shoulder. Ed rose to his feet, and turned his frustration and blame to the Doctor.

"If you knew more than a country Doctor, you could have saved her," he said bitterly.

"No one on this earth could have done more than I did," Davis stated. He directed Ed to the table.

"Ed I need your help in filling out the death certificate. The time of death was about 11:31 AM. I will need the names of your surviving children, and your signature."

Davis produced papers on which he began to write. Ed sat opposite and answered the doctor's questions numbly.

"What name were you going to call this baby?"

"Myrtie Chloe." Ed softly replied remembering the name he and Chloe had selected.

There were more questions about the family which Ed answered When the Doctor finished he rose and shook Ed's hand.

"I will send men from Sedgwick to remove your wife's body as soon as we get back to town." Doctor Davis packed his bags and waited for Ed to drive him to Sedgwick.

Before Ed left with the Doctor, he asked Mrs Crow to take the children to the Crow home. Amy said that she would and added that she would return to see that everything was cleaned. The children had gone to the bedroom where they stood beside the body of their mother and wept. Katie took her mother's hand and felt the cool absence of life. Amy called to them and soon they were on their way to the Crow farm. About an hour later Amy went by the Homan farm to see if Mrs Homan could help her, and together they returned to the Fosters where they sadly cleaned the body and the bed. Each woman stopped often and wiped away tears.

Driving to Sedgwick was a sad experience for Ed. Two thoughts were in his mind.

"Why God, why? Why now, God?" He asked the Doctor those questions, but Davis was at a loss for an answer.

"Why did she have to die now? She done so well as the West Sedgwick teacher, and our family was doin' so well."

At this time Davis put an arm around Ed's shoulders, but remained quiet for a time.

"These things happen and I never know why," the Doctor replied. "I do know that you must go on with your children, especially now that you have a new baby girl."

For a time the only sound was the noise the horse and buggy made on the dry trail.

"In all my years of practice I don't believe I have had to fill out a death certificate and a birth certificate in the same day," the Doctor stated as they arrived at his office. "Ed, I want you to know that I respected your wife a great deal, and I feel great sympathy for you."

Dazed and silent Ed nodded, but seemed to be walking in a dream. He followed the Doctor while he made arrangements to have Chloe's body removed from the Foster home. The Doctor went to the Reverend Ford, and Ed accompanied him. The Reverend agreed to preach the funeral eulogy and asked Ed a few questions which he answered briefly. He could give no information regarding the future of his children and only nodded in tacit agreement when the Minister said he would talk that over with the ladies of the Church.

In late afternoon Ed returned to a silent and empty house where all things seemed to be in order, but there was deep sorrow and loneliness there. He wandered from room to room, and finally sat alone in darkened silence beside the bed where his wife had died.

Chapter Twenty Three

Three days later a sad and frightened father with four weeping children stood at their mother's graveside while The Reverend Earl Ford gave the eulogy and read the Twenty Third Psalm. His closing prayer named the five children who had lost their mother, and Ed who had lost his beloved wife. The wooden casket was lowered into the grave as the small group of neighbors came and spoke their condolences to Ed and the children. Prairie hardened settlers with tears came and silently nodded as they shook Ed's hand. Amy Crow stood with the family holding the new born baby. After the ceremony the children solemnly gathered around her to see their baby sister. Slowly Ed moved to the group and accepted the baby, quietly turned and handed her to Carrie. Mrs Taylor came and told the group that a luncheon had been prepared for them at the at the Community Church.

"The ladies of the church asked me to tell you of their sorrow at this time," she said. "Your wife was greatly loved by all of us, and her passing is a great loss to the Community. Come to the church when you are ready."

Ed nodded that he would as the funeral entourage departed the cemetery. Workmen were standing by to close the grave as the saddened family stood at the graveside until Carrie brought them to the reality that it was time to leave.

"Papa, we must go now," she said.

Ed roused from his reverie of sorrow, and saw that they were the last people at the cemetery. Katie led the way to the buggy and the family made its way to the Community Church. After they had eaten, Mrs McAllister, who had helped serve the luncheon, asked Ed to meet with The Reverend Ford and a group of community ladies who were concerned about the future of the family. She led him to a small room where Amy Crow, Reverend Ford and two other ladies Ed did not know were seated in a semicircle.

"We do not wish to intrude in your sorrow, Ed," The Reverend began, "but we feel there is a matter of your family's well being that must be discussed, and that there are decisions that must be made."

Reverend Ford paused, as Ed sat in stiff silence.

The Pastor had been hardened to his own feelings of sympathy through many years of bearing sad news. The method he had chosen to bring the unfortunate to face their dilemmas was to repeat what he had said and then get to the difficult decisions that must be faced.

"We all understand your bereavement at this time," He stated, "but there is the question of the need for you to make decisions about your children."

He looked around the group and the ladies of the Committee nodded approval as he continued, "We, of the Benevolence Committee, recognize your circumstances. We know that you will be unable to continue living in the West Sedgwick School facilities now that your wife has passed on, and we are aware that for you to return to your one room dugout with your five children is impossible."

He paused waiting for Ed to respond, but Ed glanced at each of the nodding ladies and said nothing.

"Our concern is the five children that are now your sole responsibility," he continued. His words and manner suggested that the Benevolence Committee had already reached a decision. "We can find temporary homes for the children with families in the Community, but you must contact relatives and friends for their more permanent homes. If you have not thought about the urgency of this problem, our Committee is prepared to assist you in the placement of your children with willing families in the community."

Ed lowered his head and his shoulders slumped as though he were pondering a problem for which he did not have an answer. Amy Crow came and put a hand on his shoulder.

"I can take care of Carrie, Katie, Willie, Florence and little Myrtie for a week or so, and I will gladly do that, but you must realize that we all have our own families to look after." Amy patted Ed's shoulder and returned to her chair.

The Committee members nodded their heads in agreement as Amy sat down. There was an expectant silence in the room as the Committee waited for Ed to speak. Ed said nothing.

"Do you have relatives or friends nearby who would be willing to take one or two of your children?" Reverend Ford asked.

"No," Ed stated softly, "I suppose I could ask my mother to stay and help Amy Crow with the children for a while."

Committee members frowned indicating their feeling that Ed did not understand the magnitude of his problem. The Reverend Ford rose and extended his hand to Ed as he spoke.

"You know that time is of the essence for the children and for you, Ed." Ed did not shake the offered hand. "We feel that two weeks should be time enough for you to get your children settled in good homes. If you do not communicate your wishes to us in three weeks, we will take that to mean that you were unsuccessful and we will meet with you again for the decisions we must make." The Reverend again offered his hand and Ed shook it.

The Benevolence Committee rose, which signaled that the meeting concerning Ed's dilemma was finished for the time being. The Reverend motioned that Ed could leave the room and he silently left the room.

True to her word Amy Crow gathered the children and took them to her home. Ed drove back to the West Sedgwick house that his family had shared at the School. There were lonely echoes of happy and sad memories in that house for him now. The words he spoke to himself seemed to echo off the barren walls. He could not sleep in the room where Chloe had died, nor did he wish to remain in the house that night. Dismally he returned to the dugout where he unhitched his horse and turned it into the corral without removing the harness. He dazedly walked around the whole land that was the homestead, not realizing the passage of time or what he needed to do. About two in the morning he arrived at the haystack where he lay down and slept. In the morning Tom Kaschke came and found Ed asleep. Tom roused him and the two men drove to the West Sedgwick School where they met John Crow. John and Tom helped him move his family possessions to the dugout.

"This place is kind of small for a family," John said as he walked into the dugout. "Too bad the prairie fire destroyed the frame part of the building."

John changed the subject. "Amy and I are glad to have your children and their grandma at our house. She helps with the children, and Amy needs her, what with the added work with the children"

Central City Grandma had come for the funeral and had remained at the Crows with the children since then. "Amy wants you to come for Sunday dinner tomorrow, and your mother needs to talk to you about the children," John added.

The prospect of having a discussion did not appeal to Ed, but he knew he could not refuse the invitation.

"I'll be there," he replied without enthusiasm.

He arrived at the Crow home at noon the next day. His mother had always been one to get to the point, and before the meal was over she brought up the welfare of the children.

"Before I left Central City, I talked with two cousins who were willing to take one little girl." Julia said. "One of the families is a distant cousin of Edith Norton The husband's name is George and the wife's is Hazel. They have no children and would be willing to take baby Myrtie. The other family is a Swedish family who live in Stromsburg, Nebraska. They had a girl about Katie's age who died a year ago. Their child was about the same size as Katie and was blonde with blue eyes similar to Katie's. They would love to have Katie in their daughter's place. Two older Norton spinster ladies have said they would be willing to accept Carrie."

When Ed nodded but did not verbally respond, she continued.

"As far as Willie is concerned, I was not able to find anyone willing to take him in."

Again Ed nodded, but made no reply.

"Regarding Florence, I have no idea where she can go. The families I talked to were not willing to take a two year old."

"Chicago Grandma wrote that she would be willing to talk about that when she arrives a week from today," Ed stated.

"Should I write the Nortons that we have agreed that Carrie, and baby Myrtie will be placed with them?"

"I suppose I have no other choice," Ed replied. There was despair, weariness along with defeat in his tone.

Chicago Grandma arrived on schedule, and Ed and his mother met her in Sedgwick.

"What have you decided about the children?" She asked when they were in the buggy on the way to the Crow farm.

"Carrie and the baby will be placed with my distant cousins at Central City, Nebraska," Julia stated. "Katie will be with a Swedish family in Stromsburg, Nebraska where she will take the place of a daughter who died last year. We have not found a home for Willie."

"Willie will stay with me." There was a firmness and finality in Ed's tone which had been lacking since Chloe died.

"I'll be happy to have Florence in my home as Franklin and I just have Cora with us." Myrtie stated. "Cora will soon be married. Franklin's new commodities business keeps him busy, and I would love to have a young child in our home for company."

During the next week, Carrie, Katie, Florence and baby Myrtie were housed at the Kaschkes while their bags were packed, and they were made ready to travel to Central City, Nebraska. On Saturday their belongings were loaded in the wagon and Ed drove them along with Central City Grandma to the train station in Sedgwick. Tearful goodbyes were said and they were on their way never to be united again as a complete family. Chicago Grandma and Florence left for Chicago the next week.

There was no real place for Willie to sleep at the dugout, and Ed seemed not to care about fixing anything for meals except pancakes for breakfast and biscuits and gravy for their other meals. Tom Kaschke was the first to observe that there was no companionship between Ed and Willie, and that Ed treated him worse than he would a hired man. When Tom tried to talk to Ed, he was told that it was nobody's "damn business." Tom thought Ed's problem was related to Chloe's death and stated that he felt Ed should talk to someone about that.

"My feelings about my wife's passing are none of anybody else's business, and I would just as soon that you don't bring that up again."

Community concern over Willie spread as Ed took him to work for valley farmers. These men had sons of their own whom they would not put to work the way Ed did Willie. When anyone tried to talk to Ed about the need for a boy to be a boy, and that he should not work Willie the way he did, they received the same kind of rebuff Tom Kaschke had.

"Willie is my son. I don't tell you how to treat your boys, and I'd appreciate it if you would keep your comments to yourself."

"I don't ask my son Jordan, three years older than Willie, to do what you make Willie do," Tom told Ed one day when he saw Ed and Willie pitching hay like two men. Willie had tried to lift a forkful of hay that was too heavy for him and Ed berated him for being "no good for help."

"Ed, I'm tellin' you Willie is just a boy. You expect him to do as much as you do, and if you watch, you can see that he ain't strong enough to do such heavy work," Tom said.

"Tom, how I treat Willie is nobody's damn business. I told you before about interferin' in my business Now leave me the hell alone."

Two years went quickly by with neighbors talking of the lack of understanding between Ed and Willie. Things were different for Amy Crow. At every opportunity she invited Willie to stay with their family, and treated him as one of her own children. She knew that it would only cause Ed to turn against her if she tried to talk to him about Willie, so she never mentioned her feelings to either Willie or Ed. For his part Willie tried every way he knew to please his father, even to doing chores before Ed came home.

Amy had continued to invite Ed and Willie for meals with their family, and she unobtrusively tried to get Ed to talk about his feelings to no avail. In the meantime, she wrote to Chicago Grandma expressing her concern for these two forlorn souls, and to Ed's surprise, Chicago Grandma arrived at the Crow's.

A foreclosure notice had been posted on the Foster homestead because Ed had failed to pay his taxes. It became imperative for him to go to the County seat or lose his homestead. He felt that he had no choice, but to leave Willie at the dugout to do the chores for the one day he decided to take care of the taxes. He asked Chicago Grandma to come and stay with Willie while he was away. When Amy Crow heard of his plans, she told John that a twelve year old boy should not be given that kind of responsibility. John decided to talk to Ed.

"My boys are more used to handling horses than Willie is," John Crow stated, "and besides they are older than Willie."

"John I want Willie to learn how to work like I had to," Ed replied with surliness.

"You told me that you were fourteen when you went to work on your Uncle Johnny's farm," John said. "Willie is two years younger than you were. Anyway, I have seen you work the horses he will have to take care of, and they are not gentle enough for a twelve year old."

Ed was adamant and would not agree that Willie would need help. John and Amy discussed Ed's attitude later and decided that he had silenced them. Chicago Grandma stated her feelings the evening before Ed departed.

"Ed, I don't feel comfortable with Willie having to do the chores," she said, "especially the way John and Amy talked about it. Shouldn't you have asked Tom or one of John Crow's boys to come and help Willie?"

"I've had Willie with me nearly every day since Chloe passed away, an' I think I know pretty well what he can do. I know the neighbors talk about how I treat him, but I want Willie to be tough enough to take care of himself if anythin' happened to me."

"I think you are making a mistake," Grandma said, "but he is your boy, and I am only his grandmother. I will do the best I can to take care of things while you are away."

Ed left early the next morning.

Willie was able to do the morning chores without incident. Grandma stood outside the corral fence and watched as Willie led each horse to the watering trough, and waited with him while he milked the cow. She helped him pitch hay to the livestock, and feed the chickens. Ed had told Willie to let the horses stay in the corral for the day and Willie and Grandma watched as the animals fed and roamed around the corral. They spent the rest of the day enjoying one another's company as they walked out on the prairie and Willie told about the prairie flowers and animals they saw.

"How did you learn the names of all these things?" Grandma asked in wonder at his knowledge.

"My mother taught them to me." Willie replied. "Mama would walk with all of us and teach us. Even at night we would go outside and mama taught us about the stars."

"You must have loved your mother very much."

There was a long pause before Willie spoke, and when he did there were tears and a sob.

"I loved my mother more than I ever told anyone," Willie replied.

"Do you miss your sisters?"

"Yes," Willie answered quickly. "I wish we could be together again real soon. We are not a family anymore."

"It must be pretty hard for you living alone with your father."

"Yes, it is." Grandma could see that Willie was trying to be composed. She drew him into her arms and he put his head on her breast and sobbed out his sorrow. She hugged him until his sobbing ceased, and he withdrew from her embrace.

"I try to do what papa wants me to," he said, "but I know I'm not as strong or tough as he wants me to be."

"Your father is a good man. He hasn't gotten over his wife's death, nor have I my daughter's death, but when he can see that God knows what is best, then he'll settle down. Right now he only sees the blame and sorrow he feels for Chloe's death. Do you believe in God?" She asked gently.

"Yes I do," Willie replied. "Mama taught all of us to believe that God sent His son to save us. I wish papa believed that too."

"Maybe he will someday."

Grandma and Willie spent the rest of the day visiting and walking around the homestead. Though Willie had always been quiet in her presence she found him to be articulate about his sisters and his mother. She enjoyed listening to him as he related the way his mother taught school and the things she did for the Community. She was interested to hear that he had been bitten by a prairie rattler, and that his sister, Carrie knew what to do. He told about their pony and the dog named Shep and the fun the children had with them. Evening came and it was time for the chores.

Willie methodically went about throwing hay to the livestock. He carried two forkfuls to the center of the corral and had gotten the third. As he walked away from the feeding animals, the most recent horse Ed had traded for suddenly kicked without warning. The hoof hit Willie squarely just below his left shoulder blade. Willie pitched forward and lay bleeding and gasping for breath while that horse bit and kicked other horses in a fit of wild rage.

"Willie, oh Willie," Grandma screamed. She went to the Gate and rushed to the place where Willie lay. The horses were biting and kicking along the corral fence.

"I tried…grandma…I tried." Willie said and lapsed into silence.

Grandma Myrtie lifted him gently and took him inside the dugout where she laid him on the bed. She made him as comfortable as she could. She knew he had broken ribs because he was bleeding and frothing from the mouth, and she hoped that she had not caused greater damage to his wounds by carrying him to the dugout.

"I had no choice" she repeated to herself, "there was nothing else I could do. Poor, poor Willie."

All during the night she kept cool cloths on Willie's brow. She was afraid to remove his shirt lest she injure him further. His bleeding had soaked his shirt and began to soak the bed. Grandma alternately wept and prayed until she heard a horse ride into the yard sometime before dawn. She met Ed at the door.

"Ed, Willie was kicked by a horse," she stated wearily.

"Where is he?" Ed asked.

"He's in the bed." Grandma was sobbing softly.

Ed went into the dugout and knelt beside the bed in the dim lamplight. Grandma stood beside him. Willie groaned and mumbled something they did not understand. He opened his eyes and saw his father, and tried to lift himself from the bed, but he could not.

"Papa…I tried…to do what…you said." He grimaced as he reached his hand out to his father. Ed grasped the hand and held it to his lips, tears streaming from his eyes.

"Son…I'm…sorry," he could say no more.

Willie's grip on his father's hand loosened. His breathing stopped and there was no other sound but the sobbing of his father who had knelt beside the bed and grandma standing beside him.

For a long moment Ed stayed beside the bed and sobbed in agonized grief.

"I'm sorry…God how sorry I am…It's my fault…"

Chicago Grandma knelt beside him. She put her arm across Ed's shoulders and softly prayed. When she finished she stood and drew Ed to his feet. For a time they stood weeping in shared grief. Finally Grandma tried to give further comfort to him.

"Ed, I can't tell you how sorry I am. Don't be too hard on yourself. No one could have known this would happen. We must go on. There are things we must do. Have you put your horse away?"

Ed shook his head that he had not.

"While you take care of your horse and the chores, I'll see to Willie. The cow was not milked last night and there are chores to do. We must notify the Doctor as soon as we can." She stopped speaking as though there was nothing more for her to say.

Ed moved to do the chores as though he were a robot and could not think for himself. When he was finished, he returned to the dugout and quietly sat down forlornly giving the impression there was nothing else to do. Chicago Grandma gave him a cup of coffee and a buttered biscuit. When he finished, he went outside and hitched Dusty to the buggy and they left to make arrangements for another Foster funeral.

At the funeral service neighborhood children spoke of Willie as a quiet boy who was a good boy to play with because he was always fair. The children who accompanied the funeral procession openly wept for their lost friend. No one spoke about the circumstances of Willie's death, and few came and expressed their feelings to Ed. Nebraska relatives wired condolences with their regrets that they could not attend the service because of the urgency of farm needs. Chloe's mother returned to Chicago after Willie's funeral, and a broken, morose and uncommunicative father returned to the dugout where his son had died.

Tom and Berta Kaschke could see the figure of a man moving about at the Foster place, but Tom remembered the rebuff he had been given and did not venture to see how his neighbor was doing.

Chapter Twenty Four

It was as though Ed hibernated after Willie's funeral. Few neighbors saw him, and fewer called him for work. When he did go to a farm to work, he was surly and sorrowful. Berta Kaschke renewed her concern for him, but Tom refused to have any part in showing kindness to him. Berta felt that Ed needed someone to talk to, but Tom was the one who rebuffed Ed. Berta would not let Tom continue to react in that way for very long.

"Tom, we can't just leave Ed alone in that dugout prison he has made for himself." Berta urged one day.

"Seems to me he has turned away from every friend he ever had. I don't see why I should spend time with a man who don't give a damn about old friends," Tom replied.

"When I was a girl in Ohio, one of my uncles acted the same way when his wife died. One morning my father went to talk with him and found that he had hanged himself in the barn," Berta answered. "I think more of Chloe than to risk doing nothing and letting her husband do that. I want you to take me over to the Foster dugout every morning so we can see that he is all right. True, we owe him nothing but friendship."

Tom reluctantly agreed, and every morning when he was not busy, he drove her to the Foster place. They built a fire and made coffee, and Berta served buttered biscuits for all three. At first Ed accepted the coffee, but refused the biscuits. Berta would not permit one of her children to refuse eating, and she was determined to see that Ed ate at least once a day.

"Now see here, Ed Foster, no one blames you for anything that has happened in your family, and there's no reason that you should blame yourself. I know that Chloe would see that you ate at least once a day, and I can do no less."

For several minutes Ed sat with the coffee cup in his hands, and said nothing. Tom rose, approached Ed and put a hand on his shoulder. Ed bowed his head, and wept bitter tears all the while gasping phrases that expressed his inner feelings.

"My fault…Chloe Myrtie. Doc told me dangerous…too weak. She wanted every child. Should have stopped with Franklin…My God…my God…poor Franklin…My fault…my fault…Poor Willie…"

"Willie was a fine boy, Ed," Tom hoped to lift Ed's spirit. "It's a damn shame. No one could've stopped that horse. Nobody can tell what a horse will do."

"Tom, I had no choice," Ed stated as he lifted his head and seemed to be seeking understanding. "I shouldn't've left Chicago Grandma alone…Poor, poor, Willie."

"I could've come over, Ed. You know how I feel about neighbors helpin' out."

"I know, and I respect you for that. Tom when I traded for that horse, the trader told me he was gentle with children. How could I know that he was that wild?"

The bond between Tom and Ed grew stronger over the next two years. Slowly Ed began to accept the Kaschkes' hospitality, and began eating the evening meal with them. When Tom needed extra help, he called on Ed, but Ed seldom left the dugout without Tom. He lived as a recluse, and never spent more than a few minutes with anyone who stopped by. Even John Crow was not exempt from Ed's rejection on his last attempt to lift Ed out of his "blues."

"Ed, I just want you to know that Amy and I care about you," John stated on his last visit to the dugout.

"John your wife was in the meetin' at the church where they decided that I couldn't take care of my family." Ed stated.

"Yes, I know," Tom replied, "but you got to realize that you couldn't keep those girls here in this dingy dugout. Carrie was near the age of becomin' a young woman, and as far as the church people could see, you had no way to take care of a new born baby girl."

"It was nobody's damn business but mine," Ed replied. "Carrie was old enough to take care of Florence and the baby with Katie's help. Willie would've been all right. Those meddlin' women and that hypocrite preacher forced me to give my family to people I didn't know. I can't forget that"

"Ed, I've been the best friend to you I could be," John replied, "but I'll be damned if I'll let you speak that way. My wife Amy was a member of the Benevolence Committee an' they did the best they could for your girls. Looks to me like you could have done better by Willie yourself than you did."

Ed was silent for a time before he replied. His face whitened in anger and he clenched and unclenched his fists.

"Leave me the hell alone," Ed shouted in cold fury. "If I want to talk to you about what I do or have done with my family, it'll be a cold day in hell. All of you do gooders in the community know what's best for me, and I'll thank you to keep your opinions to yourself."

"I'm sorry you feel that way," John said as he mounted his horse. "I'm sorry you have turned your back on the people who could help you the most." John rode away without saying another word.

Two years turned to three and Ed's contact with anyone other than Tom and Berta was by mail. During those years he received letters from Carrie and Katie, and he answered them. Each letter he received was a reminder of his helplessness to change his family's situation. He barely functioned as a human being until he received a letter from Katie that roused him to action.

Stromsburg, Nebraska
May 5, 1905

Dear Papa,

  I am going to run away unless you come and bring me home. I know that I am old enough to take care of myself. I can't stand to stay here another week.

  Please write and tell me if you can come and get me. I will wait until next Monday.

I remain your daughter,
Katie Foster

Ed knew that Katie meant every word she had written, and he determined to let no time pass without letting her know what he planned to do. He arranged with Tom Kaschke to take care of his chores and left early the next morning to go to Sedgwick to catch the train for Central City, Nebraska. He sent a telegram to Katie before he left Sedgwick.

Sedgwick May 9 1905 Katie Foster Stromsburg, Nebr
Will arrive Stromsburg, Friday STOP
                    Papa

When he arrived in Stromsburg, Ed went to the livery and rented a horse and buggy. He arrived at the Wegthe farm at twelve o'clock. Katie must have been watching to see when he drove into the yard. She ran to the buggy and vaulted into the seat beside Ed. She alternately laughed, cried and hugged her father. Ed drove the buggy to the corral, and Mr. Wegthe came from the barn and greeted them.

"Mister Foster, I'm glad to meet you." There was a decided Swedish accent in his greeting. "Ve try to teach Katie Svedish so she could be our little girl, but she vould not."

"I learned a lot of Swedish," Katie defended herself. Mister Wegthe did not answer her.

"You come in house. I introduce you to Missus." Ed and Katie followed Sven.

There were tears in Mrs Wegthe's eyes as she was introduced to Ed. "All I vanted vass for Katie to be mine liddle girl. Our Katinka died six year ago. Ve thought Katie could be our girl."

Katie would not leave her father's side as he and Mister Wegthe went to tend the horse.

That done, they returned to the house where Mrs. Wegthe invited them to have lunch.

"You stay the night vith us," Mrs Wegthe stated after they had eaten, but Ed shook his head negatively before he replied.

"We want to get an early start for the drive to Nortons in the morning," Ed answered. "We will stay in Stromsburg tonight."

Ed sounded more firm than he had been for months. "Katie and I want to visit family in Central City. We will talk to them about the best thing to do, and we will let you know what we decide."

Katie had packed her things in the same suitcase which she had when she arrived five years before, and she placed it firmly in the buggy. Mrs Wegthe openly wept as they thanked her for the lunch and were seated in the buggy. They drove to Stromsburg where Ed rented two rooms. Early the next morning they drove to Central City.

Sunday there was a family gathering at the Jason Norton farm, and for the first time in more than five years, Ed and three members of his family were together. Baby Myrtie was now four and a half years old, and Carrie had become a young lady. She had finished one year of Normal School and had accepted a teaching position in a one room school near Central City. Myrtie was a lively, into everything, child who demanded her share of attention from everyone. At first Carrie was reserved and aloof from her father. Carrie and Katie talked together as long separated sisters would who had not seen one another for years.

A meeting in the bunkhouse where Ed had stayed when he first arrived at the farm brought Ed to a decision. He called the girls together and was hesitant about how to begin.

"Papa, I'm so glad you came," Carrie stated.

"Me too," Katie said, "I couldn't have stayed at the Wegthes another night. Their son, Olaf wouldn't leave me alone, and Mrs Wegthe cried every time she mentioned Katinka."

"Katie wrote and asked me to come so we could decide whether she should stay here or go back to Colorado with me," Ed told Carrie.

"Papa what I said in my letter was that I would run away if you didn't come and get me," Katie said petulantly, "and I meant it too."

"Honey I want all you girls to come live with me," Ed said, "but the way I live right now would not be a good place for you."

"It's not good for me here either," Katie stated with disappointment. "Old lady Wegthe always wants to hug and kiss me while she cries and says 'Katinka, my little Katinka.' Olaf waits for me and grabs me where I don't want to be grabbed," she paused as a sly smile crept over her face. "One time I hit him with a milk pail when he was trying to grab me."

"Carrie, how are you gettin' on with the Norton ladies?"

"They are good to me, but they think I'm an old maid like they are. They make over old clothes of theirs for my dresses and when I wear them to school, the other girls laugh at me."

"They give me dollies," Myrtie said. "I tease them."

"What do you young ladies think we should do?" Ed asked.

"I told you what I want, papa." Katie said. "I want to go home, and live with you forever."

"Carrie, is there a better time for you to come home?"

"I want to be with you and Katie more than anything, but I must stay in Nebraska next year. I signed a teaching contract for the Platte School three miles west of here. It wouldn't be right if I didn't keep that commitment."

"I want to be with Carrie," Myrtie stated.

After Ed discussed his family situation with his mother and the Jason Nortons, he decided that Katie could go home with him, and that Carrie and Myrtie would stay in Nebraska for the next year. When Ed told his mother his decision, she berated him.

"Ed Foster, you must be out of your mind," she fumed. "You have no place to keep your family. You must rent a house before you will have a fit place for them. That dugout of yours is not fit for a prairie dog to live in. I don't see how you can stand it yourself."

If her desire had been to make Ed feel trapped by the situation, she couldn't have done it better.

"There's one thing for sure," he said. "Katie is going back to Colorado with me."

"If you rent a house in Sedgwick, I will come and be your housekeeper," Julia stated. "But I certainly will not allow you to take any of your children if you intend to keep them in that foul smelling home you call a dugout."

Ed felt the old tightness in his throat, just as he had when he was a child and his mother turned her back on him when she left him in Vermont in the home of her father.

"I know that Mrs Crow or Berta Kaschke would be glad to have Katie with them until I can get a place for us." Ed stated. "I showed Berta Kaschke Katie's letter and she blessed my comin' to bring her back. She will temporarily take her in and be glad for her."

Privately Ed made it a point to find time to talk to his mother about decisions that were his and his alone to make.

"Mother, I want you to know that I have certainly appreciated everything you did for Chloe and the children," Ed said with sincerity. "I am glad to listen to what Jason an' Edith think, an' I want to know your advice. There's one thing I want you to know. I make the final decision for my girls."

Ed knew that his mother was upset at those words, and in order to avoid a long drawn out scene, he added. "I respect you as the children's grandma, an' when I put you in charge of them, I'll back you all the way when you give them orders, but right now I'm in charge of doin' what I think is best."

"Ed Foster," Julia's face was flushed with anger and her hands trembled as she continued, "I never thought I'd see the day when my upstart son would show such an attitude toward me." Tears came to her eyes. "I will say no more about what you do with your girls."

Central City Grandma left the door open for further discussions in the future as she added, "unless you find you need me to help raise them, and that's final."

"I appreciate that," Ed stated inwardly smiling because he knew "final" did not mean final.

Before Ed and Katie left for Colorado, Katie wrote a letter to the Wegthes telling them that she was returning to Colorado with her father. Two days later Ed and Katie boarded the train in Central City, Nebraska and returned to Sedgwick, Colorado.

During the year Katie was in Colorado, she spent three months with the Kaschke family, three months with the Crow family and four months with the Homans. Toward the end of the year Ed rented a small house on the edge of Sedgwick where he could keep horses. For Katie it was the most pleasant time she had experienced since she had returned to Sedgwick. She had found girls her age in Sedgwick and began spending time with them. Many evenings Ed would return home to find a note saying Katie was visiting her friends. He soon realized she needed more supervision than he could give and wrote his mother asking her to come and be his housekeeper mentioning that Katie needed a woman in the house.

In the summer of 1906 Julia, Carrie and Myrtie came home to Sedgwick, and any thought Ed may have had for a peaceful life was shattered. Julia Foster had never learned to adjust her thinking to anyone. She had learned to be silent when she lived with relatives, but she lacked patience, and she had never encountered children who were independent in their behavior and attitude as were Katie and Myrtie. It seemed to her that Carrie was the only one who had a settled personality. Katie's year of freedom enhanced her attitude of outspokenness and extreme independence. The two of them together was like pouring oil on a fire, and before long there was open warfare between them. There was no asking for permission in Katie's mind.

"I'm going to meet my friends now," Katie said as she was at the door ready to leave.

"Katie Foster, you're just like your father. He would never listen to a thing I tried to tell him," Grandma replied. "I want you to stay and help Carrie with the housework."

"I can't," Katie replied. "I told Helen Buckman I would come to her house." Saying that Katie slammed the door and left.

"That girl will come to no good end," Grandma predicted to no one in particular. "She's sowing a whirlwind and she'll reap nothing but trouble."

That evening when Ed returned from work on the Jumbo reservoir, Grandma stated her feelings heavy with disapproval for his handling of his daughter.

"Katie is the most difficult child I have ever met," she complained. "She tells me she hates me and that I am not her boss. When I try to correct her misbehavior, she tells me she will tell you and that you will let her do as she pleases."

"I'll talk to her about it," Ed replied.

"Talk…that's all you ever do." There was total fury in Julia's voice. "What that girl needs is a good thrashing. You are afraid to do what needs to be done, and, if you give me permission I 'll thrash her until she realizes that she must change her ways."

Ed tried to direct her attention to another problem.

"They're settin' up the ditch camp two miles east of town tomorrow, an' I'll be needin' to leave at daybreak," Ed said. "Katie an' Carrie can come and cook. We'll set up a tent for them to sleep in. That should give you a bit of peace and quiet."

"Ed Foster, you must be out of your mind. I won't allow a granddaughter of mine to cook for a crew of tobacco chewing, God swearing, vulgar horsemen." Grandma was doubly indignant. "See that a tent is set up for me and I'll come as the cook. Carrie can come help me, and live in the same tent, but you'll have to look after Katie and Myrtie. In my day Children were taught to respect their elders."

"Hell," Ed was livid with anger. "In your day a child wasn't human. "You didn't give a damn whether I lived or died when you left me in Vermont when I was four or five."

"It's finally out in the open," Julia stated. "You have harbored these hateful feelings for me all these years. I won't stay a minute longer than I have to if that's how you feel."

"That's fine" Ed said coldly. "I'll hitch the team up and get you to the railroad station tomorrow mornin.'" The next morning Julia's words were of self pity and criticism of Ed.

"Edward, I am surprised that you turn me out like this. I will not get in touch with you unless you apologize. You seem to have forgotten that I am your mother."

On the trip to the depot Ed realized that old hurts had not healed. He decided to try to make their parting as congenial as possible, but he could not find words that would ease the long standing friction between himself and his mother.

As she boarded the train, she told Ed not to see her to her seat or help her with her luggage. Awkwardly Ed and his three daughters stood on the wooden platform like three forlorn statues. Ed had the feeling that he would not see her alive again, but said nothing as the three watched the train move slowly away.

At the ditch camp several teamsters were eager to help nineteen year old Carrie with the cooking. Katie and Carrie made a good working team, and they were able to teach Myrtie the rudiments of cooking. Summer passed quickly and fall came. Carrie insisted that Katie enter school in Sedgwick, and Ed agreed. Katie entered ninth grade in the wooden building that was Sedgwick High School. A month after school started the girls held a conference with their father about events that had transpired since their mother had died.

"It is so good to be here with you, papa," Carrie began.

"For the first time in a long time I am where I belong," Katie said. "I have always belonged with you, papa."

"I love you, papa," Myrtie said sweetly.

"There is somethin' I need to say to all three of you girls."

"What do you want to tell us, papa?" Carrie asked.

"Nobody will ever know how sorry I am about Willie," Ed stated. "The worst thing I ever had to do was to git over blamin' myself for his death, but inside I feel that I caused his death. I was so wrapped up in myself after your mother's passing that I forgot he was just a boy"…a sob caught in Ed's throat as he continued. "I can never be forgiven for that…"

"We know you loved Willie," Carrie stated. "We loved him too, and we love you and Grandma."

The girls surrounded their father and put their arms around his shoulders. Grief that they had not allowed themselves to show swept over them, and for a time no one spoke until Carrie summarized her views of past events.

"Since mama died, all of us have been upset, but now we need to try to become a family. I'm sorry Grandma left the way she did, but I understand the deep feelings you have had about her. I know that I will write to her from time to time."

"I know Grandma wanted the best for me," Katie said, "but I needed to see my friends."

"When I was your age," Ed replied, "I thought all women were like my mother. I never remember that she showed me that she loved me. Maybe, I will be able to forgive her sometime…but not now"

There was silence as the girls stepped back from their father.

"Your mother was the best person I have ever known," Ed stated only partially in control as he sobbed again for a time…"I miss her more than I can say…Now I know that she was teaching me as well as you children when she read from the Bible…since her passing…I have been reading her Bible for myself. A verse she used to tell me has come to mean a lot to me…'If God be for us, who can be against us.'"

"There are two ways to look at life, he said. "One way is to be afraid of an angry God, and fear His judgment. The other way is to look at the word 'salvation' as God's way with people…I know that all is not right in the world, but each person, including us, must find God's salvation in their own way. God is in control, and 'all things do work together for good' to those who love him and for those who see his call for their lives. For a long time I saw pain and sadness every where I looked, and when your mother and Willie died all I could see was pain." Tears were streaming down Ed's cheeks.

"I was in so much pain when your mother died I let people send you girls away. For a long time I couldn't think right about that."

"Papa we're together now." Katie said.

"We will do our best to be a family," Carrie stated. "Mama taught us to know God and to believe in his son, Jesus, just as she did. He has given me comfort and I trust Him for my future."

Katie and Myrtie both said "me too". The girls sat down in front of Ed as he continued.

"You girls will soon be settin' up lives of your own. I pray that you will know what a man is in his heart before you marry. Be very careful of any man who shows by his actions that he has a mean and selfish heart. I want you to find men who can love you as much as I loved your mother. Hold such a man in your heart of hearts forever." He paused in deep thought. He raised his head and searched their faces for signs of understanding. They nodded their heads "We cannot know the sorrows and joys that are ahead of us, but I have a deep sense of peace about you girls, and it's because of what your mother meant to us. She gave her strength for us, and you girls could not have a better ideal to follow. Even in death her faith has given us comfort."

For a time Ed sat in silence as tears flowed down his cheeks.

"I only ask that we cherish her faith, and her memory as long as we live. I finally learned what her faith meant to me. I want you to live by it, too."

"We will papa," the three girls spoke as one with the brightness and sparkle of youth who could not foresee their own destinies. Nor could they know their futures would follow the life styles of those who had gone. They did know the joy of faith their mother taught them.

About the Author

Robert Connerly was the youngest child in a family of seven. Until the age of fourteen the family farmed on irrigated farms in northeastern Colorado. At an early age The Connerly children were put to work in the beet fields and in tending livestock. There were many experiences similar to those described in "Settlers' Prairie." Traditions of early day homesteading and survival on the prairie were discussed freely in first hand accounts of uncles, aunts and grandparents who were homesteaders before irrigation came to the region. Connerly served four years in the Army during WW II with two and a half years service in the Pacific arena. After that experience he completed his education and earned a Doctorate degree in the field of Education. He careered in education and retired as a School Psychologist after thirty-seven years.